12/01

D0501992

A Cold

CHRISTMAS

Also by Charlene Weir

Murder Take Two

Family Practice

Consider the Crows

The Winter Widow

A Cold
CHRISTMAS

Charlene Weir

Thomas Dunne Books
St. Martin's Minotaur
New York

THOMAS DUNNE BOOKS.
An imprint of St. Martin's Press.

A COLD CHRISTMAS. Copyright © 2001 by Charlene Weir. All rights
reserved. Printed in the United States of America. No part of this book
may be used or reproduced in any manner whatsoever without written
permission except in the case of brief quotations embodied in critical
articles or reviews. For information, address St. Martin's Press, 175 Fifth
Avenue, New York, N.Y. 10010.

www.minotaurbooks.com

Library of Congress Cataloging-in-Publication Data

Weir, Charlene.
    A cold Christmas / Charlene Weir.—1st ed.
        p. cm.
    ISBN 0-312-26931-5
    1. Wren, Susan (Fictitious character)—Fiction. 2. Police—
Kansas—Fiction. 3. Police chiefs—Fiction. 4. Policewomen—
Fiction. 5. Kansas—Fiction. I. Title.

PS3573.E39744 C64 2001
813'.54—dc21
                                                        2001041981

First Edition: December 2001

10 9 8 7 6 5 4 3 2 1

TO CLARA KI AND SARAH LOUISE

Acknowledgments

Boundless thanks to Susan Dunlap, who said a book could be created from a manuscript of complete confusion.

Heartfelt gratitude to Avis, Pat, Barbara, and Dana for continued encouragement in the face of depression and sheer panic, and to my children for many things, mostly for being my children.

Special thanks to Suzanne Schwartz, R.N., F.N.P., who continued to answer all my medical questions patiently and graciously.

And, of course, thanks to my editor, Ruth Cavin, my agent, Meg Ruley, and my copy editor, Ravin Gustafson.

A Cold

CHRISTMAS

1

It's just a lousy cold, Caley told herself. I can do this. I'm indispensable. I'm the organist. No organist, no rehearsal. Eyes that wouldn't open more than halfway made everything fuzzy around the edges. Like the man standing at the side of the church. When she blinked, he vanished and she couldn't see him anywhere. The day-old coffee hadn't been a good idea. It had tasted odd, and the caffeine wasn't helping. She felt a little queasy.

Caley James picked up her feet carefully as she moved across the parking lot. Not because the surface was icy. It wasn't. It was perfectly dry concrete with mounds of dirty snow bordering the edges. But her feet were numb and she seemed to be weaving. The frigid air caught her breath and squeezed pain through her sinuses.

Hampstead was experiencing the longest cold spell in the history of local weather. Brutal cold for eight days in a row and expected to remain that way. Her old car had a heater that reached tepid on its best days, which were long past. Her head felt enormously too large and sounds ballooned up as though through deep water.

The church, an imposing structure of native limestone, looked cream-colored and inviting on summer days. On cold winter days like today, with rippled clouds of gray above, it was drab and forbidding. The back door always stuck, so she yanked on it and almost fell on her face when it was opened from the inside by Evan Devereau.

"... money missing from the donation baskets," Reverend Mullet, in the hallway, was saying.

Evan nodded, distracted, his mind likely on the music.

The warmth of the robing room made her cheeks sting. She started to stamp her feet to stir up some feeling in them, but lightning bolts of pain forked through her head on the first tap.

"You don't look good," Evan said. As choir director, upon his shoulders fell the duty of arranging the Christmas choral music. "You sure you're up to this?"

"A snap." Since her kids were home alone, she hoped he wouldn't drag out the rehearsal.

He eyed her judiciously, hung his heavy coat over a hanger, and jammed it between all the others in the closet. Reddish hair cropped to a crew cut, easy manner, Evan Devereau was a wizard at coaxing glorious sounds from untrained voices—and he was one of the most completely good men she'd ever known. When he took her to the emergency room that time she'd cut her leg, he waited with her. That was more than her ex-husband had done when their baby was born. An impending sneeze sent her plunging frantically through pockets for a tissue.

"You don't have a cold," Evan said, "you have the flu. You can't play like this."

"I'm fine." If she didn't play, she didn't get paid. If she didn't get paid, the kids didn't get Christmas. She tossed her ski jacket over a chair, but didn't remove her scarf. It wasn't so warm in here after all.

In the church proper, a single light high in the ceiling shone down on the huge hanging cross of burnished brass. It lit up the altar far below, white altar cloth and blue parament for Advent, silver candlesticks and wine cups. Dark red carpeting ran down the center aisle to rows of pews waiting in the shadows. She could barely make out the silhouette of a solitary man sitting in the rear.

As she slid onto the organ bench, her page turner took one look at her and scooted as far away as the bench allowed. When Caley looked again, the man in the back was gone. Watch it, she told herself, you're turning into a nut cake. She rubbed her cold fingers, switched on the organ and then the light over the music rack. The choir members were shifting in their seats, clearing their throats and bringing themselves to attention. She played the prelude, pulled out a few more stops, and sailed into the oratorio. As the tenor rose to sing, she pulled out a mixture of stops.

"There were shep-herds at night in that same country, a-biding in the fields . . ."

Caley soared on the magic of the music, rising to crescendo, falling back to pianissimo, moving right into andantino for the soprano.

"And sud-den-ly there ap-pear'd a mul-ti-tude of the heav'nly host unto them . . ."

When the soprano finished, baritone Osey Pickett rose. He was just getting into stride when a tall slender woman with dark hair slipped quietly into a back pew.

She was Susan Wren, Hampstead's police chief. Come to arrest me for strangling a pipe. Caley felt giggles bubbling in her chest. I'm not choking it, Chief. It already hissed when they hired me. Honest. I asked them to fix it. We can't afford it, they said. Play around it. You don't need it that often. Ha. I need it all the time. Like now.

". . . with the an-gels all prais-ing God, prais-ing God and say-ing . . ."

Poised on the organ bench above the choir, in dizzying heights of shimmering air, she plunged into the music of Saint-Saëns. Her feet galloped across the pedals in racing bass. With a surging combination of reed stops, her hands scrambled to catch up.

Sound crashed from the pipes, ricocheted around the dark

wood, sparked across stained-glass windows, raced up lofty curves of the barrel vaults, and . . .

Susan Wren was moving toward the slumped organist before the sound even died away. Osey, coming from the choir loft with the choir director, nudged the page turner out of the way.

"Caley?" Evan said.

"Stand back, Evan." Susan put her fingertips at the corner of Caley's jaw. Pulse strong, rapid. Skin hot. She lifted Caley's eyelid; the pupil reacted normally.

"Osey, see if you can get Dr. Cunningham."

He tossed straw-colored hair from his eyes and loped off in his long lanky stride.

Caley's eyelids fluttered, opened, closed, then opened again. With bewilderment she stared at the choir clustered around her, all peering down. Had she died and been laid out in a casket? When she tried to sit, her eyes lost focus. Susan pushed Caley's head between her knees until she made small protesting sounds.

Osey returned and said quietly to Susan. "Doc's on the way."

Susan nodded. Flu had felled another. Half her officers were flat out with it. A crime wave sweeping through town would have the bad guys outnumbering the good guys. If the stricken didn't start recovering soon, there'd be no way she could resign. Deserting ship with only the dispatcher left to take the helm wouldn't cut it.

"Oh, God," Caley said, seemed to remember where she was, and closed her eyes.

Osey grinned. "I reckon you got his attention with that music."

"I've never heard you play like that," Evan said.

"I think I'll go home now." Caley struggled upright with some help from Susan, swayed a bit, and blinked her eyes. "Whoa."

"I'll take you," Evan said.

"Evan," Susan said firmly, "go back to rehearsal."

4

Reluctantly, director and singers, with the exception of Osey, trooped back to their seats.

"Let's get her in the robing room," Susan said to Osey.

Five minutes later, Dr. Baylis Cunningham bustled in, looked at the patient, listened to her chest, peered into her eyes and ears, told her to say Ah, took her temperature, and pronounced flu, dehydration, and slight malnutrition. "Make an appointment to see me at the office." Cunningham bustled out.

"I'll get her home," Osey said.

"You go rehearse. I'll do it."

Susan helped Caley into her ski jacket, guided her out to the pickup, bundled her in, and clicked the seat belt snugly around her.

"Give me your key and I'll see that your car gets home."

"The gray Ford over there." With shaky hands, Caley detached a key from the key ring.

"Where do you live?"

"On Hollis, straight out from Eagle's Pond."

Susan took a left on Eleventh and a right on Campus Drive. The streets were dry, thank God. Hampstead was settled in a cluster of small hills, and when the streets iced over, it was a nightmare.

The sky was a solid gray with not even a paler spot to suggest the sun existed up there somewhere, and the temperature had not risen enough to melt the dingy snow left over from the last snowfall.

Christmas was everywhere. Wreaths on doors, decorated trees in front windows, reindeer capering across front lawns, sleighs and Santas on rooftops. Colored lights on outdoor trees, along eaves, and wrapped around mailbox posts. 'Tis the season.

"You come to rehearsals," Caley said.

Susan nodded. Finding solace in the Lutheran church would bring forth much guilt-invoking, you-let-me-down sorrow from her Catholic grandmother, if she knew. "I like the music," she said.

In the dimness of the empty church, frantic thoughts stopped chasing one another and her mind grew still and light. It was the only place where she could get away; no one bothered her unless a dire emergency arose.

Eight days ago an offer had come from her old boss in San Francisco. "We've got us something of an unusual situation here," he'd said. "Money is all of a sudden spearheaded to shake some life into cold cases. I need a seasoned investigator to clear a few, zipzap-you're-under-arrest quick, and rework some of the more high-profile."

A failure of hers had ended up as a cold file. It still haunted her dreams. A baby, beaten to death, tiny body covered with cigarette burns.

"It's a two-year job. You interested?"

Arctic in Hampstead and sixty-two in San Francisco? No contest.

"Think about it," he'd said. "Take all the time you want. Till the day after Christmas."

She hadn't needed three weeks; she hadn't even needed three seconds. When she'd stopped tap-dancing up and down the walls and begun planning, her officers had started dropping with flu.

That meant she couldn't leave immediately, and it gave her time to think. Thinking made her realize it wasn't quite so simple, and she'd started juggling pros and cons. In Hampstead, she was in charge. Boss. A heady feeling. She'd grown used to it, discovered she liked it. She'd met people here who would be hard to leave. Her husband was buried here. Her father was in San Francisco. They'd get into the same old nose-to-nose fights they always had. And the most troublesome question. Could she simply slide back into her old life? The job was only for two years. Then what? Finally give up and go to work for her father's law firm because it was easier than fighting him? Hope her old boss could find money to hire her full-time? The call had come eight days ago. She had two weeks left to decide.

Caley started shivering. Susan looked at her—face flushed, eyes glassy—and turned up the heater.

"You come to hear Osey sing," Caley said, her tone almost accusatory. She was an attractive young woman, late twenties, shoulder-length hair, light brown with a slight wave, oval face with a pointed chin and innocent amber-colored eyes.

"Yes." O. C. Pickett was one of her detectives. In appearance, nothing but a lanky hayseed, not too bright. A farm boy. Whoever thought that was badly mistaken. Osey had a mind like a steel trap and a photographic memory, useful talents for a cop. He also had the ability to meet people and instantly be an old friend, another good talent for a cop. And he had a baritone voice that lifted the heart. It always amazed her when she heard him sing.

Caley James lived just past an abandoned paper factory in a three-story wood-frame house diminished by giant walnut trees, the leafless branches dark against the gray sky. It sat at the end of a long driveway and looked held together by a coat of white paint about to give up the fight. Perfect setting for a Gothic novel.

"Thank you for bringing me home," Caley said as Susan pulled up the driveway and stopped at the back of the house.

"Please don't come in with me."

"I'll just—"

"No. I have three kids."

"I've seen a lot worse than anything three kids can do."

"You don't know," Caley said darkly.

"I need to make sure you get inside safely."

"I'm fine." Caley released the seat belt and opened the pickup door.

Susan slid out, nipped around to the other side, and took a firm grip on Caley's arm. "I'll walk you to the door." She braced herself against the freezing December wind.

"Only the door? Promise?"

"Promise." Susan helped her across the driveway, avoiding the icy patches that hadn't been cleared after the last snowfall. When snow isn't shoveled, it gets trampled, then it turns to slush that turns to ice at the next temperature drop. She'd learned that to her sorrow. "Just let me—"

"You promised." Opening the door a narrow few inches, Caley edged around it into the kitchen.

Susan let her go, telling herself to check up later. In this kind of cold weather, cops did welfare checks to make sure the elderly or ill were all right. In ordinary times, she would just add Caley to the list, but with everybody out sick there were no welfare checks. One old woman had frozen to death in her own living room. Susan didn't want another tragedy.

All I have to do, Caley thought, closing the door behind her, is get to my bed. Not even that far. The couch. Miles to go before I sleep. A gargantuan sneeze almost crumpled her. She dabbed at her nose with a soggy tissue. Freezing in here. Tripping over curling linoleum in the kitchen, she went through the dining room and into the living room.

All three of her children were lined up on the couch, covered to their chins with quilts, watching television.

"I told him we weren't supposed to," Adam said. "We'd be in trouble when you got back." Adam was the middle child, the eight-year-old.

"I turned it on," Zachary said, a shade defensively, always truthful. Twelve, the responsible one.

Bonnie, the baby, at six, didn't say anything. In fact, she didn't look so good. Her face was flushed and her eyes droopy.

"It's warmer this way," Zach said. "And Adam got fidgety." His younger brother couldn't sit still for more than two minutes unless it was in front of a television set, where his brain went immediately to flat line.

"The Littles needed something to do," Zach said, from his superior age of twelve.

"Hi, Mommy." Bonnie was Caley's cuddler and usually available for a hug. Now she simply sat listlessly watching gunmen chase each other through an empty office building.

"Hello, love." Caley kissed her daughter's forehead, touched one cheek and then the other. Warm. Oh, damn.

"Zach, for goodness sake, why didn't you turn the heat up?" They tried to keep it down because even with the extra job at Basslight Music, she couldn't afford the gas bills. "We don't need to freeze to death."

"Mommy, are we going to freeze to death?"

"No, darling, of course not."

"I did," Zach said. "All the way. Nothing happened."

"Why didn't you call your grandmother?"

"She called right after you left and said she was going . . . shopping, I think. Anyway, you weren't going to be gone long. I could handle it. I didn't start a fire because I knew you'd spaz."

Caley squinted at the thermostat, twisted the dial all the way down and then all the way up. She did it again. Dumbly, she stood there as the enormity of the situation made its way through to her brain. The furnace didn't work. The worst winter since Kansas became a state—when was that? Eighteen something? The furnace was dead.

Clutching her coat tight at her throat, she clumped down the rickety basement steps and peered at the metal monster. Like everything else in the house, it was old. It sat silently in its spot in the corner like a dumb beast too tired and abused to go on.

"Damn it!" She kicked it.

". . . got released," Zach was saying. "And dangerous."

"Zach, what are you talking about?"

He sighed. "Grandma called right after you left."

"What did she want?"

"I don't know. Some stuff about this guy being dangerous and you should be careful and not let in any strangers."

Back upstairs, in the kitchen, Caley flipped through pages. Furnaces, furnaces. "What was Ettie talking about?"

"I don't know. You know how she is." Her ex-husband's mother was a mixed blessing, great in some ways, but given a topic she was a nonstop talker.

"Where's that flyer that came in the mail?"

Zach put his finger on a flyer tacked to the corkboard over the phone. "When it came I put it here just in case." Shanky's Furnace and Air Conditioning.

Caley rubbed her eyes, then punched numbers and explained her problem.

A sympathetic female voice said someone would be out within the next two hours. It would cost seventy-five dollars for him to take a look at it. Seventy-five dollars?

"We could build a fire," Zach suggested.

She put her arms around him, pulled him close, and kissed the top of his head, probably smearing germs all over him. What would she do without this child? This calm sensible child, too adult for twelve. Keep yourself under control and don't panic so much, she said silently. It wasn't fair to him.

He brought in wood, arranged it in the fireplace, crumpled newspapers, and within minutes had a fire going. Even Bonnie perked up a bit with logs cheerily crackling away.

Two hours and twenty minutes later, rescue arrived. He was thin inside a bulky black jacket, thin face with a comma-shaped scar like the letter C on his left cheek, high forehead, blondish hair, and blank deep-set hazel eyes, "Tim" stitched on his shirt pocket.

As she started down the basement stairs, Bonnie scrambled over and flung small arms around her waist. "Mommy, don't."

"I'm just going to show him where the furnace is."

"Don't go!"

"Bonnie . . ."

"Nooo!" Tears trickled down Bonnie's round cheeks. "Please, Mommy. You won't ever come back. Like the witch in Hansel and Gretel. You'll be burned up."

"That was an oven," Adam said scornfully.

"He's gonna hurt you."

"Of course he won't, darling. He's here to fix the furnace so we can get warm."

"He has funny eyes," Bonnie mumbled, sticking to her guns.

He did, Caley thought. Goat's eyes. Hazel, intelligent, knowing, and taking in everything. When she was a child, she'd owned a book about a troll who lived under a bridge. The evil troll had eyes just like the man she was about to take into her basement.

She gathered up her daughter, kissed the flushed face, and brushed light hair from her forehead. "You sit here. I'll be right back."

She turned on the basement light and stepped back to let him go first, not wanting him behind her.

A flicker of malice stirred in his eyes before he turned and trotted down the steps.

She pointed out the furnace, against the wall under the dirty narrow window. He placed his toolbox on the cement floor, removed a furnace panel, and crouched to shine a flashlight at its innards.

She huddled on the bottom step, hugging the banister. Never before had the dim lighting down here bothered her. There were only two bare ceiling bulbs sending fingers of light into the darkness spreading under the entire house. Junk was piled everywhere: boxes, old furniture, a rusted bicycle, broken toys, a doll buggy, a crib, a desk—maybe that could be cleaned up for Zach—file cabinets, chairs, a dining table. A good place to hide something, she thought. Like a body.

Tim banged away, said it needed two new pieces, and banged some more.

"Mommy!"

The edge of panic in Bonnie's voice had her racing up the stairs. In the kitchen, the little girl stood in the center of spilled orange juice that soaked the front of her clothes, dripped off the table, and puddled in a widening circle around the dropped jug.

"Go change your clothes," Caley snapped.

Bonnie's bottom lip trembled and tears filled her eyes.

Oh, God. "I'm sorry, love. It's all right." She gave the child a one-armed hug, kissed her, and patted her on the fanny. "Get something dry on. It's all right."

Nothing was all right. She'd just yelled at her baby, she had orange juice all over the kitchen, and she had a weird guy in the basement. Tears prickled at her eyes.

"I'll take care of it, Mom," Zach said.

"Zach—" Hang on, don't snivel. "You are a great kid. Thanks."

She found Bonnie in the bedroom, shivering so hard she couldn't manage the buttons on her shirt. Caley peeled off the wet clothes, slipped a dry sweatshirt over the little girl's head, gathering pale hair loose from the neckline, and pulled on a pair of sweatpants. She carried Bonnie into the living room, sat on one end of the couch, and wrapped a quilt around both of them. She hummed softly. Adam, still mesmerized by television, sat on the other end.

Horses galloped across the television and guns blazed. Struggle as she might, she still dozed.

Gradually muscles, tensed to protect her from the cold, began to relax as warmth crept in like soft spring air.

She dreamed.

God, with a mass of fuzzy white hair and the repairman's eyes, put her in an elevator and pressed a button labeled HELL. The elevator descended. When it reached bottom, the doors opened to gigantic, roaring, leaping flames. Hands grabbed her arms and legs, swung her back, and pitched her in.

"Mom! Mom, wake up!" Zach shook her shoulder. "We got a problem!"

"Adam?" She shot up. "Bonnie?"

"They're fine. In the bedroom. Mom, the furnace won't turn off."

"Turn it down." She slumped back against the lumpy couch.

"It is down. It doesn't matter. It keeps roaring."

She untangled herself from the quilts and got to her feet. Hot hot. The room swayed. It had gotten dark while she dozed. Somebody had turned on all the lights. Adam, maybe; he didn't like the dark. She headed for the basement.

"Mom, he's gone."

"Gone," she repeated stupidly.

"Wake up, Mom. We have to do something."

She shook her head, then wished she hadn't.

"Call them." Zach handed her a bill. She owed six hundred and eighty-five dollars.

"Call. I'll open windows."

She punched in the number on the invoice and, rather shrilly, explained the situation to the male voice on the other end of the line.

"It's the blower," he said, superior male to ditzy female. "Takes several minutes before it shuts off."

"It's been several hours and nothing has shut off."

"I'll send someone out first thing in the morning." Bored unworried voice.

"No," Caley said. "*Right now*. He just left. Get him back here."

Pause. "I'll try his pager."

She slammed down the receiver, used ticking seconds to track down a number, then called Kansas Power and Light.

After she explained a second time, a female voice promised someone would be there within an hour.

"Hour? We'll be on the way to mummified in an hour."

"I'll put a rush on it."

Caley disconnected and called another number, relieved when the phone was answered. "Ettie, would you take the children for a while? The furnace isn't working."

"Of course. I'll be right there."

Caley had the Littles and Zach, their breaths steaming in the cold air, waiting on the kitchen porch when their grandmother drove up. She bundled them into the car and waved as they drove away.

Feverish, shaking, coughing, aching in every joint, she switched on the outside light over the garage door and waited in her car for KP and L—or for the house to blow up, whichever came first.

13

Before either of those things happened, headlights poked up the driveway, a van parked in the circle of light outside the garage, and the repairman got out.

She scooted from the car and went to meet him. Shaking in the cold, she ran up the porch steps, opened the kitchen door, and let him in.

He smiled a creepy little smile that froze her hand as she reached to close the door behind them.

2

$\mathcal{T}$ime ticked by on long seconds. His blank eyes watched her, knowing her fear, amused by it. The kitchen seemed too bright, the ceiling light shined down on bowls of soggy cereal in puddles of milk, a loaf of bread spilling out slices, and a jar of peanut butter with a knife stuck in it. Blobs of red splattered the tablecloth. Clumps of strawberry jam, she assumed, not a foreshadowing of gory smears from her body after he hacked her up with a carving knife.

Distant music and singing: "She cut off their tails with a carving knife."

"Ms. James?"

She squeezed her eyes shut, blinked.

"You all right?"

"Fine." She calculated how fast she could get to the door before he grabbed her.

"You seem a little upset. Would you like me to leave?"

Leave? With the furnace roaring away burning expensive gas, and the house like Hades even with the windows open?

"I'll call a doctor," he said, voice bland, nothing in his eyes.

"No. No, I'm fine."

"You sure? You look a little frail."

"Sure. Yes."

"Well—" He waited a moment. "I'll go take care of the furnace, then."

"Yes." She was losing it. As bad as Bonnie with her fairy-tale imagination. Caley slumped in a chair, put her elbows on the table, and propped her head in her hands.

She could hear banging, followed by ominous silences. Her head throbbed like a jungle drum, and she envisioned him dancing, half-naked, skin glistening, around the furnace. Oh, Lord. She tracked down the Advil, tried to shake two capsules into her palm, and half the bottle came out. She dumped the handful on the table, isolated two, and gulped them down with somebody's leftover orange juice. She grimaced at the bitter taste.

When the doorbell rang, she jumped, sloshing juice over her hand. "Damn." Get a grip. She rinsed her hand in the sink, ripped off a paper towel, and headed for the living room.

Pulling aside the disintegrating lace curtain over the half-moon of window in the door, she saw her ex-husband on the porch, the light shining on his curly hair. Tall, blond, and handsome, looking like he'd just come in from the range in his fleece-lined suede jacket, ankle boots, and tight-fitting jeans. He didn't look any different than he had three months ago when she'd thrown him out, taking on this derelict house herself with three kids and no money.

She jerked open the door.

"Hi, Cal." Big smile. He stepped forward to come in. She blocked his way.

His smile turned to hurt. "Aren't you glad to see me?"

"I can't even remember when I was last glad to see you. What do you want?"

"I'd like to come in."

"No."

"Come on, Cal. It's freezing out here."

She closed the door.

"Caley?" He knocked, then leaned on the doorbell.

She opened the door a few inches.

"It's really cold." He looked charming and sexy.

Her manner softened. "Would you like a cup of coffee?"

"That'd be great," he said with relief.

"There's a convenience store six blocks that way and two blocks right. If you jog you'll stay warmer."

"I have to talk to you."

"We are talking. Similar to the last time. How long ago was that? Three weeks? Eight weeks?"

"Couldn't we go in where it's warm?"

"It's not *warm* in here, it's the Sahara. The furnace stuck. You want to pay the repair bill?"

"Of course. I'll write a check. How much do you need?"

She knew what his checks were worth. "If you have money why didn't you use some of it to take Adam out on his birthday?"

"I explained that."

"Yeah, well, when you're eight and your dad says he can't take you like he promised, you don't really understand the line 'Something important came up.' " She crossed her arms. "It never was a very good line anyway." She shivered and rubbed her arms.

"Let me in, Caley. I want to see them. They're my kids too. In fact, Zach is—"

"They're not here."

"Where are they?"

She hesitated, then sighed. They loved their father, and in his own way he loved them too. It was just that his way was limited. He made promises he didn't keep, and it broke their hearts. Zach was beginning to expect it and prepared himself for disappointment. He no longer believed the rosy plans his dad told him about, the ball games, the picnics, the movies, the drives to Kansas City. Zach just kept quiet and waited, but she could see the misery in his eyes when none of the glorious plans materialized. Adam, though not yet burned enough to accept it as the norm, was starting to get the picture. But Bonnie loved her father with no hesitations, got thrilled to bubbling when he laid out some special plan. When he didn't come through, she was devastated and inconsolable. Caley didn't want to badmouth their father, but she hated to see them so hurt and had taken to throwing in a few cautionary words. Like, "That'll be wonderful if . . ."

Mat stood there blowing on his hands and shifting his weight from one foot to the other. "Listen, Caley, I have to talk to you. It's important."

"Oh, really. Important to whom?"

"What?" He was getting a mite impatient with her. "What's the matter with you? Something has come up—"

"Come up? Again? You really ought to get some new material." She closed the door.

"Caley!" He pounded, then jabbed the doorbell.

After he got tired of pounding and yelling and stabbing her doorbell, she took her woozy head and her aching bones and clumped down the basement steps.

Awfully quiet. She peered under the banister. The furnace sat with its outer panels removed and pieces of its insides spread on the floor. Where was Tim the repairman? Took it on the lam through one of the narrow, grimy windows? Hiding? She really did have to get rid of all the junk down here. Ugly old furniture you wouldn't have in your house, ugly old pictures you wouldn't have on your walls, boxes and boxes of junk left by the previous owners—and maybe the owners before them and the owners before them, for all she knew.

"Ms. James?"

She spun around, heart flying up to her throat, beating so hard she couldn't breathe.

Tim had crept up behind her with a live snake, the biggest blackest maddest snake she'd ever seen.

18

3

$\mathcal{T}$he scream got tangled in her throat and came out in little *uuh uuh uuh uuh* sounds.

He had one hand just behind the snake's head—its mouth was open, its tongue flickering—and the other hand at the end of the tail. In between it coiled and writhed and twisted itself around his wrist.

Faster than she could see, it jerked its head loose and sank white fangs into the ball of his thumb.

Cursing, he grabbed the head and, holding it high, he dashed behind her and fed the snake into a white wicker hamper. He slapped down the lid and propped his butt on it, resting one hand on either side.

"I'll call 911." She was halfway up the stairs.

"Not necessary."

"You'll die."

"Naw."

She crept back down the stairs.

"It's just a black snake. Harmless. Good to have around, really. They take care of rats."

Rats? She looked around the basement.

He studied the beads of blood on the ball of his thumb, then sucked them.

She shivered. "Where did it come from?"

"Hibernating over there." He nodded toward the hot water heater. "Got a bit irritated at being disturbed. Can't say I blame it. How do you feel when you get yanked out of deep sleep?"

"So far I've never bitten anyone." She eyed him closely, expecting him to drop dead. A great big black snake had been down here since last fall? And the kids hadn't seen it? They were all over this place. One of them could have been bitten. She'd never seen that hamper before, either. Could he have brought in the snake inside the hamper? Why, for God's sake, would he do a thing like that? Just because she hadn't seen the hamper didn't mean it hadn't been here. With the jumble of junk down here, half the slithery creatures of Bambi's forest could be here and she wouldn't notice. Rats? Maybe it was time to clean this place out.

"I could use a rope," he said calmly. "If I get up it'll get loose."

"Rope. Right. Rope." She peered around blankly.

"On the wall over there." He nodded toward the wall behind her.

Coils of rope of different sizes hung on pegs driven into a board on the wall. He knew more about this basement than she did. She snatched one coil and brought it to him.

"You might hold the lid while I tie it down."

"Yes. Right." She didn't like being that close to him, but to her surprise he didn't smell of fire and brimstone, or even sweat and dirt. He didn't smell of anything more horrifying than soap.

He trussed the hamper up like a package about to be mailed.

"What are you going to do with it?" she asked

"I'll take care of it."

"Right." She had a vision of him eating it as a midnight snack. How had he found it? Had he been clambering through junk? Looking for what? Hidden treasure?

He finished up a knot and plopped the hamper at the foot of the steps, then went to kneel in front of the furnace. Paying some kind of homage to the furnace god? The roar of all that expensive fuel was fierce. He leaned in, did something, then backed away and sat on his heels.

She heard a click and, much to her relief, the roar dwindled. "Will it go back on when it's supposed to?" She had visions of going through the whole process again.

He gave her that scary smile that didn't reach his eyes. "Yes, ma'am."

Go then. Go go. He replaced the panels, packed up his tools, and picked up the white hamper using the rope as a handle. She stood way back and let him climb the stairs. In the kitchen, she opened the door, watched him cross the small porch, go down the five steps, cross the driveway, get into the van, and back out. From a living room window, she watched him drive away. When she was sure he wasn't going to come creeping back, she called Ettie and said she'd be right over to pick up the kids.

Mat had the children, Ettie said. He would bring them home. Mat had the children? Why did Mat have the children? Her head couldn't figure that out. She took two Advil and waited. And dozed. And waited. And dozed. And waited.

When they finally came, it was way past the children's bedtime. They were overtired, high as launched missiles and wild from excitement. With a disapproving look at the mess in the living room, he said, "See you tomorrow." Caley only had time to sputter before he was gone.

"Daddy's taking us ice-skating." Bonnie danced in circles, joy spilling over. She looked much better.

Caley caught her and took off her coat. Bonnie no longer felt hot.

"And then we're having lunch and then we're going to a movie. And I get to pick where we have lunch."

"Yeah!" Adam punched the air, pulled off his gloves, threw them at the ceiling, and flung his coat after them. "I get to pick where we go skating."

Zach was quiet, but she could tell he was excited too. "What do you get to pick?" she asked him.

"The movie."

How clever of Mat. He knew Zach would find something the Littles would both accept and that way Mat wouldn't have a fight on his hands.

It took her hours to get the Littles in bed. If Mat didn't show tomorrow, she would personally kill him.

When she finally got everybody settled, she threw her creaking, achy self into her own bed and dropped into sleep. She kept waking because she couldn't breathe. Finally, she stacked pillows, propped herself up on the headboard, and dozed. The phone, ringing at six-thirty, jolted her up from the first sleep she'd had all night. The scheduled organist couldn't make it. Flu. Could she take over the services?

"Sure," she croaked.

Sitting on the edge of the bed, she held her hands against her throbbing temples. Right. I can do it. A hot shower helped aching bones, but when she left the steamy bathroom, she started shivering. Teeth-chattering, bone-shaking chills. She downed more Advil. I can do this, she told herself. Of course, you can. Get dressed.

No problem deciding what to wear. She always wore the same clothes, church services, concerts, choir performances, weddings, funerals. Long black skirt and white blouse. No time wasted dithering about what to wear, and lots of clothes weren't necessary. She always looked either professional or devout, whichever was required. Would she be warm enough? Maybe she should wear long johns under the skirt.

Wrapped in one of Mat's old flannel robes, she padded into the kitchen for coffee. Adam slammed in right behind her. If he was awake, the other two were also. He saw to it. Bonnie came next, looking totally recovered. Caley felt her forehead and sighed with relief. She wouldn't have to tell her daughter she couldn't go with her father today. Assuming he turned up.

"What time is he picking you up?"

"Ten. That's what he said." Zach was not totally convinced either.

"Mommy, I got here first." Bonnie tussled with Adam.

"I did!" Adam shouted.

"It's mine."

"Hey!"

Bonnie and Adam were in a shoving match about who got to sit in the only chair Caley had gotten around to refinishing. She shrieked at them, sent Adam to one end of the table and Bonnie to the other, and plonked herself in the prized chair. She drank coffee. Bonnie and Adam squabbled over who got the Cheerios first.

When she left for the church, she told Zach they could watch as much television as they wanted as long as there was no fighting over what to watch. They were to take turns choosing. "Right?"

"Right, Mommy," Bonnie said.

"All *right*," Adam said.

"We'll be fine, Mom," Zach said. "Don't worry."

In the hour between services, Caley dashed home to check on the kids. It was after ten and Mat hadn't put in an appearance yet. Bonnie was making him a Christmas card, Adam was watching cartoons, and Zach was working complicated math puzzles on the computer. Mat still hadn't shown up when she had to leave for the second service.

He'd better get here.

As soon as she played the last note of Handel in the postlude, she raced home.

The house was empty.

With a huge sigh, she lay on the bed and buried herself in blankets. She dozed, she dreamed, she heard gunshots, she thought of Adam watching television. She slept. She roused to silence, then remembered the kids were with Mat and sank back into oblivion.

4

$\mathscr{R}$oy Dandermadden walked just short of a trot. The cold air bit into his lungs, and he breathed like a steam engine, partly from moving so fast, partly from anticipation. With this weather nobody would wonder why his collar was turned up and his hat pulled down over his face, or why he was practically jogging. They'd think he was just trying to get out of the damn cold like any reasonable man. He'd parked four blocks away and now he was sorry. Not only was he freezing his nuts off, but nobody comes to a motel without a car, for God's sake. Not if they're traveling and want a place to stay overnight. Walking just called attention to himself and shouted out loud what was going on. He should have thought this through a little more before calling Cindy. That was his problem these days; he didn't think.

He never did think good on his feet. If he'd had time, he'd have worked it out better, but Lillian sprung it on him right after church. She was taking Jo and Mandy and they were going to Kansas City for Christmas shopping. They took off without even inviting him, not that he would have gone, but it would be nice to be asked once in a while.

He had plenty to do at home. Get a head start on grading

term projects and get them out of the way. But the thing was, he'd wanted to spend some time with Jo today. Maybe take her to a movie or something. She was eleven and growing up so fast it took his breath away. Mandy, already seventeen, was into her own things.

Lillian hadn't said squat as they got in the car, and when he'd mumbled something about grading papers she'd looked at him like he was sprouting corn on his head and closed her lips in a thin line. He barely had time to say drive carefully before they were gone.

And there it was, a God-given opportunity. When they had backed out the driveway, he waited a few minutes to be sure they weren't coming back for forgotten purses or lost gloves and then called Cindy, doing some figuring as he waited for the phone to be answered. An hour there, an hour for return, plus at least three hours for shopping—and with Mandy along, probably longer— that gave him a minimum of five hours.

"Hi," he said when Cindy answered. "Okay to talk?"

"Yes." Her husband, assistant manager of a supermarket, was working today.

With the clock ticking, the only place he could come up with was Oskaloosa. Small enough that any unknown car coming into town would have a cop checking the license number. How stupid could he be? They should have met in Topeka.

Seeing each other at the high school had been agony, her teaching English and him teaching geography, and pretending nothing was going on, but after school let out for Christmas break, it was even worse. Now he didn't see her at all unless he ran into her at the drugstore or somewhere, and they didn't dare say more than hello.

One disastrous time he'd gone to her house. He felt like a louse after, but it just happened. By chance they were both at the library. Her husband was working and she was supposed to be at her sister's in Baldwin City. At the last minute, her sister was called in to work.

Roy worked hard all the time. Didn't he deserve some happiness in his life? All he ever did was work to pay bills, work to pay bills. Was that all there was to life? He loved Lillian; she was a good wife and a good mother. He didn't want to hurt her. He hated himself for what he was doing, and he told himself again this was the last time.

He ducked under the elm branches hanging over the narrow walkway and counted numbers as he went past doors. At number nine, he raised his fist to knock and a horrifying thought flashed through his mind. What if the door opened and Lillian was inside? What if this was a trap: telling him she was going shopping, then doubling back to catch him. Paranoia. He wasn't cut out for this sort of thing. Besides, if that were the case she wouldn't take Jo and Mandy.

This had to stop. Then the thought of never holding Cindy again was more than he could bear. It would be different if Lillian was a terrible wife, but she wasn't. She didn't nag, she didn't cheat, she kept the house in order. She kept herself looking nice. He still loved her.

But there was Cindy. He couldn't help himself. That time at her house they were just going to be together a while, have a cup of coffee. In the kitchen he'd put his arms around her. She felt so right, lips soft, body good. Holding her tight against him, he buried his face in her hair and kissed the back of her neck. When he heard a noise and looked up, he saw the furnace repairman watching them through the glass pane in the kitchen door.

They sprang apart like guilty teenagers. The bastard never said a word, but his knowing eyes put two and two together quicker than a calculator, and amused malice crossed his face. Later Roy found out the son of a bitch's name was Tim Holiday. He waited for Holiday to make some kind of blackmail overture. Sure enough, a few days later the guy called. He wanted to come and see him. Roy said no way. Holiday said Roy's wife might like to know what was going on while she was working. Finally, Roy said okay. What else could he do?

Roy was prepared to blow the guy's head off. That was all he could think of. He had no money; what little there was, Lillian knew all about. She took care of the budget and paid the bills. She kept track of every penny. If their savings account suddenly turned up missing funds, she'd spot it immediately. There was piss-all in it anyway.

And then the guy only wanted to ask questions about Mat James. Come right down to it, Holiday was weird. Swear to God, the bastard gave Roy the creeps.

He tapped lightly on number nine and Cindy was in his arms as soon as the door shut behind them. He inhaled a deep breath of her sweet scent. They kissed long and hard. God, he'd missed her. She kept his life going; without her—

"Any more trouble from Holiday?" he asked when they drew apart.

"Not a word," she said. "Oh, Roy, I've missed you so much. I love you." Her eyes glistened. "If you ever left me, I don't know what I'd do. I'd die, that's what. I'd just die."

"Cindy, listen, maybe we—"

She clung to him. "Don't tell me this is wrong. I know it's wrong. I know we have to stop. It's just that you are the only good thing in my life. I don't know what I'd do if—" She kissed him fiercely.

He'd been going to tell her this was the end, he couldn't see her again. It was going to break his heart, but he couldn't continue cheating on Lillian. If she ever found out, she'd poison Jo against him, tell the girl her father was a no-good bastard. He'd go to any length to see that didn't happen.

Since he was here. One last time. He slipped his hands under Cindy's soft yellow sweater and cupped her round sweet breasts, teased her nipples with his thumbs. She gasped. For a moment, he saw his younger daughter's shocked face, then he was lost in Cindy's sweet passion. If Lillian responded to him like this, if she even gave him a hint she liked the feel of his body— She liked to cuddle, but she never said sexy things like Cindy, or that she appreciated him. She never reached out for him. If she had, maybe he wouldn't be here.

When his heart stopped slamming against his ribs, he lay on his back, shoved another pillow under his head, and stared at the water stain on the ceiling shaped like the state of Alaska. He had one arm around Cindy, and her head rested against his sweaty shoulder. Cindy, beautiful Cindy. What the hell was he going to do?

"Roy?" She leaned up on one elbow to look at him.

He grunted.

"Tell me what you're thinking."

He growled, hugged her, and playfully bit the tip of her nose. "You, you gorgeous thing."

She giggled, jabbed his ribs, and planted a quick kiss on his chin. "It's Lillian, isn't it? You were thinking of her."

"I don't want to hurt her."

Cindy sighed. He stroked her back.

"It gets me too," she said. "All the sneaking around, meeting in motels, having to leave separately."

"You want us to forget it? Never see each other again? Except at school in the hallways and the parking lot?"

"No! I don't know what I'd do if I couldn't be with you. It's just— Life is such a mess. And I have to go home to Harley. If he ever knew I was seeing you, he'd kill me."

Roy gently rubbed her bare shoulder and slid his hand up and down her arm. He didn't know what Lillian would do. Probably take Jo and Mandy and move to the ends of the earth, make it as hard as she could for him to see them. He couldn't allow that.

"Roy?"

"Yeah?"

"What if Tim Holiday tells people about us?"

"We'll just have to see that doesn't happen."

* * *

29

"Hey, Harley, if you can take off to go screw your wife, why can't I? I just got married. You've been married since God created the earth. Aren't you supposed to be tired of it by now?" Jimmy hung his coat on a hook and slid his time card into the machine.

"What are you talking about?"

"My wife saw your Jeep outside that motel in Oskaloosa." Jim leered. "Or was it somebody else's wife you were boffing?"

Harley felt a hot rage start in the pit of his stomach. It spread through his chest, rose to his throat, nearly choking him, and filled his head with black tar. Taking deliberate steps, he left the store through the rear door.

Standing at the sink in his kitchen, he poured bourbon in a glass and tossed it off, poured another and downed that as quick. After pouring the third, he was calm enough to sit at the table and sip it.

An hour later he heard Cindy drive the car into the garage. She looked startled to see him. Setting her shopping bag on the table, she shrugged off her coat.

"Harley? What are you doing home so soon?"

He rose from the chair.

"You're shaking. Are you sick?" She came toward him, wifely concern on her face.

Drawing back his hand, he slapped her with an open palm, all the force of his body behind it. The sharp crack and the tingling in his hand brought joy.

She cried out, fell back against the wall and slid to the floor, a hand over the red splotch on her cheek. A thin line of blood trickled from her mouth.

He stood over her. "Where were you?"

She looked up at him, her eyes wide. She smelled of fear. He breathed it in with a sense of fulfillment.

"Whore." He slapped her other cheek. "Where were you?"

She cringed, tears dribbled down her face. When she tried to crawl away, he grabbed a shoulder, jerked her up, and threw her back. Her head bounced against the wall. "Answer me!"

"Shopping—" She scrabbled sideways, trying to get away. "Christmas shopping. There was a big sale at—"

"Liar!" Clutching a fistful of her sweater, he yanked her up and slammed her against the wall again.

She covered her face with her hands. "Harley, what's the matter with you? Stop. Please stop."

"Who is he?" He smashed a fist into her ribs.

"Harley—"

"Who?" He hit her again. And again.

"Harley—" she whimpered.

"Who?"

He pried her hands from her face and hit her in the mouth. "Who?"

She cried. Her face was smeared with snot and tears and blood. "Who?"

She struggled to get away.

He kept hitting, feeling the satisfaction of her fear and relishing the sound as his fists connected with her flesh. "Who?"

"Tim Holiday," she whispered.

5

—

$\mathcal{C}$aley woke to total darkness, gasping for breath. Confusion reigned as she groped through a mind so deprived of oxygen it wouldn't come through with data. She switched on the bedside lamp and immediately squeezed her eyes shut against the stabbing pain, leaving ghost images on her retinas. Her nasal passages were totally clogged, forcing her to breathe through her mouth, which was so dry her tongue stuck to her teeth. She felt run over by a truck. What time was it anyway? She squinted at the glowing red numbers on the radio. Six o'clock?

She'd slept all afternoon. No wonder she felt like road kill. Longest afternoon nap she'd had since God made her a mother. Come to think of it, maybe it wasn't God. She seemed to remember blond curls and hot breath and eager hands. It wasn't like Mat to manage a stay with the kids this long. One two-hour stint was usually his limit. Stumbling to the kitchen, she flicked on the light and grabbed a glass from the cabinet. She filled it with water and gulped, experimented with her tongue by running it across the inside of her upper teeth and then the outside. Ah, it slipped along as it should.

What had she been eating that left this taste residue? Refrigerator surprise? She drank another glass of water, then crept into the living room and gently lowered herself to the sofa. Too roughly and she might lose some valuable part of herself. Like her head.

Even though scratched like a road map, the hardwood floor, stained dark, showed every speck of dust, smear of mud, and crumb of whatever the kids had been eating. Dust curls huddled in corners and under the chairs, two wing chairs with frayed brown-and-yellow fabric. They were as shabby as was the Victorian sofa she sat on. Ragged lace curtains hung over windows smeared with sticky fingerprints. The walls had once been painted white, but she'd never gotten around to repainting. Or to adorning them with anything. Maybe she should put up a couple of those ghastly old paintings in the basement. If she cleaned them a little, maybe they wouldn't look too bad. The Christmas tree in the corner brought cheer to the room, colored lights and a lot of the ornaments made by the children, some saved from years back. She wrapped the sofa quilt around her shoulders and waited for Mat to bring back the kids.

Each child had a separate room, but the Littles left papers and crayons and games and puzzles and electronic games and tanks and dolls and action figures and books littered over the living room floor. It looked what's called lived in. Or what Mat called a mess and why don't you clean it up.

Beginning to worry beyond limits, she went to the kitchen and picked up the phone, then couldn't remember the number. Finally it floated through the sludge in her mind and she called her mother-in-law. While she counted rings, she realized the house was pleasantly warm, no longer an inferno and no longer freezing. Good ol' Tim had come through just like he said he would. After eighteen rings, just as she was on the verge of hanging up, the call was answered.

"Ettie, are the kids there?"

"No, dear, they're with their father." As though Caley were some nit who couldn't keep track of her own children.

"They should have been back at three."

"I'm sure they're fine. They're with their father," Ettie repeated, as though that meant safe and sound.

"They were supposed to be home hours ago."

"I'm sure they're having such a good time, they don't want to come home."

"But—"

"I'm dripping all over the rug and my bath is getting cold. Good-bye, dear."

Caley paced the house, yanking at her hair and running her hands through it. Pausing at the ancient mirror in the hallway, she gazed at herself, black circles for eyes, red nose, hair standing on end. *Portrait of a Madwoman.*

At six forty-five the phone rang. She pounced on it.

"Mom?"

"Zach, what's wrong? Where are you?"

"Level off, Mom. We're just about to have a pizza."

"This late? Where's your father? Let me talk to him."

"Uh—he went to order food. Don't worry, Mom, everything's cool."

It was nine forty-five before Mat got them home, Bonnie asleep over his shoulder, Adam stumbling alongside glassy-eyed with fatigue; even Zach was dragging.

Mat said he'd call tomorrow and sped off before she could gather enough wits to form sentences from all those words she'd chewed on while she was waiting, the ones about responsibility and common sense.

"What did you do today?" she asked Bonnie as she peeled clothes off the limp child and pulled on pajamas.

"Everything," Bonnie breathed happily, snuggling into her pillow as she was covered up.

Caley tucked Adam in, made sure the blankets were tight around his shoulders, and kissed his forehead. "Did you have a good time?"

"Grr-rate! We got to shoot Dad's gun. 'Night, Mom."

Gun? She wanted to shake him awake and examine this gun

business. Instead she went to tuck in Zach, who complained repeatedly that he was too old. She did it anyway. It's for me, she always told him.

"Adam said your father has a gun." Try as she might, it sounded like an accusation.

Zach sighed. "Yeah."

"And?"

He sighed again, reluctance in every molecule of expelled air. "Don't go into liftoff, Mom. We went to a shooting gallery. Targets. You know?"

She hung on to all the furious words zinging around in her head. It wasn't Zach's fault his father was an idiot. "Were you any good?"

"Better than Adam. Bonnie was hopeless. She didn't like the noise, even with earmuffs." He waited. "You going to yell at me?"

Caley smiled. "You, no; your father, yes." She kissed him and then went to her bedroom, replaced her clammy clothes with a sweat suit, and dragged her aching bones to bed.

It was a night congested with dreams about Mat and a gun, shooting the shadowy man who had appeared at church, shooting the pharmacist as he handed her medicine that allowed her to breathe, creeping into the house and shooting them all in their beds.

Blood flowing down the basement stairs brought her bursting up, shedding sleep like water. She panted. Oh, boy, she really had to stop watching all those late-night movies. Her throat was so raw she couldn't swallow, her head throbbed, and she was dripping with sweat. How long did this damn flu last? She was startled to realize daylight was seeping in around the window shade.

Bonnie breezed in and announced, "There's an evil prince in the basement."

Caley moaned. Was she up to playing one of Bonnie's games right now? "Who is he?" she asked.

"He kidnapped the princess and hid her away."

"Oh," Caley said. "That wasn't very nice. What happened?"

"You need to do something, Mommy."

"About what?"

"Finding the princess."

"The evil prince will probably tell you if you ask nicely."

"He can't. He's dead." Bonnie went into a complicated story about the good prince, golden horses, and a castle far away. Caley's mind drifted.

"Aren't you going to do something?" Bonnie demanded.

"What were you doing in the basement at— What time is it?"

"I went to get my bear. The black one that Adam took and threw down there. He grabbed, Mommy. Aren't you going to do something?"

"Uh—I'm sure he didn't mean it."

"Not Adam, the evil prince in the basement."

"He'll go away."

"I told you, he can't," Bonnie said. "He's dead."

"Bonnie, love—"

"I saw him. He's dead."

Caley rubbed her forehead with her fingertips. "Sweetie, Mommy really doesn't feel very good right now. Could we play another time?"

"I'll tell Zach," Bonnie said, and skipped off.

Caley heard Zach grumbling, then galumping down the stairs. She closed her eyes.

After a few seconds of silence, a hushed voice floated up. "Mom?"

6

—

"What?" Caley called out before her soggy mind registered something alarming in the word mothers answer automatically a hundred times a day. Mom, where is my other blue sock? Mom, do I have to brush my teeth? Mom, I can't find my library books. Mom, there's a hole in my shirt. This time there was alarm and tension in the word. It was Mom, help me, this is more than I can handle. She snatched the robe lying at the foot of the bed and swirled it around her shoulders as she ran for the basement stairs. "Zach?"

"Down here," he said, his voice reverting to eight years old.

Heart thumping, she padded down the steps.

"Bonnie was right." Zach was standing on the bottom step.

On a step above, she peered over his head. *The evil prince is dead.* She pulled herself together. Loosely. That was as good as it got. The metal furnace panels had been removed and a man lay facedown in a puddle of blood on the cement floor, head and both hands jammed into the furnace.

Her stomach twisted. The room started to dim. Suck it up, Mom!

"Stinks," Zach said.

She took his shoulders and turned him around. "Upstairs. Go."

He turned back. "What if he's not dead?" Zach whispered.

"Turn off the heat," she said, "then call 911. Tell them"—
There's an evil prince in the basement with his head in the furnace—
"there's been a serious accident." She gave his shoulder a gentle
shove.

Oh God, oh God. Careful to avoid the blood—it looked dark
and sticky—she touched the ankles. They were cool and she felt
no give as she closed her hands around them. They didn't feel
human. She pulled gently. He wouldn't move. He must be dead.

Just in case there was some life somewhere, she jerked hard.
The man slid back and there was a squishy clunk as his head hit
the floor. *Aahhh aahhh ah.* She backed away.

His size and shape were like Mat's, but the hair—the small
patch that was unsinged—was different. Wasn't it? Darker. It
couldn't be Mat. Could it? What the hell happened down here in
her basement? Nerves tingled on the back of her neck. She looked
around. Who did this? Could he still be here? She raced up the
stairs, slammed the door shut behind her, and locked it.

"Mom?"

She whirled around. "Oh, Zach. Did you call?"

"Yeah. You okay?"

"I'm fine."

"Why'd you lock the door?"

"Uh—so the Littles wouldn't go down. Where are they?"

"Adam's watching television."

That child's mind was probably permanently damaged from all
the television he'd been allowed lately.

"Bonnie's in her room playing with her stuffed animals."

It seemed a long time but was probably only a few minutes
before she heard a siren. She went to let in the cavalry.

Susan, at her desk, was trying to work a miracle, something along
the order of loaves and fishes. Less than half her personnel were

38

able-bodied. She was trying to cover too many hours with too few people. They were working double shifts, some sick on their feet and covering jobs they didn't know. George was out, Parkhurst was out, Detective Brown was out. Both Sergeant Wily and Sergeant Ross were out. Thank God for Osey. Otherwise only patrol personnel remained. Double shifts or twelve-hour shifts made them all exhausted and more vulnerable to this damn virus. One more officer had called in this morning with a temperature of 103. Would this ever end, oh Lord?

Her plans were put on hold. The first trip back since she'd moved to Hampstead three years ago, and her chances of going didn't look good. Her mother would be upset and her father furious. He'd probably been sharpening his knives since she informed him she was coming, working on his arguments. Damn and blast. She hadn't told either parent of the offer from Chase Reardon. Her father would pressure her to take it, thinking if she were around for that two-year stint, it would be easier to coerce her to stay permanently. Her mother would step in as buffer, to keep them from ripping shreds from each other.

The phone at her elbow rang and she grabbed it. "What!"

"Just got a 911 call from Zach James," Hazel said. "On Hollis Street. Accident, possibly fatal. I thought you'd want to know."

"Sorry I snapped. I was afraid you were going to tell me there'd been another burglary." They'd had a rash of them lately.

"Not yet, but the day is young."

James? James the church organist who was so sick? Something happened to her? "I'm going," she told Hazel.

"I thought you might."

Please, God, don't let Hazel get sick. She was working eighteen-hour or double shifts, holding the place together. She'd worked late last night and was back early this morning. The budget needed looking at. Some money somewhere had to be squeezed out to get her an assistant. Maybe if they gave up toilet paper. Memo: Bring your own, if you expect to use any.

Grabbing her uniform parka, she shrugged it on. When she

stepped out into the parking lot, the cold bit into her lungs and made her gasp. The wind caught her full-force, swept back her hair as though she'd been caught in a hurricane, and flapped the bottom of her parka. Damn wind was always blowing at you, no matter which direction you were headed. She turned her face from its icy edge, trotted to the pickup, and slid in.

Get gas, she reminded herself for the second time. The pickup turned over slowly in protest and finally fired up. She eased out of the lot, so the vehicle wouldn't die before it warmed up. The sun was shining in a pale winter sky, and Hampstead was cheery with seasonal decorations. The downtown area was five blocks long and two blocks wide. Store windows displayed ski scenes with elves sliding down mountains, Bob Cratchit working at his desk, Joseph Mohr quickly scribbling off the words to "Silent Night" before the Christmas Eve service. If she remembered correctly, the organ hadn't worked and the carol was written for guitar.

She turned right on Hollis and went out to the James house. An ambulance, rear doors open, sat in the driveway. Oh, shit.

Patrolman White opened the door for her and dipped his head slightly. "Chief." Mid-twenties, short blond crew cut, and round apple cheeks. He looked more like a Boy Scout than a cop. "In the basement. Osey's done the steps and the railing, so it's okay to go down."

Two paramedics lounged at the kitchen table. One gave her a shake of his head. Definitely not good. On the basement stairs, she looked at the scene. Metal panels removed from the furnace, man facedown in a puddle of blood, arms stretched straight ahead, fingers burned.

Small entrance wound high in the back and slightly to the right. Shot. Accounted for the blood. Small smudge on back of neck. She went down and stepped closer to the body. What she'd thought was a smudge was a tattoo of a spider. Her gaze slowly scanned the basement filled with old furniture, junk, old garden tools, and piled-up boxes.

She stood beside Osey, who, with arms crossed, was waiting

for the medical examiner to arrive and pictures to be taken. The usual mildewy smell of all basements was overridden by the sickly smell of burnt flesh.

"His head and hands were in the furnace," Osey said.

Strange, she thought, that the hands were in the furnace too. The killer must have tried to make him impossible to identify.

Gunny Arendal was crouching on the floor next to a jumbled pile of boxes, taking gulping breaths.

"What's he doing?" she asked.

"Trying to gain enough control to take pictures. You want to make a bet whether he can or not?"

Right now a bet against Gunny's even pulling himself off the floor looked like a sure thing. Gunner Arendal was a civilian, a journalism student at Emerson College, hired to take photos for the PD. His work was excellent, gigantic leaps above what they had been getting from whatever officer was snagged to do it, but he did tend to turn green at the more ghastly subjects. Like severed limbs or decapitation after an automobile accident. She couldn't blame him. A man with his face burned off wasn't something you ran across every day. She assumed the body was a man from the clothing, the general size, and the build. She hoped the poor man had been dead before the flames got to him.

"Doc Fisher's on his way," Osey said. "Riley's outside seeing what he can find."

Riley had no experience in field investigations, but in these perilous times . . . "Pictures, Gunny," she told the kid sitting in a curve, arms around bent legs, forehead resting on his knees.

A slight mention that she would do it if he'd hand her his camera had him pulling himself off the floor and snapping shots. He had to stop now and then to close his eyes and take a few deep breaths.

"The little girl found him," Osey said. "Around seven this morning. Bonnie. She's six."

Susan slipped on a pair of latex gloves so she wouldn't accidentally leave anything foreign at the scene. "Is she upset?"

41

"Doesn't seem to be. She says he was an evil prince. Apparently getting shoved face first in a furnace is rightful punishment for an evil prince. Her mother's pretty shook up, though. I couldn't get much out of her and I didn't want to push it. I was afraid she'd lose it."

"Where is she?"

He pointed up. "First bedroom off the hallway. She's herded all the kids in there and has them scared half to death by the way she's acting."

"Crying, hysterical, what?"

"No, ma'am. Calm, kind of like wood, and very very pale. More like ashen."

Officer White stuck his head around the doorway at the top of the stairs. "Doc Fisher is here."

Owen Fisher, a barrel-chested man with an abundance of white hair and startlingly dark eyebrows, lumbered down the steps.

"What took you so long?" she said.

"I was Christmas shopping with my wife. It's the season, in case it escaped your notice." He stood still and looked long at the body. Most men she knew would be happy to be called away from shopping, but not many would be thrilled to be called away to view a body with its head in a furnace and the acrid smell of burnt flesh in the air. Bodies were Fisher's life. He was happy to be called from anything, even deep sleep, to see a body in any condition, the grislier the better. Simply a greater challenge, as far as he was concerned.

"How long has he been there?" Fisher asked.

"We're waiting for you to tell us," Susan said. "He was found at seven."

"Enough pictures?" Fisher asked.

Susan nodded.

"Let's get him back a ways and turn him."

Owen Fisher and Osey pulled the body farther from the furnace and turned him face up. Fisher whistled softly. Osey turned slightly pale. Even Susan felt a little queasy. She could hear Gunny

42

rapidly swallowing the excess saliva that collects just before vomiting.

"If you contaminate this scene," she said, "you're fired."

He put down the camera and fled.

The dead man's face had been burned to a grotesque blistered mass of something inhuman. Intense hatred or an attempt to keep his identity from being known?

She was horrified by the viciousness of the act and somewhat dismayed at her selfish thought that she couldn't leave town with a homicide on tap. Reardon's job offer would be pushed to the back of her mind.

"Somebody sure didn't like him." Owen opened a black medical bag, got a thermometer, and sliced into the liver to take the body's temperature, peered at the face and pinched the skin on one arm.

"How long has he been dead?" Susan said.

"You always ask."

"Right. Give me a guess. Then you can cart him away and do your chopping."

"Twelve to eighteen hours, I'd say. The temperature down here will have to be factored in."

"How did he die?"

"Well, that's a puzzlement, isn't it? I'd say gunshot right through the heart. Should be easy enough to verify once I get him on the table."

"Gunny?" Susan called.

"Uh—yeah?" Gunner's voice came from the top of the stairs.

"Camcorder."

Gunny clattered down the stairs and did a camcording of the basement. Osey gently eased the wallet from the victim's back pocket, got fingerprints, and then opened it.

"The driver's license says his name is Tim Holiday," Osey said. "Fourteen dollars in bills, twenty-eight cents in change, and one credit card with the same name."

Susan left them to it and went upstairs. In the bedroom, she found Caley leaning back against a stack of pillows, unmoving and, as Osey had said, extremely pale. Bonnie was crying. Adam was watching his mother, warily. Zach was sitting on the edge of the bed methodically kicking the heel of a black and silver western-style boot against the floor.

A jumble of stuffed animals was pushed to the foot of the bed. A cardboard box held a pile of toys with tanks and action figures prominent. Clothes covered the floor. Bookshelves spilled over with books. Pictures of soldiers and spacemen were tacked to the walls.

"I need to talk with you," Susan said to Caley. "In the kitchen."

"I can't leave them."

"They'll be fine. We'll just be in the kitchen."

"No, Mommy." Bonnie threw herself on Caley's lap and wailed. "Don't go."

Caley looked at Susan as though to say, You see.

"They'll be fine," Susan repeated. "I'll make sure of it."

Zach, the twelve-year-old, gave her an accusing look. "You're the police chief," he said.

"Yes."

"Aren't you supposed to see that this kind of stuff doesn't happen?"

While it wasn't exactly logical, she got his point. If a stranger could be killed and mutilated in their basement, how could he trust her to take care of his siblings? Susan didn't know enough about kids to come up with an answer. She went to the kitchen and told the paramedics they were free to move the body as soon as Dr. Fisher gave the word, then called the department.

"Hazel, I need somebody, anybody, over here. Could you find a female officer to stay with three kids while I question the mother?"

In ten minutes Luke Demarco marched—and *marched* was exactly the word—into the kitchen. Oh Lord, Hazel, wasn't there anyone else? Anyone? Demarco was ex-military, tall, dark hair cut short, thin face with a square jaw, broad shoulders tapering to a narrow waist. Lean, mean, and hard. What would he do to three already traumatized kids?

"Follow me," she said, and led him to the bedroom. She told him to watch the children and told Caley to come with her. If Demarco was surprised or annoyed, it didn't appear in his wooden expression.

In the kitchen, Caley blinked like she was just coming out of a spell and looked around. She reached for the empty glass coffee carafe. "Would you like some coffee?"

"I'd like that very much," Susan said as she sat at the table, not because she wanted more caffeine jangling through her bloodstream but to give Caley a familiar task to do. While her hands went through a routine that didn't need thinking about, her nerves could slow and she might loosen her tight control, maybe get her color back to normal.

After the coffee dripped through, Caley pushed a mug of very black liquid across the table and sat down with her hands wrapped around a second mug.

"Tell me about the man in your basement," Susan said.

"Who is he?"

"You don't know?"

"How can I know? I couldn't see his— Is it Tim?"

"Tim?" Susan repeated.

"That's the only name I know. The furnace repairman. It was on his—" Caley vaguely waved her fingers across her chest.

"Tell me about him."

"I don't know anything, except he is—was incompetent. Terrible. He had to come back a second time to get it right. He—" She seemed to remember the man was dead and she should be respectful. "When did he die?"

"We're waiting for Dr. Fisher to do an autopsy. He can tell us more after that. Probably sometime yesterday afternoon."

Caley turned pale again. "You mean he was here, down there, all night?"

"Where were you yesterday?"

"Church." Caley gave her a weak smile. "How's that for an alibi?"

"All day?"

"In the morning. I played for the services."

"Both eight and eleven?"

Caley nodded.

"What did you do between services?"

"Came home to check on the kids. They were fine, waiting for their father to pick them up."

"What time did he pick them up?"

Caley scratched at a hole in the vinyl tablecloth. "How did he die?"

Usually that was the first question asked. "We don't know yet."

"Wasn't it an accident?"

"Dr. Fisher will be able to help."

Caley scratched her hand down her face as though wiping away the vision of a man with his head stuffed in her furnace.

"It's just— He was kind of creepy. Looked like he would drool over books about Ted Bundy."

"What do you mean?"

Oh—he just—" With one finger, Caley smoothed the edges of the hole. "He looked like those pictures you see of psychopaths who killed dozens of people and you wonder why anybody would let them get close enough to— You know."

"You let Tim in."

"Well, I was expecting him. I called to get the furnace fixed and he came. We were freezing." She started to get up. "I have to check on my children."

"They're fine," Susan said. "Officer Demarco is with them."

Caley almost smiled. "I hope he's brave and strong."

"The bravest and the strongest." Susan didn't know about giving three innocent children over to Demarco. Would he terrorize them so much they'd have to tell it to some shrink thirty years from now?

"This man was creepy . . ." Susan prompted.

"Yeah. I thought it was just the way he looked, you know. Like being nearsighted or having brown hair. He just looked—weird. Then there was the snake."

"Snake?" What the hell kind of case was this?

Caley explained, and added, "Black snake, he said. Harmless."

"You had never seen, the children had never seen, this snake in the basement?"

"Never. Believe me, I would have had it removed."

"Would the children have told you about it if they had seen it?"

"Well—"

"What?" Susan said.

"Zach would have told me. The Littles— Adam might have found it interesting to just have it there, so he could study it, and Bonnie . . . she loves everything. Not only furry things, but birds and insects and— She'll barely let me kill a mosquito. If she thought it might be hurt she wouldn't have said a word. She's apt to weave everything into some story in her mind. Fairy tales with spells and wizards and princes and—she might have decided the snake was someone a wizard had cast a spell on. Who knows what she might have thought."

"What time did you get back from the second service?"

"About twelve-thirty."

"Where were the children?"

Caley bristled. "They were with their father."

"His name?"

"You don't believe me? I don't blame you. It's a rare occurrence. Henry James."

"Excuse me?"

"My ex-husband. His name is Henry Matheison James. Affectionately known as Mat." Caley pressed the heels of her hands hard against her temples. "My head is going to explode. Is it all right if I take some Advil?"

Susan nodded. She asked for the name of the company Tim Holiday had worked for and why Caley had called that particular place. "I'll need to talk with the children."

"Not unless I'm there." Caley stared at her, fangs showing, claws extended.

"I'll be very careful," Susan said. "I won't hurt them."

"Not without me." Caley said.

"Of course," Susan said, but only because she had no choice. Children were usually more forthcoming without their parents. With a parent present they said only what they thought the parent would approve of.

All three children were crawling around on the floor in Adam's bedroom, picking up bits of paper or dirt or debris. Caley's eyes widened in amazement. The room that had been in shambles was now perfectly neat, toys all put in boxes and stacked on shelves, clothes neatly arranged in closets, books lined up according to size.

"Hi, Mommy," the little girl said. "We're playing Marine."

"He wants to see nothing but elbows and assholes," Adam said in a voice as deep as he could make it.

Susan looked at Demarco and choked on a laugh. Caley looked at him with awe. He stood at attention, face expressionless. "It gave them something to do while we waited," he said.

Susan asked them if they'd ever seen the repairman anywhere before. At school or ice-skating or the library.

"You mean the evil prince?" Bonnie asked. "He was trying to steal the princess."

"School's out till January," Adam informed her.

Zach seem worried, but Susan thought it was concern about his mother. She'd try to speak with him when he was alone, but on the whole she thought there was nothing any of them could tell her.

Adam had nothing to say, except he thought it was cool to have a dead guy in his basement. Susan felt it was something he was eager to relate to his friends. Bonnie told a convoluted tale about a beautiful princess who lived in a castle and rode a golden horse. One day the evil prince made the horse stumble and he kidnapped the princess. A handsome man with a little girl of his own saved the beautiful princess.

Susan gravely thanked the children, apologized to Caley for any inconvenience, and said she might be back with more questions. She nodded at Demarco to come with her.

From the living room window, Caley watched Chief Wren and the other cop get into separate cars. When they were gone she found Bonnie in her own bedroom.

"Bonnie, did your daddy stay with you all day yesterday?
"Sure."

"The whole time? Even when you were having lunch?"
"Uh-huh."

"And when you were ice-skating?"
"Yeah. Except when he came back here."

Caley took a breath. "Why did he come back here?"
"I forgot my gloves."

"Was that in the afternoon?"
"Sure."

Just about the time the man in the basement was getting himself shot?

7

—

$\mathcal{P}$auline Frankens pulled back one edge of the lace curtain that crisscrossed her front window and made sure that so-called police officer took himself off. Police officer! Look at him, Ollie.

The big longhaired cat, curled up on the sofa, opened one benevolent green eye and gazed at her.

"Does he look like a police officer to you? Looks like a leatherneck to me." Pauline giggled at the awkward feel of the unfamiliar word in her mouth. "Oh dear, do you suppose we're watching too much television, Ollie?"

The cat stretched himself out to his full length, made a quick twist to his other side, and curled up again. He covered his nose with his plumy tail as though he would have no more to do with the subject.

"Well, he's not at all like that sweet Osey Pickett. We would have talked with him, wouldn't we, Ollie? Lord's sake, I went to school with his grandfather. Or was it his great-grandfather? Must have been great-grandfather. Makes no difference, at least we know who Osey is. And a good boy even if he did go and become a cop." Pauline giggled again at using a word she wouldn't say to anyone but Ollie. "I always thought it was because he wanted to wear a uniform and impress the girls. Because, let's face it, Ollie, he isn't the most handsome of boys. Looks kind of like a scarecrow, when you get right down to it. And there he is wearing ordinary clothes again anyway.

"Maybe I should have told that man, Ollie. Do you think I did the wrong thing by not telling him what I saw? It's just that I'm sure there's a simple explanation. I'll discuss it with Ida Ruth. She'll know what to do."

Letting the curtain fall back, Pauline picked up the cat, hugged him under her chin, and listened to him purr. When she placed him back on the afghan put there to protect the sofa from his hairs, he immediately curled up again. She limped to the wooden rocking chair, adjusted the cushions, and sat down. Taking the baby blanket she was knitting from the needlepoint bag at her feet, she peered at it critically.

All the activity at the old Ellendorfer house told her something had happened there again. Maybe she should have let that fierce-looking man in so she could find out what was going on. Except he wouldn't have told her anything.

Silly old fool, jabbering on to yourself. Would it have hurt your pride to let the man in? That's why you didn't. All this talk about leathernecks, just nonsense. Though he did look mean. It was all because her beautiful ceramic figures on the tables and shelves and the pictures across the piano had a little dust. And her lovely crewelwork pieces that gave her so much joy.

God bless this house
All those that dwell therein,
And every guest who comes
Its humble walls within.

She'd been lazy this morning, reading Dickens in bed instead of getting her breakfast and her work done. It had been so long since she'd read him, and her arthritis had been kicking up so bad lately she just hadn't wanted to get up. Now she had to wait to find out anything. "I'm getting slothful. It's a sin, Ollie. Don't let me do that anymore."

Her fingers knitted away as she watched the house across the street. It had a curse on it. "Not that we believe that kind of nonsense, Ollie." Tragedy fell on anyone foolish enough to live in it. Ellendorfer, who built it, hanged himself in the barn. Garage now. Then the Lewises bought it. He disappeared the day after he and his bride moved in and was never seen again. She lived in that big house and grew old all by herself. Until one day they hauled her away completely gaga. After that the Jolmans with all those children. They weren't there very long. The children kept getting hurt or sick and Mr. Jolman broke his leg and Mrs. Jolman ate some bad green beans and then the youngest child got diphtheria and liked to die. After that they moved. They said it just wasn't worth it. Then the Malleys. Just the two of them, there was. Lived in the place perfectly happily for years and folks thought the curse was finally broken until one day he up and shot her dead, then shot himself.

Pauline had tried to tell handsome young Mat James that it wasn't a suitable house for a family. He said he needed a large place and he could afford this one. Pauline had explained it was so cheap because nobody would live there. Caley and the three young ones moved in, but Pauline never saw Mat much. She knew the first time she met him he was one of *those* kind. Handsome doesn't make up for dependable. If she was any judge, and she was one who could tell just by looking, he was worth no more than yesterday's sunshine. She didn't think he even gave that poor girl money to feed and clothe the four of them.

Caley said she could take care of them, she didn't need him, but it must be hard. And such a sweet thing. She was always checking up to make sure Pauline was all right and getting things for her from the supermarket and sending the oldest boy over to help her.

All along, Pauline knew in her bones, something bad would happen and now here it had. She wished she knew what it was.

"Well, we can't sit here all day while work's to be done." She stuck the knitting in the bag and struggled to her feet. "First, we'll have to get rid of this dust and then we'll have to vacuum the carpet."

Ollie slid off the sofa and slunk from the room. He didn't like the vacuum cleaner and sheltered under the bed until it was safely back in the closet.

Susan left Osey in charge of the crime scene and headed back to the office, stopping at Pickett's service station for gas on the way.

"Anything going on?" she asked Hazel, who was eating vegetable soup at the computer.

"Nothing, thank the Lord. Can you watch this for a minute?"

"Sure."

Hazel returned with another bowl of hot soup, which she gave to Susan. "Something besides junk food. The vegetables are from my garden. It'll help keep the flu away."

Susan thanked her and took a sip. Mmm. Good. "Why on earth did you send Demarco to watch three kids?"

"He'd just come in. Looking a little wobbly, but he was here. Why? Did anything happen?"

"He whipped them into shape in no time. I think Caley James wants to hire him as a nanny. Anything from Parkhurst?"

"Not a peep."

"Damn."

"Demarco called to say he covered the entire south side of the street and got nothing. He'll turn in his reports at the end of his shift. There's an old woman directly across the street that he thinks you should see. She wouldn't talk to him."

Susan took the soup to her office and ate while she went through the stacks of folders on her desk.

The phone rang and she picked it up.

"I just thought you'd like to know the mayor's on the way," Hazel said.

Great. "Do you know what he wants?"

"He didn't say."

"I'm out talking to a witness." Susan hung up, slurped the last of the soup, and took off.

Pauline was just rewinding the cord on the vacuum when the door-bell rang.

"Police Ch—" Susan said.

"Of course you are," Pauline said. "Come right in out of the wind."

She was a small plump woman in her eighties with a cloud of white hair, a kind wrinkled face, and pale blue eyes. She wore a lavender sweat suit and striped black and lime green socks. She smiled a welcome.

Demarco probably hadn't used his charm, Susan thought sarcastically.

The room was exceedingly hot. A white afghan with brightly colored granny squares was spread across the sofa and an orange cat was spread across the afghan. It blinked at her. The room was made small by too much furniture. Tables and shelves were crowded with ceramic figures of Victorian girls, flowers, cats, and bunnies. Hanging by the front door was stitchwork that read:

A blessing upon your new home,
A blessing upon your new hearth,
Upon your newly kindled fire.

"My grandmother made that," Pauline said. "I hung that up when I moved in as a young bride sixty years ago. If you don't like cats, just push him off," she added.

The cat tightened its upper lip to reveal long sharp fangs. Susan decided she'd just sit down right here on the other end of the sofa.

"Another tragedy at the Ellendorfer place, I see," Pauline said. "Who died? Not Caley, or one of the children? They're all right, aren't they?"

"They're fine. Why do you think someone died?"

Pauline looked exasperated. "I may be old, young lady. And I may totter, but I still have a brain. I saw the body being put in the ambulance. They aren't completely covered up unless they're no longer breathing."

Susan smiled. "Yes, someone died."

"Who?"

"His name was Tim Holiday. Did you know him?"

Pauline thought a moment, then shook her head. "No. Who is he?"

"He came to repair the furnace."

"Oh, yes, he was there many times. I was beginning to think she was sweet on him. How did he die?"

"He was shot." Susan kept the business with the burned face and hands to herself. "When did you see him?"

"Because it's so painful for me to get around I spend a lot of time right here in this chair." She patted the arm of the rocker. "And I look out the window. You probably think I'm a nosy old lady."

Susan loved nosy old ladies. They saw things nobody else noticed and were a font of information. "Of course not," she said.

Pauline grinned. "Yes, you do, dear, but that's all right, it's true. At this stage in my life I feel it's my right to be nosy. I saw this young man five or six times, maybe more. I didn't count."

"When?"

"Well, let me see. Two nights last week, I mean fairly late, after the lights were out for quite some time. That's why I thought young Caley was seeing him. I said to myself, I hope that ex-husband of hers isn't the jealous type. I know they were divorced, but it's one thing for a man to run away from his wife and another to let some other man have her. Not that I approve of affairs, but things are different now and I don't approve of that ex-husband of hers either. A good man stays with his wife and children and provides for them."

"What nights did you see Tim Holiday?"

"Thursday and Friday for sure."

"Did Mrs. James let him in?"

"I don't know about that. He went in and out the basement door. She's a nice young woman," Pauline said, in case Susan should judge her harshly.

"I agree," Susan said.

"She gave me this outfit." Pauline looked down at her sweatshirt. "She said it was stunning and I did *not* look like a silly old lady. It would be just the thing to keep me warm. She's right about the warm part."

Susan smiled, understanding why Pauline liked Caley James even though Caley might be carrying on with the furnace man. "What other times did you see this man?"

"Saturday afternoon, and I thought, Good, they're no longer being sly about it. Then he came back again Saturday evening."

"What about yesterday?"

Pauline hesitated for the blink of an eyelid. "Sunday afternoon is the day I play bridge, so I wasn't watching between four and seven. Starting at four gives the others time to have Sunday dinner and get it cleared away. Of course, it doesn't matter with me because I no longer have a family to see to. There's just Ollie and me and he doesn't require a full Sunday dinner. Is that when he was killed?"

"Did you see him at all last night?"

Pauline frowned. "Here, you're not thinking she had anything to do with it, are you?"

"We need to check everything," Susan said as though there were some tedious rule she had to follow. She gave Ollie a pat, rose to leave, and thanked Pauline, adding that if she had more questions she'd be back.

As Susan jogged across the street to the James house, she could feel Pauline's eyes on her back.

Pauline turned from the window and frowned at the cat. "Oh for goodness sakes, Ollie, I'm getting so forgetful. I did see something. I was so worried about that sweet Caley I didn't even give it a thought. Do you think I should tell that nice young policewoman?"

Ollie didn't have an opinion.

Pauline shook her head. "I'm sure it was nothing, just the door being opened to let him in, and anyway it was in the afternoon."

Ollie vigorously washed a paw.

"Quite right, it's of no importance. I'll see what Ida Ruth thinks."

Zach answered the door. In his black and silver boots, he was two inches taller than Susan.

"I need to see your mom," she said.

"You were just here," he said. "She's in bed. She's sick."

"I'm sorry, but it's important."

"Zach?" Caley called. "Who is it?"

"Police," he said.

Caley, wrapped in a fleecy robe, came up behind him. Shivering, hair tangled, eyes unfocused.

"Only a few questions," Susan said.

Caley nodded, told Zach to let her in, and padded in stockinged feet to the kitchen. "Coffee?" Caley asked.

"No thanks." Susan sat down at the table.

Caley filled a mug from the carafe and, holding it in both hands, sat at the table. She looked like she wanted to put her head down and go to sleep. She took a sip and looked at Susan, struggling to keep her eyes open. "What now?" she asked wearily, and then went into a coughing fit.

Susan waited until it was over. "How many times was Tim Holiday here?"

"I told you. Twice. And he wouldn't have been here the second time if he'd done it right the first time." She put her elbows on the table and propped her head in her hands.

"Mrs. Frankens said he was here six times or more."

Caley shook her head. "Twice," she insisted. She sneezed and got up to search a shelf for tissues. When she found the box, she sat back down.

"Why would she say that if it weren't true?"

Caley blew her nose. "Mistaken. She's old. Her eyes aren't too good."

"Were you having an affair with Tim Holiday?"

Caley threw the soggy tissue toward the trash basket, missed, and got up to drop it in. She plopped back into the chair and rubbed her eyes. "Did you see the movie *Psycho*?"

Susan nodded.

"Well, I wouldn't any more have had an affair with Tim Whatever than I would with that guy." Snatching another tissue from the box, now on the table, she dabbed at her nose.

"Why would he have been here when no one else was here?"

Caley started to get angry, then let it go, as though it required more energy than it was worth.

Susan threw questions at her and Caley simply let them hang in the air. She stuck with her story that Holiday had been in the house only twice.

Zach came to the kitchen door and glared at Susan. She told Caley to go back to bed, smiled at Zach and said, "I'm afraid you might see a lot of me until this is cleared up."

In the pickup, Susan got out her notebook. Shanky's Furnace and Air Conditioning was located at Tenth and Harvest. She buckled the seat belt and turned the key in the ignition. Caley claimed the victim had been in her house twice and Pauline Frankens said she'd seen him go in at least six times. Somebody was lying, and Susan didn't think it was Pauline.

* * *

Even furnace repair wasn't immune to seasonal decorations. Silvery garland trailed around the door and licentious elves danced across the glass.

A bell tinkled as she went inside. It was dim and cramped, with cluttered shelves of odd-looking things that she assumed were either furnace or air-conditioning parts. The place smelled dusty, as though last summer's air still hung around. In the rear was a Dutch door with the top half open and the bottom half topped by a counter. In the lighted office behind, an overweight man puddled over the edges of the desk chair he sat on. He struggled up, waddled over, and propped himself on the counter. "What can I do for you?"

"Are you Mr. Shanky?"

"Nope. Name's Johnson, Fred Johnson. Bought the place from Shanky when he decided to retire and move to Florida. That'll be twenty-five years come March. Never bothered to change the name. Would have had to change the sign too. It's an old business. Customers like to come back to a place they know."

"How many employees do you have, Mr. Johnson?"

"Got me five. All good men. One of them been up to something I should know about?"

"You had a call on Saturday from Caley James. She wanted someone to fix her furnace."

He consulted a ledger on his desk. "Right as rain. Any problem?"

"Tim Holiday went to fix it. Why did you send him and not someone else?"

Fred scratched his head. "Yeah, I remember. He said she was a friend and she'd be calling and give it to him."

"How did he know she'd call?"

"Can't help you there. Cold as it is, we've been having a lot of calls."

"I need Holiday's address."

Fred closed the ledger, came back to the counter, and rested his arms on it. "You mind telling me what this is all about?"

59

"I'm sorry to tell you, Holiday is dead."

"Goldarn!" Johnson shook his head. "What a terrible thing, and right at Christmas. What happened?"

"His address, Mr. Johnson."

Johnson consulted another ledger and read the address out to her. She jotted it down. "How long has he been working for you?"

"Two months."

"Where had he been before?"

"That I can't tell you right off. Got it filed away with his references."

"Did you check the references?"

"Naw. I know a good man when I see one. A cold winter like we been having, I hired him right up and glad to have him."

"Was he a good worker?"

"One of my best. Never griped about after-hours jobs or weekends. Never wanted time off for this and that."

"Ms. James said he was incompetent."

Johnson looked defensive. "I ain't had no complaints from anybody else. I stand by my work. She got a complaint, she can call me. I'll put it right. Been in this business a long time. Folks around here know me. Just ask anybody, they'll tell you Fred Johnson does the job right." Fred scratched his belly.

"What do you know about Holiday?"

"Well, I can't say that I know much of anything, as a matter of fact."

"I need a list of the people he made repairs for."

"For the whole two months?"

"Every one."

He gave a long-suffering sigh, then laboriously wrote out names and addresses in a spiral notebook, tore the page out, and handed it to her. "You ask 'em. See if I don't stand by my work."

"Who were Holiday's friends?"

"Friends?" Fred looked completely perplexed, as though friends were some odd item that only the peculiar had.

"People he was close to."

"Well, I'll tell you. He never had much to say. Kind of kept to himself like."

Susan thanked him and started to leave.

"You want his post office box number?"

"Sure," she said, wondering what might be in the post office box of a homicide victim who found a snake in a customer's basement.

8

---

*T*he wind was sharp enough to peel the skin off Susan's face as she trudged back to the pickup, parked around the corner. A sparrow pecking at frozen dead grasses cocked its head and peered at her with one shiny black eye.

"Right," she said. "It's all part of the job."

When she got to the shop, Hazel said, "Everything under control."

"What did the mayor want?" Coming in from cold air to warm air made her face tingle.

"He thinks you should ride on one of the floats in the parade on Christmas Eve day."

"You wouldn't be kidding me?"

Hazel grinned, exposing a slightly crooked front tooth. "Not about a thing like that."

"I hope you told him I'm leaving on the twenty-fourth for the first vacation I've taken since I got here."

"I pointed that out to him. He said you couldn't leave with this murder hanging over the town."

Yeah, there was that. It was only the thirteenth. Clear this homicide, wait for the flu epidemic to pass, have stricken cops jumping back to work, and make a decision about Captain Reardon's offer. Piece of cake.

She needed the job offer decision firm in her mind; if she didn't, her father would pounce like a mountain lion and tear her to shreds. If only it weren't limited to two years— She sighed. Ah yes, the if-onlys she had in her life.

At the courthouse, another beautiful old building made from the local limestone, she fought the wind for the heavy door. Once she got it open, the wind blew her inside and slammed it shut behind her. She searched for a judge to sign the warrant and found Judge Hansen was in his chambers reading yesterday's *Hampstead Herald*. She got his signature and set off for the post office at a good clip.

Two overworked employees were handling a long line of people mailing packages. "O Holy Night" came from a speaker somewhere.

When she explained what she needed, the young woman looked at her in dismay. "I was supposed to be off at one."

Everybody, including Susan, looked up at the clock on the wall. Five minutes until two.

"Go." The middle-aged man, thinning hair and a pot belly, gave a long-suffering sigh. "Get yourself all dolled up for your boyfriend."

"Thanks." The young woman planted a kiss on his cheek and danced off.

"Turn that thing off on your way out!"

The radio went silent. "Sorry, folks," he said. "There's rules. I'll get to you as soon as I can. Just be patient."

" 'O Little Town of Bethlehem' and 'Jingle Bells' all day long. It's enough to make you want to smash every colored bulb in town. What was that number?" he asked Susan.

"One three eight."

He looked through files, isolated one, tracked down the key, and showed her a file card. Name Tim Holiday, address 364 Poplar, no phone number listed. Box 138 had an ad for mail order

CDs, another for free cable installation, one for a long-distance phone service, and a brochure for Schneider Monument Company: Special and personalized designs for markers and headstones in granite, marble, or bronze. A man who chose his own headstone before he died?

"When did this come, do you recall?"

"A few days ago. Isn't that just something?" He shook his head. "Hardly any mail ever comes to this one, but he got that. Spooky, huh?"

"Did anyone else get this brochure?"

"Nope."

"Was there ever anything important?"

"Not that I recall. Just junk mail, like you see." He broke off, scratched the balding spot on the back of his head. "Although seems to me there was one letter one time . . ."

She felt a flicker of hope. A letter coming to a post office box that usually just got ads was likely to be noticed at a small-town post office.

"It had a Texas postmark, but no return address."

That didn't help her any that she could see.

Holiday had lived in an apartment above Graham's rare book and sewing machine repair shop. It wasn't open on Mondays, for either books or sewing machines. What kind of man handled both?

When Osey arrived, he handed her the key taken from Holiday's pants pocket. Just as Susan opened the door, Gunny came dashing up, cameras in tow.

"It hasn't been tossed," Osey said. "That's for sure."

At first glance the place looked unlived in, but a closer look showed that the occupier had been scrupulously tidy, owned very little, and lived like a monk. Living room, bedroom, kitchen, and bathroom with an old-fashioned claw-footed bathtub. In the early days of the business downstairs, whatever that had started out as, this space was probably lived in by the proprietor.

Susan pulled on latex gloves and waited for Osey to take prints and Gunny to get pictures.

The front window looked out on the street. She could see a man and woman coming to the shop below, whether to seek out rare books or repair a sewing machine was hard to guess. Finding the place closed, the pair turned around and went back to their car.

"Okay," Gunny said.

She thanked him and told him he could leave. When Osey told her he couldn't think of a single other place that might hold prints, she sent him to search the kitchen while she took the bedroom.

There was a double bed, tightly made up; a four-drawer chest; and a straight-backed chair. The furniture looked like it came with the apartment.

Starting with the bed, she stripped it, checked underneath, and made sure there was nothing attached to the underside of the mattress and springs. There wasn't even any dust under the bed. The chest was nearly empty. Four pairs of socks, jockey shorts ditto, two unmarked handkerchiefs. That was it.

The closet, narrow, with a bar for hanging clothes and a shelf above. The shelf was empty, not even dusty. Two brown work shirts with "Tim" in a patch on the pocket and two pairs of work pants on hangers. Two flannel shirts, one solid blue and one red plaid, two pairs of jeans and a down jacket. One pair of shoes, two pairs of boots, one well worn, the other nearly new.

Who lives like this? Someone hiding—or running.

An artist friend who lived very sparely had once told her, "If you don't need it, it's a burden." Holiday apparently lived by that rule.

The living room had a threadbare brown tweed couch, a matching overstuffed chair, and a small television set, new. Probably the sole item Holiday had bought when he took up residence.

All walls were bare and could use a coat of paint, dingy white being the prevailing color. On the floor at one end of the couch was a cardboard box with a checkbook, box of checks, receipts for paid bills, and two bills waiting to be paid. Rent and telephone. No out-of-local-area calls. The checks were printed with Holiday's name and the P.O. box number. She dumped out the books of checks. Well, now, what have we here? What she had was a bank safe-deposit box key.

There was not a single personal piece of paper. No letters, postcards, receipts for purchases, movie tickets, nothing. Why? Only because she couldn't find them? Who were you, Mr. Holiday, and why were you so secretive?

She went to see if Osey was having better luck. He was leaning against a cabinet as though it was the only thing holding him up. She looked at him closely. Oh, hell. The latest flu victim. Eyes dull, face flushed, sweating, shivering. Damn it.

"Osey, for heaven's sake. Why didn't you tell me you felt like shit?"

"I'm okay."

"The hell you are. What is this, some kind of prairie ethic? Everybody has to be stalwart and soldier on even when they have a fever of a hundred and six?"

He gave her a weak smile. "Something like that. I was fine until a little while ago."

"Can you get yourself home?"

"Yes, ma'am, I reckon I can do that."

"Get your ass in bed. Take Tylenol and drink orange juice and don't let me see your sorry face until it no longer looks diseased."

"Yes, ma'am."

He didn't move. "Well?" she demanded.

"You want me to leave this minute?"

"Exactly."

"Okay, I'll just—"

"Go!"

He left.

Who next, oh Lord? Please not Hazel. If that happens, at least, let George be back. Hazel and George Halpern had been with the department since it was a pup.

The cabinets had some canned goods, a box of crackers, a few dishes that looked as though they'd been picked up from Good Will.

Where did you come from, Mr. Tim Holiday? And why did you come here?

The refrigerator had a six-pack of beer, bottled water, ice cubes, and frozen dinners. Here was a man who kept life simple. Aspirin in the medicine cabinet. Nothing hidden in the toilet tank or any of the light fixtures.

The telephone in the kitchen was working. Pushing redial got her the library.

A stack of Hampstead newspapers lay on the floor by one end of the couch. She picked up each one and shook it, hoping for a receipt, a scribbled note, a grocery coupon, anything. She got more than she'd hoped for. Beneath the last paper was an envelope with two old snapshots. A younger Mat James and a young woman, a different woman in each picture. She turned one over, saw written on the back "121110078." Account number for the safe-deposit box the key belonged to? The second picture had a different number.

She locked up Holiday's apartment with numb fingers. The wind hit her as she stepped out onto the sidewalk. She sat shivering in the pickup waiting for it to warm up.

This block had no residences, only businesses, and most would close at five-thirty or six. It was already four-fifteen and completely dark. With a squad of seasoned investigators, she could get each place checked out, clerks and customers questioned, leads turned up, before memories faded. She didn't even have Osey.

Demarco? She didn't know what he'd done in military intelligence—an oxymoron, surely—or how good he was.

She got Hazel on the radio. "I sent Osey home. He's so sick he can barely stand. Get me Demarco. Have him call me on the cell phone. I'm going to check something at the bank, since it's open till six."

"Okay. Anything else?"

"Do you happen to know who operates the rare book store and sewing machine repair shop on Poplar Street?"

Pause. "No, sorry, but George might know. Can you hold while I try him?"

"Yes."

Minutes went by. Through the windshield, she watched a woman come from the florist's shop sheltering a wrapped bouquet of flowers. A couple went into the restaurant. "Susan?"

"Still here. How is George?"

"His wife says he'll live, even though you couldn't tell it by the way he's carrying on. He says it used to be owned by Mitchell Graham, but he died a few years ago and just recently his grandson sold the business. To a Will Baines."

"I don't suppose he knew where the new owner lives?"

"Out on Falcon Road."

Susan scribbled down the address. "Thanks, Hazel. Anything going on?"

"Not even the mice are stirring."

Hampstead National Bank was a new building on First Street, yellow brick with white trim around the windows. Inside, it had green tweed carpeting and a row of tellers behind bulletproof glass. Even Hampstead had its share of crime. Susan sat on the padded tweed armchair by the desk of the vice president.

Karen O'Maly smiled. "How can I help you?" She was a plump woman with red hair, hazel eyes, and blue slacks slightly too tight.

Susan explained why'd she'd come and showed her the safe-deposit box key.

"He doesn't have one here," Karen said.

"Are you sure?"

Karen smiled, showing the dimples in her cheeks. "Oh, yes.

He has a checking account here, but that's all. No savings, no safe-deposit box."

Susan thanked her and left. Her cell phone rang just as she was getting into the pickup.

"Demarco." Clipped. Military.

"The victim lived above Graham's rare book shop on Poplar Street," she said, just as clipped. "Hit all the businesses in the vicinity and question everybody. Owners, clerks, customers, walkers by. See what they can tell you about Tim Holiday. Get what you can tonight and go back at it tomorrow."

"Yes, ma'am. Anything else?"

"That'll do to start."

She called the Fredericks County Bank, the only other bank in town, and found the safe-deposit box wasn't there, either. Damn it. Was everything about this victim a secret?

Falcon Road ran along above the river. Will Baines's house, wood frame painted dark brown, was tucked neatly into a grove of cottonwood trees.

She parked in the driveway just behind a black minivan and climbed flagstone steps up to the rear door. A burly man in his early forties, black hair, wearing a gray sweatsuit, came to the door. He had a hand-held computer in one hand and didn't at all fit her mental picture.

"Chief Wren," she said, although she thought he knew who she was before she identified herself. "May I come in?"

He looked the type that fled out the back door when cops came knocking at the front.

He led her into a living room with a comfortable-looking couch, a braided rug in front of a stone fireplace, fire blazing, and chairs of the same vintage as the couch. A footstool sat nearby, to prop up cold feet before the fire. No Christmas tree.

Through an archway, she could see a dining room filled with computers. On the oval dining table, on the desks lining the walls, and on the floor. Screen savers flickered. Too bad. She would have liked to know what he had on those computers.

She sat on the footstool and held her hands out to the fire. "Rare books and sewing machines?"

He grinned. "You think computer people can't read?"

She couldn't get a fix on this guy. Cocky, engaging, apparently open. But her cop antenna hummed. He didn't like her here, but he didn't ask what a cop was doing showing up on his front step.

"Do you know anything about sewing machines?"

"Somehow I can't believe you came here to ask me about sewing machines," he said.

She shook her head. "I came about your tenant."

Surprise flashed in his eyes. "What about him?"

"He's dead."

Baines looked startled. "Bummer. What happened? Was it the flu?"

"He was shot. You know anybody who might want to kill him?"

"I don't even know the guy. Never says anything to me. Pays the rent. As far as I know he hasn't torn up the place."

"How long have you known him?"

"I inherited him when I bought the business."

"How long have you been here?"

"A few months."

"What made you choose Hampstead?"

"A friend moved here. I thought I'd give it a try."

"And just decided to buy a business?"

"I've always wanted a bookstore," he said.

Yeah, right, she thought. "Do you own a gun?"

"No. The man was shot?"

"Weren't you curious about your tenant?"

"Not really. As long as he paid the rent and didn't cause trouble, I was satisfied."

"Were there references for him?"

"Surprisingly, yes, since Graham's papers were a mess," he said.

"May I see the references?"

"Sure."

From a metal file cabinet in the dining room, he went through drawers and pulled out a folder. He handed it to her. The label read "Tenant." She opened it and found a single sheet of paper with "References" at the top and three names below.

Johnny Pechkam

Stu Palmer

Caley James

9
—

$\mathcal{G}$randma's here," Bonnie announced, bouncing into Caley's bedroom on Tuesday afternoon. "She brought doughnuts."

Caley liked Mat's mother well enough, but when Ettie moved to Hampstead, Caley's heart had given a clutch. It had turned out okay, and even though she hated to admit it, she didn't know what she'd do for baby-sitting without Ettie. Caley struggled to pull on her coat, then searched for her keys. Damn it, where are the car keys? Oh, here.

Ettie, trim and pert in well-fitting copper-colored pants and sweater with yellow flowers, was in the kitchen putting doughnuts on a plate. She was in her sixties, attractive, slender, with short platinum hair, Mat's blue eyes, and his charming smile. Despite having been divorced herself, she refused to accept Caley's leaving her son. "It'll work out," she always said.

"Hi." Caley stumbled into the kitchen.

"Are you sure you should be going out? You look dreadful, dear. Can't they find someone else?"

"It's a funeral," Caley said.

"Oh, I'm sorry."

"No one I knew. And I'd rather play for a funeral than a wedding any day. I hate weddings."

"Well, my goodness, why?"

"Mostly they just want any appropriate music at a funeral and they leave it up to me. For a wedding, the bride wants something, the bride's mother wants something, the groom's mother wants something. Sometimes the groom wants something. They argue. They fight. They pick awful stuff and have to be gently persuaded to use something else. They pick stuff I never heard of that I have to practice hours to learn and then they change their minds and give me a whole new stack."

"Is it for the evil prince, Mommy?"

"No, darling. It's no one we know."

"The old lady who froze to death on her couch?"

"How do you know about that?"

"Mrs. Frankens. She said no one checked on the poor old soul, and when they did, she was stiff as a Popsicle."

"Well, I don't think it was quite like that. Back around five." She kissed all three kids.

"Your mother is very stubborn sometimes," Ettie said to Zach.

He grinned. "You just have to know how to handle her." Going up the stairs two at a time, he jumped the last two and landed on his toes. He slid open the bedroom window and climbed out onto a tree branch, then climbed across to the tree house. Actually, four boards nailed between two limbs. Dad had been going to build him a tree house. Like most of Dad's promises, this one only got a start, but it was a place where Zach could be by himself and think.

He was so cold, he grabbed the old blanket draped over a limb and wrapped it around himself. Sitting cross-legged on a board, back against a branch, he tried to figure out what his dad was up to. Something. He knew from the way Dad acted all weird and mysterious and being around so much. The gun was a super shocker.

When his butt got numb, he gave up thinking, hung the blanket back over the limb, and went inside for his jacket. Zipping up the red-and-white down jacket, he stuck a knit cap in the pocket, grabbed his ice skates, and shoved them under the jacket. If his grandmother saw them she might mention them to Mom. Mom tended to worry. He ran down the steps and told his grandmother he was going to Sam's to play the new computer game Sam's dad gave him.

"Can I go?" Adam asked.

"No, dumbhead, you're too young."

"What about me?" Bonnie said.

"You're a girl." He didn't mention that Jo would be there too. Bonnie stuck out her tongue.

"Be careful, dear," Ettie said as he headed for the door.

"Back in a few." Trotting along the drive, he pulled the cap over his ears and waved to Mrs. Frankens, sitting in her window.

Boy, did he have a story for Sam and Jo. A dead man in the basement beat anything they ever told. Probably gross out Jo. Zach kicked a stone, picked it up, and slung it underhand at the telephone wire.

How long would his dad be around? All he did was make Mom yell, and he threw around promises about stuff he never did do. It was easier if he just stayed away.

Shit. Zach raced down the street. The air smelled faintly of wood smoke. The sky was pale blue with no clouds and a sun was up there somewhere. He ran the four blocks to Sam's house, on Inverness.

Sam answered the door, coat on, skates in his hand. "What took you so long?"

"You two be careful, now," his mom called.

Zach wondered if all adults were programmed to say that to kids. He promised himself when he grew up, he'd never say it to a single kid. It was dumb. Who wasn't careful?

He and Sam sped along the sidewalk, punching each other on the shoulder.

"You want to do something fun?" Sam pushed Zach's shoulder and shoved him onto the dead grass.

"You wouldn't know something fun if it bit you in the ass."

"Ice-skating."

"Oh. Wow. Sure is a good thing I brought my skates."

"Not at Eagle's Pond, you dumbnuts," Sam said. "Let's go to the river."

"You're a nut cake. That's over two miles."

"Come on." Sam took off running.

Zach had two choices. Let the retard go by himself and fall through the ice or go with him and see he didn't get hurt. With a sigh, Zach took off after him.

Jo ran down the porch stairs to meet them when they stopped at her house. "Where we going?"

"Sam wants us to drown." Zach pounded him on the shoulder.

"What?" Jo asked.

"The river."

"You can't skate there," Jo said in her superior voice. "It isn't totally frozen."

"You can where I'm going." Sam zigzagged around blocks until they reached Orchard Drive, then they followed it all the way out to Lakeview. When they finally got to Falcon Road, even Jo was ready to throw Sam onto an ice floe.

By the time Sam tromped them through trees and led them to a sheltered spot, sort of a cove near the river's edge, Zach was whacked. It was kind of neat, though. They could see houses on Falcon Road above, but if they didn't look up, they could be totally in the country. Just trees and the river with frozen patches. They seemed totally alone, until a car went by on the road above.

Zach had gotten hot scrogging along through all the trees and dead bushes and stuff. He unzipped his coat and stuck his cap in his pocket.

"Isn't this awesome?" Sam said.

"No," Jo said. "The ice is rough and rippled and it hills up where it got frozen over tree roots."

"Yeah! It's going to take maximum power to skate on this."

"You're such a jerk," Zach said. Sam had recently read an old book with the phrase "maximum power" in it, and now everything the jerkhead did, he had to do with maximum power. Zach wondered if he needed a new best friend.

"You know what, Sam? You should go to Brains R Us and pick up a six-pack."

"Let's go home and play Zodiac Plan on the computer," Jo said.

"I came to skate."

Jo looked with distaste at the hard dirt where she would have to sit to put on her skates. "I'm not skating here."

"Sam, this is stupid. Look at it—" Zach's attention was pulled to the road above. A car had driven up and disappeared from sight down a driveway. A silver Lexus. His dad had a silver Lexus. Mom didn't know anything about cars, but Zach did, and he knew how much they cost. Where did Dad get the money?

"I got to do something," he said.

"Where you going?"

"You guys go home; I'll see you later. Take my skates." Zach gave them to Sam and waited until Sam and Jo set off with Sam grumbling. When they were out of sight around a curve, Zach scrambled, climbing and pulling with maximum power on bushes and tree branches to get up to the road. He jogged to the driveway he'd seen the car turn into.

The mailbox, built into a limestone pyramid, said "Will Baines." Through the shrubbery, Zach could see the rear end of the silver car and, just in front, a black minivan. When the driver's door of the Lexus opened, Zach crouched behind the pyramid and stretched his neck to watch his father get out, bulky manila envelope in hand.

The house was wood, painted dark brown. It looked neat, kind of country like. His dad went up a bunch of steps to the porch, rapped on the door, and a guy in a black sweatshirt let him in.

Whatever his dad was doing didn't take long, because pretty soon he came back without the envelope.

"The rest?" A man's voice Zach didn't recognize, heavy with menace.

"I'll get it," Dad said.

"You better. You know what'll happen if you don't."

Dad got in his car, backed out the driveway, then goosed it and took off.

Zach wondered if he dared take a closer look at the minivan. Before he could decide, the big guy in the black sweatshirt trotted down the steps and got in it. Zach watched it leave. Who was this Baines anyway? And why was he threatening Dad?

Before he could chicken out, he went up on the porch and thumbed the doorbell. He heard it pealing away inside. If anybody came to the door, a wife or something, he'd say he was selling magazines to make money for school band uniforms. Nobody wanted to buy magazines. Candy sometimes, if you looked pitiful enough, but not mags. Nobody answered. Cupping his hands around his eyes, he tried to peer through a narrow panel of heavy glass with swirls all through it. By squinting, he could make out an entryway, a long couch, and a big window on the far side. Looked empty.

He followed a path around back to a patio-like thing and a multipaned glass door. With his pulse jumping around, he looked in. Library with shelves of books all the way to the ceiling. Wow! He'd love to get in there and go through them. He saw a fireplace and a long leather couch, coffee table in front. Desk with computer and a stack of computer printout. Right on top of the printout, Dad's manila envelope.

It was so full the sides bulged. What could be in it? Zach itched to get his fingers around it, and without exactly meaning to, he had his hand on the knob and was turning it. The thud in his chest was so loud, he probably wouldn't hear a diesel bearing down on him.

Just a look at the envelope; he wouldn't touch anything else. Just to see what Dad had going with this guy.

One quick glance over his shoulder and he was inside, breathing hard like he'd just run up a mountain. The air was thick and heavy with a faint sweet undersmell, almost like cherry soda.

He moved to the desk and spotted the gun behind the printout. Looked just like the one Dad bought. Had Baines killed the furnace guy? The cherry smell was stronger around the desk. He leaned over and sniffed, then picked up the small paper bag tucked in behind the monitor and unfolded the top. Pipe tobacco. Didn't smell half bad before it was smoked.

He put it back and hefted Dad's envelope. Heavy. The flap was closed and the little metal tabs flat. He bent them up, opened the flap, and looked inside.

Money.

Stacks of it held together with rubber bands. He slipped a thumb and forefinger inside and pulled out a stack. Used fifties. Real? Of course, real, stupid. Where would his dad get counterfeit money? Where would his dad get real money? He pulled out another stack and fanned through it. Why was Dad giving all this money to the Baines guy?

Footsteps crunched on the gravel driveway outside.

Zach stuffed the money back, dropped the envelope, and was out the door, running through shrubs and around debris on the opposite side of the house. He pounded across the road, slid through bushes, and plunged down the slope. Pressing against the frozen dirt, he listened for somebody crashing after him.

Had Baines driven away and then come back on foot? He could be waiting at the top with his gun. Moving carefully so he didn't tumble into the water, Zach made his way along the river's edge, grabbing at bare tree limbs to help himself along. One snapped, sounded like a gunshot. He tried to get as far from the brown house as possible.

Could his breath be seen if Baines watched from the road? He was puffing like a dragon. Finally, he clambered up the bank to the road. A black minivan whipped around the corner and clipped his shoulder as it sped by. He spun, stumbled, and rolled down the bank.

Brakes squealed.

He huddled against the dirt.

"Hey!"

Silence.

"HEY!"

A bulky man in jeans and a KU sweatshirt came down the bank, sliding on his heels. "You stupid or what!"

Zach pulled in air. It wasn't Baines. This guy wasn't as tall or as thick, and he had kind of thin gray hair.

"You coulda' been killed!" His jacket had the same cherry-sweet smell as Baines's office. Probably used the same tobacco.

"Hey, kid, you okay?"

"Yeah."

"Here." The man stuck out a hand.

Zach saw himself dragged up and thrown in the minivan.

"Come on!"

Zach's arm was seized and he was hauled up the bank.

"Don't go running in the road like that."

"No, sir."

With a grunt, the guy got back in his minivan. Black like Baines's, but this one had a sign on the side: "Learn to Fly. Private Lessons. Stop Wishing, Start Flying, Porter Kane," and a phone number.

Zach trudged along the edge of the road. His ears were freezing and he unzipped a pocket to get his cap.

It was gone.

Could he have lost it at Baines's house? It wouldn't matter except it had his name stitched inside.

10

———

Susan flipped through her notes until she found the list of people Holiday had worked for the week before he was killed. Unfolding the map, she jotted down addresses in some sort of order and started off for the nearest, the Wakefield residence.

The house was new, or relatively so, set in an area of similar homes, all built about twenty years ago. White, wood frame with a brick facing and a picket fence.

Christmas lights were draped over a fir tree in front, strung along the eaves and across the top of the garage. Ho ho ho. Her chances of getting home for Christmas were slim to zero, and what was she going to tell Reardon? Hold on to the job while I clear this homicide? She braced herself against the wind, trotted up the walkway, and rang the bell.

"Who is it?" A female voice called.

"Chief Wren."

Silence, then "What do you want?"

"Mrs. Wakefield?"

"Yes."

"I'd like to ask you a few questions."

"What about?"

"Could I come in, Mrs. Wakefield? It's awfully cold out here."

"I'm so sorry." The door opened to reveal a small pretty woman in her thirties, blond, dressed in rose-colored slacks and sweater. Around her shoulders, she had a pink fuzzy robe.

"Please, come in."

Her face was puffy, bruised black and blue, one eye almost swollen shut. She'd been badly beaten. "Mrs. Wakefield—"

"Cindy. Please excuse the way I look. I swear I'm so clumsy sometimes. I tripped over the cat and tumbled all the way down the stairs. Have you ever heard of such a thing?"

Yes. That or a variation thereof. Always from a woman with bruises, broken bones, teeth knocked out.

"It looks worse than it is. Please come in."

The living room smelled of Christmas from the fir tree in the corner with brightly wrapped gifts underneath. A wreath hung over the fireplace and red stockings were tacked to the mantel. Ceramic elves capered over the end tables.

"Please sit down."

Susan sat on the brown plaid couch and Cindy backed up to a matching easy chair at a right angle.

"Who hit you, Mrs. Wakefield?"

"Nobody! Good heavens, I told you I fell. You wouldn't believe how clumsy I am sometimes. It's a wonder I don't break my neck."

That might happen one day. "Was it your husband?"

"Harley? Of course not! He'd never hit me."

Susan had heard that also, scores of times. She made a mental note to check on domestic violence reports and visits to the emergency room.

"Would you like some hot chocolate?" Cindy started for the kitchen. "That's such a cold weather thing, isn't it?"

"Please, don't bother. I want to ask about your furnace."

"Furnace?" Cindy looked confused for a moment, then she was guarded and wary. "What about it?"

She went into a kitchen bright enough to make Susan blink. Wallpaper with bright yellow daisies, floor shiny from recent waxing, cabinets painted a dazzling white.

"You had it repaired lately."

"Yes," Cindy admitted. She took milk from the refrigerator and poured it into a saucepan.

"Who fixed it?"

"Oh, my goodness, you'd have to ask my husband. He takes care of all that."

She was lying. Why lie about a simple thing like that? "Shanky's Furnace?" The kitchen smelled of cloves and cinnamon.

"Maybe. I just don't know."

"Did you know Tim Holiday?"

Cindy turned pale beneath the bruises. The mention of the victim's name frightened her.

"School wasn't in session the day he came here. You were home."

Cindy's hand shook as she spooned cocoa into mugs, and a sprinkle fell on the yellow countertop, looking like freckles.

"You let him in," Susan said, as though she knew exactly what happened.

"Oh, yes, I remember now."

"Was the work satisfactory?"

"Yes, it was. It is. You can feel how warm it is."

Sweltering, in Susan's opinion. It made her feel light-headed. "What does your husband do?"

Cindy didn't say, None of your business. She answered like a nicely brought up young woman. Her husband worked at a supermarket. "I teach English at the high school." She chatted on about her students and how much she loved teaching, but that it really was nice to have a break now and then and how even so, she would be glad to see them when school started again after the new year.

"Tell me about Tim Holiday."

Cindy sloshed milk as she was stirring it, turned off the burner, and poured hot chocolate into the waiting white mugs with little

82

yellow daisies. "I don't know anything about him." She dropped in tiny marshmallows.

Susan gingerly sipped the hot liquid, trying to avoid the melting white marshmallows spreading out into a sweet goo, something she'd stayed away from since the days of roasting them over a camp fire. Cindy claimed to know nothing about Holiday, but the mention of his name had set her nerves jangling like chimes in a Kansas wind. Sweet little schoolteacher kills furnace repairman? Susan might chase that around some more if she could dig up a motive.

The furnace sat in an alcove off the kitchen, and Susan took a look at it. When she left she gave Cindy a card. "If you think of anything, or if you need anything, call me. I can help."

Susan thought she'd have Demarco talk to Mr. Harley Wakefield, lean on him a bit and mention cops don't look kindly on men who beat up their wives. Demarco was enough to scare anybody. Could Holiday have known about the wife beating? Would Harley Wakefield care if he did? Care enough to murder Holiday?

Porter Kane lived in a small pale brick house about six blocks from the Baptist church with Joseph missing from the crèche. The one-story house was located toward the rear of a *huge* lot, a detached garage to one side. A black minivan sat in the driveway, logo on the side about flying instructions. This amount of space in San Francisco would allow you to retire in style and take expensive vacations. Winter-dead grass stretched all the way back. Near the garage were two bare-limbed trees and a floodlight atop a pole. With the wind grabbing her hair, she hustled to the door and knocked.

"Mr. Kane?"

"Yeah?"

He had the look of a man who felt life had broken its promise to him. Burly, in his fifties, just under six feet with muscles gone slack from lack of exercise, thin grayish hair.

"Chief Wren. May I come in?"

The front door opened onto a small entryway that led directly into the living room, which was remarkable only for its lack of a Christmas tree. An easy chair sat within comfortable viewing distance of the television set, the small table by the chair had an ashtray with a pipe resting in it. Dust was thick over all.

"Have a seat," he said.

She sat on one end of the couch. "I need to ask you about Tim Holiday."

"I heard about him." Kane dropped into the easy chair and reached for a pack of cigarettes. "Poor bastard. You catch the son of a bitch who did it?"

"Not yet. Holiday was out to repair your furnace on the sixth."

"Right." He shook out a cigarette and lit it.

"Is it working now?"

"Yeah."

"Holiday repaired it and you've had no further trouble?"

"Nope."

He was wary of her and she didn't know why. Simply didn't like cops? Knew something about Holiday's murder? Wanted her to go because he was busy? Hiding something? All of the above? "Where is the furnace?"

"In the basement."

"I'd like to see it."

"Why you want to do that?"

"Just to be thorough." She had no interest in the furnace. Her interest was in what Holiday had seen when he repaired it.

She thought he was going to refuse, but he led her down to the basement. It was dark and cluttered with boxes of some kind of machinery.

"Light's burnt out," he said. "Haven't got around to changing the bulb."

She dutifully peered through the murk at the furnace while he kept his eye on her. Something behind those boxes he didn't want her to see? She wished she could look through them, but she had no legal right to do so. She thanked him, gave him her card, and told him to call if he thought of anything that might help.

In the pickup, Susan looked up the address of Ida Ruth Dandermadden. The woman lived in a large white house, stone walkway to a porch that went across the front and around the side, with porch swings and lounge chairs.

She rang the doorbell and waited. After what seemed a long wait, a woman dressed in pleated skirt and tailored blouse opened the door. She looked to be in her eighties, with iron-gray hair pulled into a bun at the nape of her neck, a narrow face, and a thin mouth in a firm, disapproving line.

"Mrs. Dandermadden? Police Chief Wren."

"I know who you are." Ida Ruth Dandermadden let Susan inside with the manner of the Lady of the House who would hustle police into the kitchen rather than let them enter the parlor.

Sure enough. Ida Ruth went straight to the rear of the house, bypassing the living room. In the kitchen, she asked Susan to sit down. Susan did. She knew a command when she heard one.

Ida Ruth remained standing, arms crossed over a narrow chest. Obviously the way one questioned the help.

"You had your furnace looked at a few weeks ago," Susan said.

"I did," Ida Ruth said. "Is this about his murder?"

"Do you know anything about the murder?"

"I do not."

"His name was Tim Holiday. Did you know him?"

"No."

Oh dear, Susan thought, this was going to be tiresome. "How many times did you see him?"

"Only the once when he came to see about the furnace."

"Never before or again? Around the neighborhood, at the supermarket?"

Ida Ruth loosened her stiff posture enough to ask if she could get Susan something.

"No, thank you. How was the work he did? Satisfactory? Or did you have to get him back again?"

"Perfectly satisfactory."

Susan asked questions but got nothing for her troubles. "I need to see your furnace," she said.

Ida Ruth looked startled. "Well, if you must. It's this way."

In a dark hallway, she opened a door onto an even darker stairway going down. She reached inside and flipped a switch.

"You'll see it when you go down. If you don't mind, I'll wait here. It's hard for me to get up and down steps these days."

The basement was huge and for the most part empty. There was an old wooden table, some chairs, a lamp, two trunks, a hot water heater, and a gas furnace. Susan dutifully trudged her way over to it. Yep, surely looked like a furnace. If Holiday had done more than fix it, she wouldn't know. She'd love to go through the trunks, but could think up no legal reason to do so. Had Holiday looked inside and found something that Ida Ruth killed him for? What? Skeleton of long-dead husband? Too much television. Had Holiday put something inside one that he didn't want to leave in his apartment? Unlikely. How would he retrieve it?

"Did you find it, dear?" Ida Ruth said impatiently.

Susan thought about pretending to sprain her ankle and taking one quick look in a trunk. She trudged back upstairs, thanked Ida Ruth, and handed her a card. "If you think of anything that might help, give me a call."

Ida Ruth showed her to the door. "Why did she kill him?"

"Who?"

"That James girl. I knew she shouldn't be allowed to play at church. She's divorced," Ida Ruth hissed. "And now look what she's done."

"Why do you think she killed him?" Susan stepped out to the porch.

"I may look like an old woman to you, but Pauline tells me what goes on over there and I know what's what." That said, Ida Ruth firmly closed the door.

11

———

According to the sign, the rare book and sewing machine business was open from ten to six, but when Demarco went in the place was empty. "Hey!"

An elderly man, short, with a thatch of white hair, came from a back room. He looked like a skinny Santa Claus.

"Mr. Baines?"

"I doubt you sew, and you don't look like the kind of man who collects. So what can I do for you?"

"You don't think I can read?" Demarco didn't bother to say he could also sew a rip in a trouser seam if he had to.

The man smiled, squeezing the wrinkles in his face together into a finely woven mat. "Did I jump to conclusions again? Mitch always did say I shouldn't be so quick to judge. He was the one who took care of the book side. When his grandson sold the place, I stayed on to run it for the new owner. Martin Thackeray." He offered a fragile hand. Demarco was careful in shaking it. "I repair sewing machines. Wouldn't know a rare book if it were to sit up and sing to me. You have a sewing machine that needs fixing?"

"No."

"Looking to buy a rare edition of Geert Groote?"

"Never heard of him."

"Me, neither. So what can I do for you?"

"I want to know about your tenant," Demarco said, showing his badge.

"Now, if you had a Singer circa 1926 that you wanted fixed, I'm your man, but to ask about Tim Holiday, that's all I know about him, his name. Mitchell, Jr. rented the space about three months ago. I told him not to be so hasty. Get some references and check them out. What did we know but that the man might be a smoker and burn the place down some night."

"What did you learn?"

Thackeray held out his hands and shrugged. "I don't think Mitchell even asked for any. Too trusting, that man, like his father. You might wonder how they stayed in business all those years. But I must say Holiday was an ideal tenant."

"How often did you see him?"

"I never saw him. Maybe once or twice. And I'll have to say he was quiet. I never heard a thing. No jumping around or loud music. What's this about?"

"The man's dead."

"I heard that. What happened?"

Demarco got what he could from Thackeray, which amounted to nothing. He knew the black-haired female in the chief's role only had him doing this because everybody was sick, but it was good to be back in investigation. He thanked Thackeray and went out.

Six or eight other businesses were on this block. Directly across were the medical offices of Drs. Cunningham and Barrington.

He jogged across the street and entered the building. The receptionist was young and pretty and blond, in a good position to see anybody go in and out of the apartment above the rare book store.

"Officer Demarco," he said. "I'm trying to find out . . ."

"I can't tell you anything about a patient." Her back stiffened with resolve.

"The man who lives above the sewing machine repair place," he said.

She relaxed. Sweet kid, not real bright. She'd just revealed that Holiday wasn't a patient.

"Have you ever seen him?"

She nodded hesitantly. "If you happen to look over and he's coming out or going in, you're bound to see him, you know? He was in here once."

Demarco thought he must be losing it, if he'd been wrong about something so simple. "Was he sick?"

"Not really. He asked if I knew Mat James."

"Do you?"

"I'm not really supposed to talk about that."

James was a patient.

"Otherwise, just going in or out. He was— I don't know. He always seemed so sad."

"Sad? Why do you say that?"

"I don't know. He was kind of a scary-looking guy, really, but something about him just made you think he was really sad. You know? Like he had something really tragic happen in his life."

Haven't we all? Demarco thought. "Who else have you seen going in or out?"

"No one."

"Friends?"

"I wouldn't know about that. I just never saw him with anybody."

"How often did you see him?"

"I don't know. Going in and out. You don't count, you know?"

The phone rang. She picked it up and spoke softly, "Doctors Cunningham and Barrington."

Demarco placed a card on the desk, told her to call if she thought of anything.

Next to the doctors' office was a flower shop. It was warm and steamy inside. Christmas leaped out and grabbed him. Speakers on the walls blared out carols. Cutesy-cutesy, artsy-fartsy Santas and elves and reindeer cavorted and simpered and leered from walls and shelves and displays. Ice skaters skated eternally round and round an artificial pond. Christmas trees in white and blue and pink and silver. Whatever happened to green? Baskets of glass baubles and glittery icicles, garlands of silver and gold, boxes of angels and birds and stars and bells. It was enough to convert you to instant atheism.

"Help you?" A sour-faced female sagging into middle age, with short brown hair and a busy attitude, jabbed lollipops into a large Styrofoam wheel.

"What do you know about Tim Holiday?"

"Who?"

Demarco planted himself at her side and waited until she looked up at him over the tops of her glasses. Obviously, his face didn't please her any more than his voice had. Any little kiddies wandering in here would probably go shrieking out and have nightmares.

"He lives across the street above the sewing machine repair shop."

"What makes you think I know him?"

"Do you?"

"No."

"You ever seen him?"

"Maybe."

"How often?"

"How do I know? I'm busy. So if you'll just go bother somebody else, I'd appreciate it."

He resisted the sweet thought of slapping her around. Cops were discouraged from that. "He's been killed. I'm investigating his death."

"The poor bastard. What was he up to?"

"Why do you think he was up to something?"

She gave him her full attention. "Stands to reason. You're here, aren't you? On the run, was he?"

"What makes you think that?"

She stared at him. "Here you are with your asinine questions. You think I'm so mashed out on Christmas I can't think straight?"

"Was he ever in here?"

"Once. Wanted a bunch of daisies sent to . . ." She stopped mutilating the Styrofoam to think. "Aw, now, who? Oh, yeah. Caley James. Only reason I remember is because he asked questions."

"What kind of questions?"

"Like did I know where she worked and did she work full-time. I told him I deliver flowers, not information. I sent the daisies with a blank card."

"Why blank?"

"Because he didn't put anything on it. Not even his name. Now, if you don't mind, I'm busy." She resumed jabbing lollipops into innocent Styrofoam.

"Merry Christmas," he said on the way out.

In the picture-framing shop, a small tree decorated with colored lights and tiny picture frames sat in the window; silver strands of festivity were draped over the pictures on the walls. He asked about Holiday and learned the young woman who owned the place had never seen him and didn't know anyone lived above the sewing machine place and was that legal? She had space above her shop and could she rent that?

Demarco told her to check with the city.

The waitresses at Spinner's restaurant had seen Holiday a few times. He ordered take-out food, picked it up, paid, and left. He'd been in the bakery and bought doughnuts. He'd never been in the nursery, nor had he partaken of the services of the hair salon.

Irritation itched at Demarco to go back with no information, but that's what it looked like he'd have to do.

He sat in the unmarked, thought a minute, and then fired up the motor. At the department, he sought out Digger, the computer wizard. Digger's office was a small windowless room with rows of overloaded shelves sagging under bulging folders, books, and computer printouts. Computers, printers, copiers, faxes, and machines

Demarco couldn't identify were squeezed together, allowing just enough room for Digger's desk. He could barely be seen over the stacks of paper surrounding him.

"See what you can find out about Tim Holiday."

"I'm busy," Digger said.

He always said that. The only way to get what you wanted was to wait him out. Demarco was good at waiting. He stood by the desk and looked down at Digger until the guy looked up.

"I'll get to it as soon as I finish this stuff I'm working on."

"It's the homicide victim."

Digger slapped the paper he held onto the top of a teetering pile of folders. Demarco waited to see if the whole thing would topple. He wondered if Digger could sort it out if it did.

"You want me to do this now? Look at all this stuff I have to get to."

"Now," Demarco said.

Digger stared at him, then sighed. His fingers played over the keys. A few minutes later, the printer came to life and spewed out papers. Digger handed them to Demarco. "Now, can I get back to work?"

Demarco gave him a distracted thanks as he read.

Well well well, he thought. *Chief* Wren should find this interesting.

12

Zach was used to the cold. Living in Kansas made you used to any kind of weather, and he'd lived here most of his life. He wondered sometimes what it would be like to live in Seattle, where his mom came from. It rained most of the time. Mom missed the rain, and she missed Seattle. When Zach pointed out it rained in Kansas, she said it wasn't the same. In Kansas, the rain came with thunder and lightning and hail and tornadoes, scary stuff. In Seattle, it was sometimes soft, sometimes hard, but seldom thunder and lightning, seldom scary. Zach liked thunderstorms.

He sure could use his cap; his ears were getting numb. Hours had passed since he'd told Sam and Jo to go home. They'd be inside now, warm, having supper probably like nothing had happened. It was completely dark, maybe getting on toward six.

How dangerous was the mess his dad was in? Dangerous enough that he'd bought a gun. Baines had a gun. The dead guy'd been shot. Whose gun? Dad's? Baines's? At least Mom'd been keeping doors and windows locked since the dead guy. Mostly. The Littles weren't very good at remembering. And the house was so old, sometimes windows looked locked and weren't. Maybe they could just pack up and move to Seattle.

Why did he feel so guilty? All he did was sneak into some-body's house. Big deal. The door wasn't even locked.

He trudged up the long driveway. Hey, count the good stuff. It hadn't snowed. The driveway didn't need shoveling. That was good. And weeds weren't growing through the cracks. That was good.

Yeah, right. Those were the only two good things in his life.

He went around back and climbed up to the tree house. Ollie, Mrs. Franken's big orange cat, was sleeping in a corner. "What are you doing here? Don't you know it's warmer in your house? Dumb cat." Zach stroked him and listened to the loud purr. His bedroom window looked locked, but it wasn't. The lock was so old it wouldn't catch. He slid the window up and climbed inside. Unzipping his jacket, he shrugged it off and hung it way back in the closet. After sitting on the bed for an hour or two or ten or ten years, he went downstairs.

Mom, at the stove, looked up from the pot she was stirring. "Zach, what's wrong?"

Probably saw guilt in big red letters on his forehead. "Nothing." He went back upstairs.

"Zach?" His mom came in. "What is it?"

"There's a lot of things to do in this world." He threw out the first dumb thing that came to his mind. "With so many people doing so many different things. I don't know where I want to go. I can't even think of what I want to spend my life doing."

She put an arm around him. What would she do if he told her about Dad and the money?

"You know," she said. "You have an advantage most people don't have."

That confused him. She was lots like a butterfly. Thoughts flitted through her mind and lit this place and that.

"You have, you know." She sounded like she was trying to convince him. "You're smarter and you've grown up quicker than most. Partly it's your father's fault, but a lot of it's mine, I'm sorry to say. I should have been better, a more mature mom. You think things some adults never get around to. What I'm trying to say is, you don't have to know this minute. Where you are right now is— the best thing to do is just be there. Enjoy it as much as you can. I know things aren't easy, but try to let life just unfold for you. What'll happen is things pretty much work out if you let them. You know? If you don't get in their way and you try to think good thoughts when you can and do good things when you can."

Was there some good thing he should do here about Dad and the money that he couldn't think of?

She put both hands on his shoulders and looked into his eyes. "Zach?"

He tried a grin. "You have to think I'm smart; you're my mom."

"What kind of nonsense is that? Everybody thinks you're smart."

A distraction was needed here before she went into cosmic worry.

"I went off and left Sam and Jo all alone on Falcon Road. How smart is that?"

"Where's Falcon Road?"

"Over by the river."

"What were you doing way over there?"

"Looking at the river." And seeing Dad give some guy named Baines a lot of money. Did Baines kill the furnace man? Would he come back here and hurt Mom or the Littles?

"Since Sam has lived here all his life," she said, "and Jo is a pretty bright girl, I expect they have enough sense not to fall in the river. I've made spaghetti. Let's go eat."

13

$\mathscr{R}$oy Dandermadden watched his wife. She was curled up on the couch, her face drawn and weary. He hated to think he'd contributed to her tiredness. She was doing the nine to five while he was free for Christmas break. Well, hell, it wasn't as though he had nothing to do, and he was getting meals together for supper. Not that he was much of a cook, but that meant she didn't need to do it.

He was managing to have time with Jo. Even at eleven, she was already slipping away from him. Mandy, seventeen, was spending all her time with friends and giving him excuses when he wanted her to do something with him.

"I don't see why you don't call her," Lillian said.

Because he didn't think his mother would go for it, that's why. Lillian thought it made sense, and he, honest to God, didn't know what they were going to do otherwise, but . . . He sighed.

"Tired?" Lillian's voice had an edge to it.

Lately, she'd been sharp instead of her usual sweet self. Did she know about Cindy? No, she couldn't. Even if she were to wonder . . . And why would she wonder? They'd been too careful, he and Cindy. Since her husband beat her so awful, Roy hadn't even smiled at her in the supermarket. He wanted to go and rip the skin off Harley, the bastard, but Cindy said it would only make things worse. He tried to get her to go to the police, but she wouldn't. So there they were. Cindy at home with that son of a bitch Harley and him sitting here with Lillian, who sent sharp-edged sarcasm in his direction. Ain't life grand?

Roy rubbed his face. Dishes needed doing. He might as well get to it. Mandy was supposed to, but as soon as supper was over, she'd disappeared into her room. She hadn't used to be that way, only since Lillian started acting like he was a leper. Where was the damn remote? After a long search, he found it under the paper and clicked on the television.

Lillian put down her book. "Have you even called her?"

"Not yet."

"Why not?"

"Lillian—"

"What?"

"She won't go for it," he said.

"She wouldn't give you any money to help her granddaughter go to Stanford? The child has a partial scholarship. All she needs is some help."

That "all she needs" was a mite misleading. It amounted to some thousands.

"The thing is, Lillian, Mom believes in people making their own way. She thinks making it easy for kids is bad for them. It makes them not appreciate what they get." There was a lot more to it, but he didn't think Lillian would care to hear that, either.

"Give her a call, Roy. You're her only child and she has lots of money. It isn't as though that money won't come to you anyway when she passes on."

Even knowing the call was a bad idea, Roy went into the kitchen and picked up the receiver.

"Mom? How you feeling?"

He listened through a long chain of ailments. "Well," he said when she ran down. "The thing is, Mom . . ." He didn't want to do this. He knew she wouldn't go for it. "I needed to ask you about the fall."

"What fall? I didn't fall."

"No, I know you didn't. I mean next August. Mandy's graduating in the spring and going off to college." He hesitated.

"I'm aware of that. You think I don't keep track of my granddaughters? Will you just go ahead and say what it is you want to say and get it over with? The way you go dithering on is as bad as your Aunt Rosie was before she died."

"The thing is we could use some money to send her to college."

There was a cold silence. Roy knew he shouldn't have said anything.

"Roy Dandermadden, you knew when that girl was just a little thing that she was bright as a button and would be ready for college at this very time. You should have been prepared."

"We are. It's just that everything is very expensive and we did have to live along the way—"

"Your daddy Billy Forrester and I worked hard all our lives to provide for you. Now it's your turn to do for yours. I don't believe in handing things on a platter to young people. It's not good for them. They need to work for it, just like your daddy and I did."

Mostly, the money came from Billy Forrester Dandermadden's daddy, but Roy didn't point that out. "I realize that, but—"

"I never did understand why she wanted to go all that far away anyway. California? We have a very fine college right here in Hampstead."

"Stanford is an excellent school, Mom. She's been given an opportunity very few people get."

There was another frosty silence.

"Okay, Mom. I'll see you Tuesday, then."

"Don't be late, darling."

"I won't."

He didn't have to say anything to Lillian when he went back

to the living room. One look at him and she knew. "Your mother said no," Lillian stated.

"I knew she would." He sprawled on the couch and clicked the remote.

"She is the most selfish old woman. After all you do for her. Over there all the time, fixing this and fixing that, and her granddaughter needs—"

"Let it go, Lillian."

"I'm not sure I will. Ida Ruth Dandermadden is a selfish, tight-fisted, mean old woman and she better watch her step or someday she just might get a great big shove."

14

Shortly before eight, Susan went back to the shop to see if there was anything going.

"Hazel, what are you still doing here? Get yourself home! You've got to take care of yourself. Without you I'd have to pack up and leave. Find someone to take over and get some rest."

"Not to worry. There was another burglary. Other than that, it's so quiet I'm sleeping while I sit here."

"Where was the burglary?"

"Quail Creek Road."

"What was taken?"

"Two gold watches, a camera, and cash."

"Please tell me we got something on this bastard."

"Nope." Hazel yawned.

"How long have you been on duty?"

"Eeh, not even twenty-four hours," Hazel said. "An old hen like me doesn't need sleep."

"Sure, desert me. Serve me right for all my sins to be thrown into the lion's den. And if that doesn't make sense, nothing much does these days."

"You might go home yourself. I don't want you sick, either. It'd get really lonely around here. Couple of phone calls came. I put them on your desk."

When Susan got to her office with a mug of coffee, Demarco was waiting.

"Chief," he said in his snide way.

She took a tired breath, a sip of very strong black coffee, sat down, and put her feet up on the corner of the desk. Demarco stood at attention in front of it. She rubbed her temples with thumb and fingertips, wondering if she should say, At ease, Sergeant. Had he been a sergeant? For all she knew he'd been a general in charge of the whole damn Marine Corps. Did Marines have generals? "Sit down," she said.

"I'd rather stand."

She looked at him, took a breath to say Sit or you're fired, and told herself she couldn't afford to lose him. "What did you find?"

He took out his notebook. "Holiday bought groceries at the supermarket. He rarely said anything beyond 'Fine' if he was asked how he was. If he has friends, I haven't found them. All the businesses in that area are closed at night with the exception of the restaurant. Holiday was in there a few times, bought food to take out. Holiday went to the library a lot. Thackeray—the guy who works at the rare book place—saw him there.

"Holiday asked the flower shop woman about Caley James."

"Asked what?"

"Does she work, where does she work, what times does she work? Does she have any friends? Who are they?"

When she was with the San Francisco PD, Susan had worked with officers who didn't like her, who didn't like females in the department, who didn't like females. Demarco seemed full of all three. Her old boss, who started out with the second, slowly came around. In eleven days, she had to let him know her decision about his job offer.

"One other thing," Demarco said.

She waited.

"Nothing turns up on the name Tim Holiday anywhere. Driver's license is fake. Credit cards are fake. He doesn't exist."

"What?" Susan let her boots fall to the floor with a thud. "What have we got here? A killer who doesn't want the victim identified and a victim who doesn't want to be identified?"

"That's what it looks like."

"Can you explain this?"

"No, ma'am, I can't. Witness protection comes to mind, but Digger didn't run into any flags when he was playing with his computer. There just wasn't anything."

"Holiday could have been running," Susan said, and told Demarco about the bare apartment. "Or hiding."

Demarco nodded. "If so, he knew how to set up a fake ID. And why would the perp not want him identified?"

"Both mixed up in some criminal action that, if we learned about it, would lead us to the perpetrator."

"Yes, ma'am. That would indicate something serious enough to risk a murder charge."

She rubbed the ball of her thumb from the bridge of her nose up her forehead. "You got any ideas?"

"Only that Holiday might have been a felon and would have been arrested if we had his name."

"Yeah, but it doesn't explain why his face and hands were burned. Revenge? Hatred?"

"Or," Demarco said, "finding the vic's identity would lead to his partner in crime."

"I've sent the prints Osey got from the apartment to the FBI. Maybe they'll tell us something."

"Maybe," Demarco said. He marched out. She wondered if he marched to bed every night and to the bathroom in the morning. Would Parkhurst ever get back?

Of the three phone messages Hazel had mentioned, two were from the mayor. He wanted Susan to be one of the reindeer on the Santa Claus float in the Christmas parade. Crumpling both, she tossed them at the wastebasket. They fell in. Since she'd been chief, her basket success had gotten a lot better. The third said Ettie Trowbridge wanted to talk with her.

She grabbed her coat, told Hazel she was making one stop and then going home. "You all right until Marilee gets here?"

"Right as rain."

"Would you admit it if you weren't?"

"No," Hazel said with mock horror.

"What is it around here? A sin to get sick?"

"Grievous," Hazel said.

The sky was black velvet with zillions of bright stars looking like part of the Christmas decorations. She shivered as she huddled over the steering wheel, waiting for the pickup to warm enough so it wouldn't die when she drove off.

Dark streets, lighted windows, decorations everywhere, crisp cold air. Small quarter of new moon. Christmas card stuff.

She felt nostalgic and weepy. Good Lord, what was the matter with her?

Stores were open for shoppers who seemed out in droves despite the cold. She hadn't yet done any shopping, which meant parents, a zillion nieces and nephews, and a few old friends to get something for. For the friends, she thought something from Kansas. What that might be, she didn't know. Cow chips, maybe?

She was tired and irritated. This homicide wasn't going anywhere and she'd just learned the victim didn't even have a name.

Ettie Trowbridge, Caley James's mother-in-law, lived in a small neat brick house with white trim and a deep porch across the front. It sat on a wide lot with large houses on either side, making it look only half grown.

Ettie, in her early sixties, was small and slender, her platinum hair cut short and styled in loose curls. She looked perky, dressed for the season in green pants and fleecy red tunic. The house smelled of cinnamon and brown sugar. Recently baked cookies? Nice grandmotherly thing to do, though she didn't look the grandmother type. She looked more the hiking and skiing type. The television was on slightly too loud, but Ettie picked up the remote and clicked it off.

"So nice of you to come," Ettie said. "I'd offer you some coffee, but if I drink it this late it keeps me awake all night. A gracious hostess would offer it anyway and simply not drink it. I will, however, offer herbal tea. Would you like some tea?"

"That would be nice." Susan wondered what Ettie wanted.

"Let me take your coat."

Susan turned it over and followed Ettie into the kitchen.

"I'm worried about Caley." Ettie put water in a teakettle and set it on the stove.

"Worried?"

"She has this nasty flu—and no wonder, as cold as it is. I never realized how cold it got here. How do you stand it?"

Susan smiled. "Where are you from, Mrs. Trowbridge?"

"Texas," she said as though it were on the other side of the world. "And please call me Ettie. How do people survive here?" The teakettle made a discreet little shriek and Ettie poured boiling water into the teapot.

"It doesn't get cold there?"

"Not like this."

"It's usually not this bad, I'm told."

"Oh, yes, I've heard that from everybody. If it's going to be this dreadful, it could at least snow for the children." Ettie poured tea into china cups with pink roses and passed one to Susan, then put chocolate chip cookies still warm from the oven on a plate.

"I make them for the children," Ettie said. "I'm not good at baking, but cookies I can manage."

"How long have you lived here?" Susan broke a chunk from one, the chocolate still gooey, and popped it into her mouth.

"Four or five months. I'm here because of the grandchildren. I had no idea how strongly I'd feel about them."

Why had Ettie wanted to see her? "What do you know about Tim Holiday?"

"Oh dear, is that the poor man who was killed? I just wonder how that will affect the children. Probably give them nightmares."

"How well did you know him?"

"Know him? Goodness me, I never even met the man. I can't imagine a young woman as pretty as you as a police chief. What made you take up this kind of work?"

That couldn't be why you wanted to see me. "What do you know about Holiday?"

"Not a thing. I keep telling Caley she should get out of that dreadful old house. Just look what happened."

"Did she ever mention Holiday to you?"

"No." Ettie sipped tea. "You probably wonder why I asked you to come."

Right.

"This is difficult and I do wonder if I should mention it at all. Did Caley tell you someone is following her?"

"Who?"

"Well, that's just it. She's never sure it's real, or at least that's what she says." Ettie sighed. "I do wonder if it's all in her mind."

"You think she made it up?"

"Well— I love her dearly, but she has a strong imagination and she is awfully scattered."

"Did any of the children ever mention that they were bothered or frightened by someone? Or see anyone around?"

Ettie shook her head. "This is awkward. I hesitate to say anything, but what if it was that—that man who was killed?"

What if, Susan thought. He'd apparently asked about Caley. Maybe he'd been stalking her.

"Oh," Ettie said with exasperation, "Mat needs to get out of that tiny little place he's in and find someplace where they can all be together. Someplace decent."

"I was under the impression they were divorced."

Ettie brushed that aside. "A misunderstanding. They'll sort it out. Mat's in a little financial pinch at the moment, but when he gets it taken care of, they'll be all right."

Susan wondered if Caley thought that.

"I worry about her," Ettie said. "I worry about the children. Sometimes she doesn't have the sense God gave a goose." Ettie sighed. "Maybe it's all just nothing. Her imagination. And, of course, if it was that poor man, the one who was killed, then there's no more problem. Oh, I don't know. I felt I simply had to tell you."

Susan thanked Ettie and took herself back out in the cold.

When she turned into her driveway, she saw she'd forgotten to leave lights on again. The house stood in dark uninviting gloom under the big walnut trees. She drove into the garage, closed the door, and, head down to avoid the wind sandpapering her face, hurried toward the kitchen door.

Before she could get it open, she heard footsteps and turned to face whoever was coming up behind her.

15

$\mathcal{S}$usan?"

"Oh, Jen, you startled me. What are you doing out so late?"

Jennifer Bryant, a twelve-year-old who lived a few houses down, was slated to take care of the cat while Susan was away.

"Does your mother know where you are?" Susan asked. Mrs. Bryant wasn't all that crazy about Susan for complicated reasons.

"Yeah," Jen said. "I only came over to give you some stew and stuff I made."

"Wow, Jen, thanks. You want to come in?"

Jen hesitated. "I guess not. Are you going on your vacation?"

"I hope so. Remains to be seen."

"Someone was here earlier," Jen said.

"Who?"

"Don't know. I saw him come up to the door. I guess he knocked. Anyway, he waited a second or two and then left."

"Was it a male?"

"Pants and jacket. I couldn't really see."

"Big man? Small man? Fair, thin? What?"

"Kind of tall, ski jacket, so I don't know if he was skinny or fat, but I think not fat."

"What time was this?"

"Not too long ago. Maybe an hour."

"Okay. Thanks, Jen." Susan waved as Jen scooted down the driveway and cut across the lawn next door on her way home.

Juggling the stew pot, a paper bag of she knew not what, and a bowl of salad, Susan stuck her key in the lock. Perissa the cat was waiting, yammering about serious neglect and starvation. Right, first things first. She fed the cat before she gathered the mail, then flipped through it as she listened to messages on the answering machine.

Three hang-ups, a call from her father asking when her flight got in, one from an old friend in San Francisco wanting her to call, and one from Fran, who said she'd have to call off their dinner, she felt lousy with this damn flu.

Susan dropped the mail in the office off the living room and picked up the phone. Fran's number got her the answering machine and she left a message of sympathy and reassurances that she would stop by in the next day or so to see if anything was needed.

Since the house was spotless, it must be Tuesday. Mrs. Dorr arrived every Tuesday and cleaned and polished. She'd worked for Susan's husband for years before Susan came and had simply continued showing up after he'd been killed. Every Tuesday she made sure the house was clean.

Unlike Caley's miserable house with all its dirt and clutter, Susan's wasn't falling apart and nothing crunched or made sticking sounds underfoot. No sounds of children playing and arguing, no hustle and bustle of family life. It was quiet and empty. She was all alone in her clean, well-kept-up house.

In the paper bag, she discovered fresh rolls Jen must have gone to a lot of trouble to make. Susan was weary to the bone—head-throbbing, muscle-aching tired. She put the stew in the refrigerator and a roll in the microwave.

When it clicked off, she got a fork, sat at the table, and read the *Herald* while she ate the salad and hot roll. The national weather report said Kansas City was fifteen degrees below zero, wind chill making it minus 30. San Francisco was sixty-two. Where would she rather be? She hauled herself up to bed.

The cat woke her in the morning. Perissa, named after a half sister in the *Faerie Queene*, meant "excess." As a kitten she'd reduced the household to rubble. Much calmer now, she still woke Susan when she thought the day should begin. Poking her nose in Susan's ear even though it was still pitch-black, she purred until Susan stirred.

A shower blasted away the cobwebs and got her tiptoeing into the day. Clothes, and food for the cat, made it official. Another day had begun.

Her first stop at work was the coffee machine, then she checked the reports on her desk. Nothing about the burglar. Nothing about the missing Joseph from the crèche at the Baptist church. Nothing about fingerprints from the FBI. Too soon, she knew, but she'd hoped anyway. Who did she know with the feds?

It took a while before she remembered Morton Stoddart. He'd worked a couple of years for SFPD, then moved on to greater glory. She picked up the phone and, after being transferred from extension to extension, tracked him down at his desk. Where else? He always was a hardworking guy.

"Mort, hi. It's Susan Wren—uh, Donovan."

"No shit? What are you up to?"

"Slogging through crap. You?"

"Same. Trying to clear a few things so I can maybe be with my family on Christmas Day."

"You're married?"

"Boy, are you behind times. Two years now."

"Happy?"

"Beats single. You?"

"Widow." She didn't tell him her marriage only lasted four weeks.

"Hey, I'm sorry. I don't suppose you called to renew old times. What do you want?"

"Never could fool you."

"Hey, I'm a trained agent. We're first-class at this detective stuff. You call to collect on the debt I owe you?"

She told him she was the chief of police in Hampstead, Kansas, and in answer to his questions, she explained where Hampstead was and how large it was, then held the receiver away from her ear until he stopped laughing. "I've got a murder here and the victim is proving slippery to identify. I sent prints . . ."

"Yes?" he said warily.

"Is there any chance you can speed things up?"

"Are you kidding! It's Christmas!"

"Didn't think so. Just thought I'd ask." They spent another minute or so reminiscing about old times before she hung up.

Until she knew who the victim was, she wouldn't likely know who killed him. Leaving the coffee cooling on her desk, she snatched her coat and went out.

The library was new, built with money donated by a philanthropic woman whose parents, grandparents, and on back forever, had lived in Hampstead. It was glass and brick, up to date and efficient, but it didn't have the charm of the old one, which had been cramped, poorly lit, and didn't even have bathrooms.

A group of harried mothers with preschool-age children were trying to interest hyper kids in sitting still and listening to the nice lady reading a story. The kids wanted to run up and down the aisles dumping books on the floor.

Susan went up to the checkout counter and asked the frazzled-looking young woman about Holiday. "I can't help you. I don't know him. Beth is out with the flu. I'm temporary and beginning to think I don't know anything." She sent a black look at two little boys racing past.

"Was that the man who got killed? So sad. And so close to Christmas too. Although"—she leaned closer and whispered fiercely, mouth going from smile to sharp teeth—"I, for one, will be glad when these monsters get back into preschool."

She straightened and resumed her prim smile. "I think maybe he came in to read newspapers."

"What papers?" He had the local *Herald* stacked in his apartment, so he must have read out-of-town papers.

"I don't know. I'm sorry, I really don't. You want me to ask Beth when she gets back?"

"That would be nice."

Susan went back to the department and hung up her coat. She poured out the cold coffee and refilled the mug. With her feet on her desk, she made phone calls to banks in nearby towns, asking about a safe-deposit box in the name of Tim Holiday. Who'd have thought there'd be so many banks in so many little towns? This was the kind of grunt work she usually had flunkies doing. It was a needle-in-a-haystack kind of thing anyway. With everybody sick, everybody was overloaded and this was probably useless.

16

Zach sat in the tree house hugging Ollie. The big orange cat purred in his ear. Ollie was a glutton and a thief. Whenever Bonnie lugged him into the house, he stole anything on the table. Butter was his favorite. If Zach got lonely out here, all he had to do was bring out a cube of butter and Ollie would swarm up the tree and crouch by his knee, eyes slitted, purring like a jet engine.

He squeezed Ollie too tight and the cat made a "mrmr" sound of protest. "It's freezing out here, you retard cat. Why don't you go home where it's warm?"

He saw the black minivan again. Just like the other time, it drove by real slow. What did Baines want? It was like he was watching them. Trying to scare them? Looking for him? Looking for Dad?

Zach was glad now that Chief Wren hadn't been home last night. He'd had this stupid idea of telling her about Baines. Something Sam might have thought up with maximum brain power.

Zach felt hollow. He didn't know what trouble his dad was in, and he didn't want to make it worse. He didn't know what Baines might do to Mom and the Littles. He didn't know if spewing to the cops would make everything worse.

Pushing Ollie aside, he pulled up the hood of his sweatshirt and slithered down the tree. Before leaving the shadows of the trees, he looked for the black minivan, but didn't see it. He cut through three backyards, scaled two fences, and then went out to the sidewalk.

Head down, he jogged along. Whenever a car passed, his shoulders hunched up like they were afraid there was a target painted back there or something. He was sick and tired of the cold. Why couldn't it be warmer? Even snow would be warmer than this.

He needed a plan, some way to take care of this mess.

17

It was perfectly fine for Pastor Mullett to talk about Christian charity and those less fortunate, but Ida Ruth Dandermadden gave a lot of money to the church and just how would he feel about Christian charity if she decided to take her money elsewhere?

Billy Forrester Dandermadden had been a good man, God rest his soul. She had married him in this church and been faithful to him ever after. There were no standards today. Everything going from bad to worse. She wouldn't put up with it. Not for a minute. God's will was God's will and that was that.

None of this saying it's too bad and everybody is doing it. Next thing, we'll have divorced people in the pulpit.

We'll just see about this organist. Ida Ruth knew a few people who thought the way she did, and it was her God-given duty to set things right.

She put down the baby jacket she was knitting for the Elsons' new grandson, went to the kitchen, and looked up a phone number. With force, she punched in the numbers.

"Marsha, it's Ida Ruth. Have you had time to think about what I told you?"

"Of course I've thought about it. You said it was important, but I'm just not sure it's very kind—"

Ida Ruth tapped her foot while Marsha Arendal dithered on. Failing, poor dear.

"—and she does play real nice and she has—"

"Yes, dear, I know she can play the organ. Evan Devereau wouldn't have hired her otherwise, but that doesn't change the fact that it's improper for a divorced woman to be playing for church services."

"But, Ida Ruth, the poor thing has three children. Children need to be fed and have clothes on their backs."

Ida Ruth took in an impatient breath while Marsha went on about nonessentials. When she could stand it no longer, she broke in. "She should have thought of that before she got a divorce. I'll call you again. I need to get ready for my quilting session. You just think about what I can do to that grandson of yours."

"Gunny? But he's a good boy! Why—"

"Just think about what I told you and what could happen if you don't do what I say."

She hung up, tucked her knitting in its bag, and trudged to the bedroom, where she added a strand of pearls to go with her crisp white blouse. It might be only the girls, but Ida Ruth liked to look nice no matter where she went. People had no standards today. Her green shawl, her quilting bag, her knitting bag, her coat, and she was ready.

So cold, so cold. She hugged the coat around her as she made her way to the garage. Was it ever going to warm up?

The car groaned and coughed and shook before the motor finally started with a roar. Must get Roy to take a look at it. While the car warmed up, she worked for fifteen minutes on her knitting. When the time was up, she tucked the knitting away and sedately backed down the drive.

Even after stopping for pastries, hers was the only car at Pauline's when she pulled up in front. The others were late again. Couldn't they understand promptness was important?

She snatched her quilting bag and went up the walk. Tapping on the door, she pushed it open and called out, "Pauline?"

"Here." Pauline Frankens came from the kitchen wiping her hands. "I was just finishing up some dishes."

"I brought the pastries. I didn't want you to stand on that knee. How is it?"

"Oh dear, Ida Ruth, I think it's better. Isn't it irritating getting old? It gets in the way of so much. Next thing we'll be quilting at the old folks home, dribbling onto the fabric."

"That sounds absolutely disgusting."

Pauline went back to the kitchen to finish the dishes. Ida Ruth followed.

"Have they arrested that woman yet?"

"What woman?"

"Don't be obtuse, Pauline. You know very well who I mean."

"No. Why would Caley be arrested?"

"For killing that man."

"Nobody's been arrested as far as I know."

"What are they waiting for?"

"I believe they want to know who did the killing first," Pauline said with exasperation.

"Somebody has to do something about that woman, and I'm not one to shirk my duty." Ida Ruth sniffed.

The doorbell rang and a voice cried out, "Yoo-hoo! We're here."

"Make yourselves comfortable," Pauline called. "I'll be right there." She let the soapy water out of the sink, dried her hands, and collected the dishes of nuts and chocolate candies.

Pauline could see that Ida Ruth was irritated with her, but she was not going to go along with her old friend's getting Caley James removed from playing in church and that was that.

Ida Ruth made it clear how she felt about "that James woman" playing the organ in church. Throughout the entire afternoon, she made it clear.

When the other two left, Ida Ruth helped Pauline straighten up. "Do you need anything before I go?"

"I don't think so, Ida Ruth. Thank you."

"Then I'll let myself out. You sit down and rest that knee of yours."

It got dark so early these days, and Ida Ruth had to admit she was tired. She had loved Billy Forrester every day of her life, and there was never a better man who walked the face of this earth, but she must admit she was just as glad she didn't have to fix his supper when she got home.

In the old days when Billy Forrester was alive, she'd have to come home and fix him a big meal when all she really wanted was a nice bowl of soup and maybe a piece of toast. Being a widow was hard, but it was freeing not to have to answer to anybody.

The back porch light wasn't on. Tsk. Now, she was sure she'd turned it on before she left. Burned out, most likely. She'd have to tell Roy to change it.

Awfully dark. Feeling carefully with her foot, she found the bottom step and groped for the railing. Too many stairs to take easily anymore. When they bought this house, she could run up these steps and think nothing of it.

Maybe it was time to sell and move in with Roy. Holding tightly to the railing, she pulled each foot up to the next step.

Just as she was congratulating herself that she was almost there, she heard a crack. The railing splintered. It gave way. She felt herself falling.

18

Bonnie plopped on the edge of her mother's bed. "Mommy?"

"Mmmm?"

"Mommy!"

"What, darlin'?"

"Don't you think you should get up now?"

Caley rolled onto her side and rubbed her grainy eyes. "What time is it?"

"Five o'clock, and Zach is gone and Adam is watching television again. I told him not to but he is anyway."

Caley wondered why she was still asleep at five o'clock in the afternoon, but it was too much for her. She snaked an arm out from under the bedcovers and circled thumb and forefinger around Bonnie's wrist. Up. Yeah, up. Her head pounded and her face felt hot. She'd had wild dreams of rapists and murderers breaking into the house. Dragging her feet to the side of the bed, she dropped them to the floor.

"Do you need some help, Mommy?" Bonnie took Caley's hands and tugged.

With supreme effort, Caley managed to get herself seated. It did nothing for her aching head. "Where did Zach go?"

"I don't know. He said he'd be back in a really short time and I should have some cereal. Mommy, I don't like Froot Loops. Could we get something else?"

"Sure. Next time I go to the grocery store." If I live that long.

"I made some coffee. Would you like some?"

"No!"

Bonnie's face crumpled.

"Nice of you, honey, but I think I'd like to get up first and drink it in the kitchen." She sat with her elbows on her knees and her hands propping up her head. What did the kitchen look like? Grounds all over, yesterday's coffee spilled, and water splattered from trying to wash the pot.

"You go get your robe on and I'll meet you in the kitchen." She groaned as she rose unsteadily to her feet.

In the kitchen, the ceiling light shined down on the mess. Maybe the only thing to do was move and let whoever came along next deal with it. She stumbled over peeling linoleum and caught herself on the doorframe. Her pounding head didn't appreciate that at all. She poured herself a cup of Bonnie's coffee. Black and thick as paving tar. Bonnie had scooped in about a cup of grounds.

"How is it, Mommy? Do you like it?"

"It's delicious, sweetie. It's just what I needed." She took a gooey sip. "Adam," she yelled, "turn off the television."

"Aw, Mom."

"Now!" Caley gritted her teeth and got up for milk, added a goodly amount to the coffee, and sat back down. "Do you think you could get dressed, Bon? I've got to go to work pretty soon."

Bonnie tipped her head to one side and studied her mother. "You don't look like you should go to work?"

Caley ruffled her daughter's curls. "I don't feel much like it, either, but who'll buy Froot Loops if I don't go to work?"

"Mommy! I told you I don't like Froot Loops."

"Right. I'll try to remember that. See what you can do about getting dressed." Caley got up, swayed a little, and caught herself on the edge of the table.

The doorbell rang. Bonnie skipped off to answer.

"Hi," Susan said. "I need to talk with your mom."

"She's drinking coffee. Would you like some?"

Susan followed the child to the kitchen. Caley James rose and cinched the belt of her robe. "Oh," she said. "Was there something—"

"A couple of questions," Susan said. "I'll try not to take up much of your time. Are the children all right?"

Caley put a protective arm around her daughter. "They're fine. Why shouldn't they be?"

"That was quite a traumatic experience."

Caley's hand tightened on her daughter's shoulder.

Bonnie looked up at her mother. Maybe because her mother squeezed her shoulder so hard.

"Go and get dressed," Caley said.

The little girl trotted off.

Caley looked at Susan, eyes dulled with fever. "What questions? I really need to get ready for work."

"Who looks after the children while you're working?"

"Ettie. Their grandmother."

"I need to hear about the man who's been following you." Susan sat down at the kitchen table, and after a few seconds Caley sat across from her.

"Tell me about this man."

Caley rubbed her eyes and took a gulp of coffee. "How do you know about—" She squeezed her eyes shut, then opened them wide.

"Tell me about him."

Caley drank more coffee. "Not following me. Here. Hanging out. Behind the garage, across the street, around the neighborhood." She rubbed her face. "A shadow. He seemed to be there, but when I looked he'd be gone."

"You only saw him watching your home? Did you report this?"

Caley started to shake her head, then winced. "I didn't think anybody'd believe me. Probably think I was crazy. People around here think I'm crazy enough as it is. And I wondered if he was camped out in the abandoned paper factory."

"What did he look like?"

"What does a shadow look like? Fog?"

"Could it have been Holiday?"

"The repair man? Why would he hover around?"

That was going to be Susan's very next question. "What reason could there be?"

"None. Unless the man was—"

"What? Unless he was what?"

Caley seemed to be trying to shake herself out of a fugue. "Nothing. I was going to say an ax murderer, but that's too scary." She rubbed her eyes, crossed her arms on the table, and rested her head on them.

"I need another look in your basement, but you needn't come. Go ahead and get ready for work."

"I'll come with you," Caley said, tight-lipped.

She went first down the wooden stairs and flipped on the light switch.

With only two bare bulbs to illuminate the entire area under the house, the basement was shadowy and dim.

"What are you looking for?" Caley asked.

"We still haven't found the murder weapon." What Susan was searching for was anything that would tell her what had happened here. She needed an army of searchers to do it right.

What she had was herself. Get on with it. She pulled on a pair of latex gloves and opened the box nearest the furnace. Old clothes, out of style and mildewed. Another box, more old clothes. Another box, old clothes. A little theater group would have a treasure trove down here. She quickly went through the box, not bothering with pockets. Bad police work, but Armageddon could arrive before she finished if she tried for thorough.

There were several boxes of old clothes, some full of dead moths as well. And some with old pictures of people who might have modeled for *American Gothic*. She found a box with no dust.

It held photo albums. She riffled through the top one and saw that some of the pictures had been removed. She hauled the box to the stairs, where Caley, huddled in a bulky sweater, sat on the bottom step. The post she was clutching seemed the only thing holding her up.

After poking around randomly without coming upon anything of any use, she went over to sit down beside Caley. "Where are the missing photos?" She showed her the pages with blank sections.

Caley took in a long breath, as though she were too weary to do it more than once. "I don't know. One of the kids? Bonnie maybe?"

"Would she remove them without permission?"

"She's a good kid," Caley insisted as though Susan had implied otherwise. "So are the boys." Caley looked up at the spiderwebs on the ceiling and pulled in another long shuddering breath. She closed her eyes.

"What were you saying?" she asked after a moment.

"The photo album. Where are the missing pictures?"

"I have no idea." She appeared to be falling asleep.

"How long have they been gone?"

"No idea."

"When did you last see them?"

Caley acted like she'd been drugged. Just when Susan thought she'd better shake her awake, Caley opened her eyes, blinked, and looked around as though trying to figure out where she was.

A long moment went by. "When I put it down here."

"This is where you keep photo albums?"

A weary smile floated across Caley's face. "I'm not very good at putting things where they should go. I've never had a basement before. It seemed a wonderful storage place. Limitless. I could just keep putting stuff down here and still—" With a hand, Caley gestured all around. "Space, space, space everywhere. I didn't know everything would smell of mildew after it had been here ten minutes."

She rubbed her eyes. "I don't think I've seen that particular album before."

"You must have boxed it up," Susan said.

"No. I may seem like a flake to you, but I'm not so far gone that I can't remember stuff. I didn't."

"Who did?"

"Mat, probably. That would be like him. To do something without telling me. He's—" Caley caught herself.

"He's what?"

Caley shrugged. "Doesn't always tell me what he does."

"How did you meet Mat?"

Caley sniffed and rubbed her nose with a shredded tissue. "I thought it was a fairy story come true. Bonnie doesn't come by it out of the air, you know. She gets it from me, all her stuff about fairy tales. I was working for Triple A in Seattle, saving money to go to college. My parents died when I was a baby and I lived with my grandmother. There was no money to send me to school. Then Mat James strolled into my life to get road maps. He was the handsomest, most gorgeous, most beautiful man with the most devastating blue eyes I had ever met."

Caley coughed, a hacking cough. "He'd taken a leave of absence from his job in Kansas City and traveled across the country. In Seattle he bumped into me, and we got married two weeks later."

"You got married after only knowing a man for two weeks?" Susan's voice held no judgment. She'd met a man and married him after two weeks. Four weeks later he was dead.

"Wait till you hear the really dumb part," Caley said. "I went back to Kansas City with him and life started. It wasn't two years before he bumped into another gullible female who gushed over blue eyes and golden curls and dazzling charm. And that was only the beginning. I kept threatening to leave; he kept begging me to stay, promising never again. We had Adam and I threatened to leave. He begged and promised. We had Bonnie, same thing. Six years later, where am I? Ha. Hampstead, Kansas."

"Why *are* you here?"

"Mat was transferred. He bought this house before I even saw it. We all moved in. I finally smartened up when he got into another affair. I threw him out. So far I'm standing firm. This place is so—" Caley put her face between her knees and mumbled to the floor as though reciting words she'd memorized. "It's a great house. A little run-down, is all. It needs a little paint and cleaning, but it's got six bedrooms and a basement for when it's bad outside, and this town is a great place to raise kids. Wait till you see it." She lifted her head. "That's what he told me before I got here and saw this Addams Family house."

"Mat was still with you then?"

"He moved us in and then I found out about the apartment in Kansas City. When I dropped by, a cute little brunette was with him. Don't say it takes me forever to learn something." She rested her cheek against her knees, wilting to the point of dropping over. "Even when he threatened to take Zach away if I went ahead."

"Take him away?"

"Zach's not mine. He was two when I married Mat."

"Where's his mother?"

"She died when he was a baby. Overdose of sleeping pills." Caley started up the stairs.

"Let me help you."

"Thanks, but I think I can make it."

In the living room, Adam was sitting cross-legged in front of the television and Bonnie was singing to a doll while she changed its clothes.

"Hey, you two," Caley said. "Did either of you take snapshots out of this album?"

"I didn't," Adam said without taking his eyes from the television screen.

"It was the evil prince," Bonnie said.

"Why would he do that?" Caley asked.

"Because he wanted the numbers on the back, of course," Bonnie said.

124

19

After calling her boss at the Basslight Music store, who heard the first croaked word and told her to stay home, Caley crawled back to bed and pulled the blankets over her shoulders.

Women were to Mat as air was to lungs. Not long after their marriage, Caley picked up signs that he was getting new air.

When she'd first met him, he claimed she was one of the love-liest women in the world, her hair was the color of dark honey with the sun shining through it, her eyes like finest cognac, her skin like porcelain, and her face like the sculpture of a goddess. When she looked in the mirror she saw chin-length light brown hair, clean and shiny but otherwise left to itself, hazel eyes, and a face without makeup. No goddess that she could see. It made her uneasy and put Mat's credibility to question. It left her feeling one day he'd meet a real goddess.

And he did that very thing.

After those first two years, tokens of other goddesses in the Garden of Eden started showing up. Caley, being the innocent doofus that she was, was too dumb or too unwilling to listen to the inner voice that was both strident and panicky. In the begin-ning there was only the faint odor of perfume. It could be the woman at the coffee shop where he stopped every morning before going to work. Her hand brushed his when she left the check. Or one of the tellers at the bank. They probably had lunch together. He gave her a quick kiss on the cheek. The clerk at the convenience store where he sometimes stopped to pick up the paper before coming home. He gave one of his fellow employees a ride.

It was a long time before one persistent voice came through. Didn't it seem a trifle odd that each and every one of these women wore the same perfume? And so lavishly it made her stink of it?

He'd started getting home later and later. Not something she'd notice in the ordinary stream of their life. He did the usual eight-to-five stint and got home around five-thirty. She didn't get off at the sporting goods store until nine. The first time she'd called and didn't get him she thought nothing, but after a second and third, the game started. Find the golden Easter egg.

None of this was concrete evidence, but her women friends began to look at her with wary eyes and shift knowing glances to each other. They'd been there, and their instincts were better than a bloodhound's at finding the buried body.

The time finally came when Caley believed them. The truth must out. So one day when Mat told her he had to work late, she called in sick to her own job. The owner of the sporting goods store, a man, had his own radar, and it bleeped immediately. He wanted to know what she was so sick with; she didn't sound sick. Cramps, she told him. She started telling him about her periods, the amount of blood and the color, and . . . He didn't stay on the phone to hear the rest.

She sat and thought about transportation. They only had one car. Mat drove it, even though his job was closer. Would she want him to arrive at work all sweaty from pedaling a bicycle? She rode the bicycle.

Her neighbor in the next apartment had said she could borrow his car any time she needed one. She'd never taken him up on the offer for a couple of reasons—number one, he was weird, and number two, she didn't know what he might want in return—but she couldn't see herself pedaling madly in hot pursuit of Mat's red Thunderbird convertible.

So she borrowed the neighbor's old blue Chevy. In shorts and tennis shoes—they were easier to drive in than sandals—and oversized sunglasses, a six-pack of bottled water on the seat beside her, she sweltered in the afternoon heat, keeping an eagle eye on the Thunderbird in the bank lot. She fanned herself with the paperback novel she'd brought. It was too hot to read. Kansas City was bordering on hell, as far as she was concerned.

Seattle wasn't like this. She tried to imagine cooling rain, but wasn't very good at it.

As she waited, and sweated, she'd examined the glove box and found it stuffed with inflammatory pamphlets to overthrow the government that had taken away all our rights. The backseat had books on how to make bombs and destroy bridges. The slogans were "Burn 'em down" and "Blow 'em up." The car, rust spots held together by primer, smelled like dirty socks. The smell and the sun were making her sick.

Bored, she tried to sleep sitting straight up. She didn't want to lean back because the seat back was sticky and she didn't care to find out what made it that way. After forty minutes, just in time to keep her brain from permanent damage, Mat came striding out of the bank, swinging his briefcase, yanking his tie loose to pull off, and unbuttoning his shirt collar. He tossed the tie in the passenger seat of the Thunderbird and took off. Bright red, not hard to follow in the afternoon sun. The dazzle almost blinded her even with dark glasses that kept sliding down her sweaty nose.

He drove south a while, then zigzagged west and came to an apartment building with two floors of apartments and apparently four apartments per floor. She parked on the other side of the street, oozed from the car like a bad spy, and slunk along in the direction he was going.

Mat, intent on seeing his paramour, didn't even look her way.

He trotted eagerly up the stairs to the second floor and rapped softly on the door of the second apartment. He leaned his head close to it.

Maybe he was whispering magic words like "Jack sent me." The door opened and the Other Woman threw her arms around his neck with an octopus grip and pressed her lips plunger-style against his mouth. Her hair, cascading blond curls, swayed with passion.

Mat's arms wormed around her; he walked her backward and kicked the door shut behind them. Well, now, wasn't that sweet? Caley climbed the stairs, albeit slower than Mat had, and checked the number. Two-one-four, with a card that read "Buller, T." Caley was pretty sure the *T* didn't stand for Thomas.

Buller, T. must read children's books. Lined up against the wall were a small cement Snow White and, even smaller, three dwarves. The other four dwarves must not have made it yet. Probably hard for cement dwarves to climb to the second floor. She looked over the railing down to the parking lot at Mat's shiny red Thunderbird.

Picking up Snow White, she hefted it in her hand and wondered if it would bash Mat's head in. As a blunt object, it had a nice feel to it. It's a good deed you're doing, Snow White. She pitched Snow White down at Mat's car. It hit with a satisfying clunk and bounced, leaving an okay dent in the red hood. She picked up a dwarf and studied it. She couldn't actually tell who it was, but it looked like Dopey. They all looked like Dopey. Unless they were all Happy with a Dopey smile. She heaved it.

This time her aim was better. A starlike crack crazed one side of the windshield.

Some guy came barreling out of the apartment below. "Hey! Whattaya think you're doing!"

"Don't worry," Caley yelled. "You're safe."

The door of apartment two-one-four banged open. Mat flew out, pants in hand, otherwise as bare as Adam in the Garden. He saw her, stopped, and stared at her, slack-jawed, goggle-eyed.

He seemed to be having trouble talking; all he could do was

stutter "Ahahahah." She could see his mind kick in and start to spin with explanations while he tried to pick one that he might throw out.

"It's not what it looks like," she said helpfully. "You can explain everything."

He nodded and notched up a syllable to "Uhuhuhuh." The blond, probably Buller, T., came out of the apartment clutching an airy filmy thing around her, blond hair in sexy disarray.

"You know how bad this looks," Caley coached, "but I'm always jumping to conclusions and don't always think."

"Caley—"

She threw a Dopey-Happy, hoping to bash in Mat's head. She hit his shoulder. Dopey landed on his foot, toppled over, and the head broke off.

"My gnomes!" Buller, T. knelt beside the decapitated blunt instrument and cradled both pieces against two large globes that Mat had, no doubt, recently had his hands on.

With Mat on her heels, Caley stomped to the last Dopey-Happy and grabbed it, trotted down the stairs, and smashed a star on the other side of the Thunderbird's windshield.

Mat groveled, begged her forgiveness, swore it would never happen again. She let herself believe him. She turned out to be pregnant, and there was Zach, three years old. He wasn't hers; he belonged to Mat.

Even at the best of times, love and pain were right up there vying for first place.

20

On Thursday morning Susan was working through two poached eggs, a sausage patty, and an English muffin at the Coffee Cup Cafe when Fran Weyland, her friend who owned the travel agency, slid into the booth across from her. "Have you packed yet?" Fran croaked.

"Ha, very funny. Did you tell me a month ago these tickets were nonrefundable? You sound terrible. What are you doing out of bed?"

"I'm better now. I said nonrefundable and it's still true."

"You don't sound better."

"Wait until you hear me tomorrow." Fran had wild dark hair, large hoop earrings, and in honor of the season, had on a bright red sweater with white reindeer. She wore her usual bunch of silver bracelets that jangled when she moved. "You think there's a chance you'll make it?"

"I have ten more days. Miracles have happened in less."

"I'm sorry. Have you told your parents?"

"Does that mean you don't believe in miracles?"

"Correct."

"I haven't told them yet. Did Tim Holiday ever get any tickets from you?"

Fran shook her head, making the hoop earrings swing.

"I don't suppose he repaired your furnace."

"No. But I did see him one day. At least I think it's the person you're talking about. Looked a little like your average serial killer."

"That's the one."

"I was slogging through the campus the other day getting my exercise and he and another guy were arguing. I probably only noticed because he looked spooky and the other guy was gorgeous."

"Description of gorgeous," Susan said, taking out her notebook.

"Blond curls, strong determined chin, straight nose, and a lush mouth with clear-cut, sensuous lips."

"Eye color?" Susan said dryly.

Fran grinned. "I only glanced at him."

"Ever seen him before? Since?"

"No. And I surely would have noticed."

"Do you think he was a college student?"

"Maybe, but he was a little older than your ordinary student."

"What were they arguing about?"

"That I don't know, but Gorgeous was mad. 'Half of it's mine and I need it. If you don't give it to me you'll be sorry!' "

Susan raised an eyebrow.

Fran laughed. "Well, that was the gist of it anyway."

"Give it to me again. Without the histrionics."

"That is what he said. 'Half of it's mine. I need it.' Or maybe 'I want it.' Then, 'We worked on it together.' The spooky guy said, 'I paid for it.' " Fran looked at her watch. "I have to go. I'll talk to you later." She dashed off in a flurry of scarves and a jangle of bracelets.

Susan took a sip of coffee. Okay. It was Christmas vacation. Half the students were off and half the remaining ones were female. That left only twenty-five hundred or so to examine for blond curls and sensuous lips. She finished her cholesterol, paid, and left.

Hazel was already back at work, she noted. Going ever farther afield, Susan plunked a stack of phone books on her desk and started calling banks for a safe-deposit box in Tim Holiday's name. There wasn't even any assurance Holiday had used that name. Who knows what name he might have used? And the bank might be in Hong Kong. She yawned, took a sip of coffee. Would she ever get peons back on the job to do this kind of thing? Work was piling up to high-rise proportions.

Before she could get started, her phone buzzed and Hazel told her that Beth had called to say she was back to work at the library though she still sounded hoarse.

Susan punched in the library number. "Chief Wren, Beth. I'm glad you're feeling better."

"Well, at least I'm on my feet. Abby said you were here the other day. Is there something I can help you with?"

"Tim Holiday," Susan said. "The dead man, yes, do you remember him?"

"Sure, he came in to read newspapers. Not local papers, but Dallas, Texas."

"What interested him about Dallas, I wonder?"

"He wanted papers from twelve years back."

That surprised her. Twelve years? "Do you remember the dates he wanted?"

"Sure do. Starting with December twenty-fifth and for some days after that. I don't remember how many exactly."

"Can you get me the same ones?"

"Well sure. Microfilm, actually, but it took a while before it got here."

"Do the best you can."

"I'll give you a call when I've got it, okay?"

"Yes. Thanks, Beth."

After a thought for twelve-year-old Dallas newspapers, she got back to the business at hand and made five calls.

On her sixth call, the voice on the other end said, one moment, please, and came back slightly longer than one moment later. "Who did you say this was?"

"Chief Wren in Hampstead."

Muffled voices in the background, then, "Yes, ma'am, we have a box under that name."

She was so startled she choked on a gulp of coffee. After a moment for recovery, she said, "I'll be there this afternoon."

The phone rang as soon as she put it down.

"Bad news," Hazel said. "Another tragedy."

133

21

Paramedics, patient strapped to the gurney, raced down the driveway, one squeezing an air bag. Susan was relieved to see that it wasn't another death. At least not yet. She stepped aside to let them get past and joined Demarco, standing by the garage, waiting for Gunny to finish taking pictures.

"What's going on?"

Demarco, uniform coat collar turned up, stood with his fingertips in his back pockets, looking impervious to the cold. A solid oak in a strong wind. "White female, aged eighty-three. Found lying on the cement walkway below the stairs. Railing down as though she'd put her weight on it and it gave."

"You think it was something different?"

"It gave, all right, but the brackets anchoring it were loosened. You can see the scratches. She fell, was unable to get help, and lay there all night."

Shivering, Susan jammed her gloved hands into her pockets.

"Her son tried to call twice last night, and when he still got no answer this morning, he came to check on her. He took one look at her lying on the cement and thought she was dead. The paramedics thought different."

Gunny, who was getting a lot of experience this cold winter, didn't look green this morning. Porch railings were a lot less messy than a corpse with the face burned away. "Where's her son?"

"His name's Roy. He's inside, waiting for you."

Roy Dandermadden, slumped on the Victorian sofa in the living room, stared down at the carpet as though memorizing the pattern of roses and leaves.

"Mr. Dandermadden?"

He started to get up.

"Please, sit."

He sat straight, hands clenched on his knees.

She tried an easy chair and found it so comfortable she had to slide to the edge to keep from falling asleep. "What times did you call your mother last night?"

He rubbed a hand down his face. "Uh—I'm not sure—eight and eight-thirty, maybe. Yeah. I think so. I didn't call again because it was getting late and I thought she'd be in bed. It's hard for her to get up and down anymore, you know? I want her to get a phone by the bed, but she feels it's an unnecessary expense. This morning when she didn't answer, I got to worrying, you know? She isn't as young as she used to be. Though she'd be all over me if she heard me say that." He gave Susan a thin smile.

"Did she have any physical problems? High blood pressure? Dizziness?"

"Well, high blood pressure, for sure. It runs in the family." He slightly loosened his clenched fists.

"Some arthritis," he said. "Makes it a little hard for her to get around, but nothing that keeps her in or anything like that. Can't this wait? I need to get to the hospital."

"Why did you call last night?"

"Uh, well, uh—I thought I'd better check and see if everything was all right. Why the hell didn't I come last night? She lay there all night." His eyes got watery. "If I'd checked up on her more— come over and—"

"Are you the only son?"

135

"Yeah. Only one period." He stared at the Christmas tree by the large front window. "Jo put it up. So she'd—" He stopped.

"Jo?"

"My daughter. Eleven. Smart as a whip and loves her grandmother. Mom didn't want a tree this year. Too much bother. So Jo— That's the way she is. Always doing for her grandmother and—" He broke off as though he'd forgotten what he was going to say.

"Do you have other children?"

"Mandy. She's seventeen. Going away to college in the fall. She loves Mom too, but she has so many things going, she doesn't get here as often as Jo."

"How well does Ida Ruth get along with your wife?"

"Lillian loves her," he said, quickly and a shade defensively.

"They had their frictions," he admitted. "I guess all mothers do with daughters-in-law. It's just they didn't see eye-to-eye on everything."

"Like what?"

"Oh—" He suddenly focused, worried she'd get to—what? Susan wished she knew. Something about his wife and Ida Ruth. Had they had a fight?

"Nothing specific," he said. "Just where things should go in the kitchen. Over the counter, under the counter. Things like that." He took in a breath with a soft sob. "Is there anything else? I need to go tell Lillian. She's at work, but—"

"Where does she work?"

"At Sanders and Son. The attorneys. She's a secretary. Been there for years."

"Do you know what your mother did yesterday?"

"I don't know. I'm sorry. I should— Why?"

"I wondered if she'd felt ill yesterday, maybe coming down with the flu that's going around."

He shook his head. "Pauline might know. They've been friends forever. Have their quilting bee every Wednesday afternoon. Both born in Hampstead, went away for years, then came back to stay.

It's a good place. Mother loves it. She has her cronies and she's important in the church. Always doing things. I need to go," he said.

"Has she had any arguments with anyone lately? Irritated anyone?"

A weary smile. "I wouldn't be surprised. She isn't the easiest person to get along with. She likes things her way, and no changing her mind once she's decided. Firm as a rock." He said this as though it were an endearing quality.

His eyes watered and he moved toward the door.

Susan let him leave, saying she'd talk with him again. Indeed she would. Something was going on under the surface that she intended to get to.

After making a few notes, she went outside through the kitchen door. Demarco was poking through the frozen stretch of ground along the side of the garage.

"Find anything?"

"Probably nothing pertinent." He held up plastic bags with cigarette butts, an old comb, and a pencil stub.

"Let's get going on the house-to-house," she said. "You take this block. I'll do the one behind."

Many neighbors were already out watching the activities. Demarco got names. Head down against the wind, she walked around the block. The lots were large and the houses well insulated. Which explained why Ida Ruth had been unable to make herself heard when she fell.

At the house directly behind she pressed the doorbell and identified herself to the middle-aged woman who answered.

"Oh, my goodness. My name's Rita Short. Please come in. What is it? Who's been hurt?"

"Your neighbor, Ida Ruth."

"Oh no, oh no. Please come in." Rita fussed around, straightening the afghan on the couch and lining up the magazines on the coffee table.

"Here," Rita said. "This chair is comfortable. Can I get you some coffee?"

"Thank you, no."

"It's already made, no trouble at all."

"Really," Susan persisted. "No."

"Well, if you're sure." Rita sounded disappointed. "Is she all right? Oh, my. It's been so cold, I try not to go out unless I absolutely have to."

Rita sat on the bench of the old upright piano that had pictures covering the top. On the wall beside it was a piece of stitchery that read,

> Hail, Guardian angels of the house,
> Come to our aid,
> Share with us our work and play.

"What happened?"

"She fell on the rear porch stairs."

"Oh, no. How badly is she hurt?"

"She's been taken to the hospital."

"I should have been checking on her. Oh, no. I'm not a good neighbor. She's not as young as she used to be and with this weather we should all be keeping an eye on each other."

"Is she a friend?" Susan asked.

"Well, not exactly, but we've lived here for twenty-five years, and she's been here all that time and then some. She isn't exactly a person you get close to. Although a perfectly good woman, I have to say. But she does have her own opinions, if you know what I mean."

"Like what?"

"Oh, she gets very upset when my grandchildren play in my yard and make noise. Children do, you know. And she doesn't like it at all that the new organist at the church is divorced. She plays beautifully. When my husband's mother passed away, the young woman played at the funeral. Ida Ruth is—well, she's sort of old-fashioned, I guess you might say. A divorce is really a sad thing, but I have to admit my own daughter is divorced. Does that mean she can't go to church?"

"Have you ever seen Caley James at Ida Ruth's house?"

"Well now, let me see. You know, I don't believe I have. But you can't really see much for the trees."

"Did you see anything last night?"

"No, that I didn't."

"Hear anything?"

"Oh dear, did she call for help? I'm just the least littlest bit deaf, and if I have the television on sometimes I don't hear anything else. I didn't even know all the commotion was going on over there until Dora called just now. She's right next door. She said there was an ambulance and police and everything."

"What time did you go to bed last night?"

"Ten o'clock, like always. Was it after ten that she fell? Poor soul. What happened?"

"Apparently, the railing on her back steps broke."

"Oh, my dear Lord." She put fingertips against her mouth. "She wasn't outside all night long in this cold? Ida Ruth isn't exactly a kind person, but I wouldn't wish that on anybody."

Susan escaped after a few more exclamations and went to the next house. No better luck there. People stayed in with the windows shut.

She didn't get anything until she got to Myrna Cleary. Middle-aged and overweight, Myrna wheezed when she opened the door. She hadn't seen anything or heard anything. "Poor Ida Ruth."

"How does she get along with her son?"

"He's awfully good to her. I see him over there all the time working on things."

And maybe loosening a stair railing while he's at it?

"Nobody gets along very well with Ida Ruth. She just isn't a getting-along-with kind of person. And she does try to run his life, I expect. When somebody is telling you what to do all the time, you're not just eager to be with them day after day, are you?"

"Did they have a quarrel?"

"Not that I know of. And I know he does come over to take her shopping and the like. Takes care of the house. Cleans the gutters and does the painting and such."

"Did you ever see Tim Holiday over there?"

"The one got hisself killed at Caley's house?"

"Yes," Susan said.

"Didn't know him at all. Don't think I've ever seen him."

"He wasn't ever here to repair your furnace?"

"No. It's been working along just fine, thank the Lord. But there was a boy a few days ago."

"What age?"

"Oh me, I didn't see him, not to take a good look at. Just a boy. He was in the backyard is how I came to notice him. Ida Ruth only has the two granddaughters, you see."

"What did this boy look like?"

"Well—" She thought. "Tall boy. He was wearing a red-and-white jacket, one of those puffy ones that all the kids are wearing these days."

"Down," Susan said. "Was he slender?"

"Hard to tell, isn't it? But I would think so." She screwed her eyes shut. "Blue jeans, I believe."

"Hair color?"

"Blond hair. Light-colored, anyway. That's about all I can tell you. Oh, except he had on cowboy boots. Black and silver, they were."

Twelve-year-old Zach James was tall, and he had a red-and-white ski jacket. He also had a pair of black-and-silver boots.

22

*U*sing the radio in the pickup, Susan checked in with Hazel. "Anything that needs my immediate attention?"

"Nope. But we had another one."

"Burglary?"

"You got it."

"Damn it!" Susan took three deep breaths. "Okay, keep White on it. I'm going to the hospital to see how Ida Ruth Dandermadden is doing and then I'm going to Woodsonville."

The hospital doors whooshed open as she trotted up. She headed for the elevators and Ida Ruth in the ICU.

A nurse was straightening the sheets and checking lines to various machines.

"How is she?" Susan asked.

The frail old woman in the bed looked as though her skin were paper thin on a face with high cheekbones and a prominent nose. Her hands, resting on the top of the white sheet, looked like gray talons. A breath rasped through her throat, then nothing, then another breath. Her chest, bony under the sheet, barely moved.

The nurse, a young woman wearing a short-sleeved yellow shirt and white pants, motioned Susan outside. She had short brown hair, bangs cut straight across, a turned-up nose, and a no-nonsense manner. The pin on her shirt pocket said Amy. "She's not good. Broken hip. Pneumonia. And a stroke. That's why she can't speak much. Her son hired me to make sure she gets everything she needs. I think after she dies he doesn't want to feel like he didn't do everything he could."

"Has she said anything?"

"Nothing that makes sense."

"Like what?"

" 'You there.' She's said that several times."

"Was she talking to you?"

"No. She might not even know that I'm here. She probably wouldn't like it if she did, poor lady. Her son told me when he hired me she wasn't the easiest person to get along with." Amy smiled. "I told him I could handle her. I'm used to all kinds."

Susan believed it. The arms under her short-sleeved shirt had a lot of muscle.

"She said, 'Boy. You, boy,' a couple of times. I can't make out much. 'No' a time or two. And 'Wait.' Like she was telling someone to wait for something, you know?"

"She's unconscious?" Susan said.

"You can't ask questions and get answers, if that's what you mean. What she can hear—" Amy shrugged. "That's another thing."

Susan hadn't expected anything different. Still, it would have been nice to have Ida Ruth explain what all her mumbles had been about.

Susan thanked Amy and headed back out to the parking lot.

Woodsonville was a small farming community with a population of 425, according to the rusted sign on the edge of town. Water tower, city park with deserted playground equipment, and a downtown section five businesses long. She had no trouble finding the bank, brick and stone with two large rectangular windows across the front.

The county sheriff with a warrant, Susan, a bank official, and someone from Internal Revenue all crowded into the vault area. Susan handed over the key she'd found in Holiday's apartment and the bank official slipped it into the lock. He had some trouble getting it open, but finally managed and pulled out the box. He placed it on a table.

With everyone watching, Susan opened the safe-deposit box. Inside, there was a Texas driver's license in the name of Fredrick Joyce with an address in Dallas, two credit cards with the same name, an Oklahoma driver's license with the name William Forbes, five thousand dollars in twenties and fifties, and some papers for accounts in the Cayman Islands. The bank official added up the amounts and whistled. He showed the number to Susan. Three million dollars.

Neither Fredrick Joyce nor William Forbes was poor. When she got back to the department, she asked Hazel to send a copy of the prints from Holiday's apartment to the Texas Department of Justice and to whatever the same thing was called in Oklahoma.

23

$\mathcal{S}$usan threw off muffler and coat, sat at her desk, and pried the lid from the coffee. Steam rose. She took a sip. Hot, not exciting. One of these days she'd make a pot of Peet's coffee, fix some bacon and eggs, and share all that wonderful cholesterol with Perissa.

Her phone buzzed and she picked it up. "The mayor on the line," Hazel said.

"What this time?"

"Since you didn't respond to his phone calls, he assumes you don't want to be a reindeer in the Christmas parade. You can ride with the Boots and Saddles."

"Did you point out that I don't have a horse, to say nothing of a boot or a saddle?" Or any of the rest of the regalia. They did the Old West motif with lots of fringed buckskin, cowboy hats, and fancy holsters sporting six-guns strapped to their waists. They also did some impressive drills that, even if she had a horse, she couldn't do on short notice.

Hazel's voice bubbled with laughter.

"Tell him that, with everyone sick with the flu, I'm going to have to direct traffic while the parade is passing by."

"I'll tell him you're not in."

An hour later, Hazel buzzed again. "Beth called from the library and said the microfilms you wanted are in."

Susan grabbed her coat and ran.

At the library, she slipped in the first film and focused the machine.

In White Water, Texas, on December 24 twelve years ago, Deirdre Noel was stabbed thirty or more times. Blood covered the bedroom walls, floors, and the stairway down to the kitchen.

Branner Noel, the victim's husband, was picked up the following day, Christmas, arrested, and put in jail. Two days later a grand jury was convened and he was indicted. No bail allowed.

The White Water paper was a weekly, and each week the bulk of it was filled with articles about the homicide, the brutality of the murder, repeated mention of thirty or more stabbings. Wounds were described and emphasis placed on the blood that started in the bedroom and ended in the kitchen. Photos of the victim and suspect were prominent.

There was also a photo of court security struggling with a man whose face was twisted in rage, identified as the father of the victim. He came into the courtroom with a handgun, intent on shooting the defendant. He was disarmed and sent home. Jesus. No mention of his being charged with anything, no mention of his name. She went through the articles a second time and made copies of each one.

Why was Holiday so interested in the murder trial of Branner Noel?

At the shop, she arranged for a copy of the court transcript to be sent to her by overnight shipping. She asked Hazel to find Demarco. Ten minutes later he stood at attention before her desk, back stiff as iron.

"Run a make on Frederick Joyce and William Forbes." She told him she'd found the safe-deposit box and what was in it.

He nodded, spun on his heel, and marched out.

She sighed. Would Parkhurst ever get over this damn flu and get back to work?

She yawned and rubbed her grainy eyes. Go home, she told herself. Soon, she promised, and put in a call to the prison where Branner Noel had been incarcerated. She asked to speak with the warden. Warden Marble was away for the Christmas holiday. She asked for the assistant warden. He'd gone home for the day. Nobody else was authorized to give out information on an inmate. She left her name and numbers—office, home, and cell phone—and requested that Assistant Warden High call her when he got in.

From Information, she learned that White Water, Texas, didn't have a police department. Putting her hands on her neck, she stretched it back until it cracked, then she massaged it. No more phone calls. Enough already. She needed to get out of here. That sounded so good, she was reaching for her coat when she pushed herself to make just one more call. She asked Hazel if they had a map of Texas.

A minute later, Hazel came in lugging a large atlas and dropped it on Susan's desk. "It's old, so some things have changed. What did you need?"

"I want to find out what county White Water is in."

Jackson County. She picked up the phone for the last call of the day, she promised herself, and got the sheriff's department in Jackson County. She explained she wanted to know about the murder of Deirdre Noel that occurred twelve years ago.

"Twelve years?"

Right. How could her weary mind explain succinctly and clearly? "A homicide that occurred twelve years ago may have a bearing on a homicide I'm currently investigating."

"Uh—well, maybe Sheriff Riggs might know something about that. He's been here that long, but he's out right now. Could I take your number?"

Of course, he was out. She recited her office number, her home number, and the number of her cell phone, then heaved herself up from the chair and reached for her coat. When the phone rang, she eyed it narrowly, but sighed and picked it up.

"Mayor Bakover on the line," Hazel said.

Susan fled.

On the way home, she stopped to pick up a pizza. Not bothering to even check her phone messages, she sat at the table with Perissa perched on one corner. Pizza, a beer, and she was sufficiently stuffed and so weary she had difficulty hefting herself to her feet.

Before she trudged upstairs to bed, she stopped at her home office to see if anything urgent was on her answering machine. Two hang-ups, a message from her father telling her to call him, and the voice of Mort Stoddart, former San Francisco cop, now with the FBI.

"Because it's the season of giving and because I remember you busting your chops to save my ass that time I screwed up and let a suspect get away, I got your prints identified for you. Don't ask me how. I'm going to be paying back favors for years. The prints belong to a Branner Noel, convicted for murder twelve years ago. Don't say I never repay my debts. Merry Christmas."

She replayed the message. Tim Holiday was actually Branner Noel, and he'd been reading about the homicide he committed twelve years ago. Who killed Holiday/Noel? Why had he been released from prison? She assumed he'd been released and hadn't escaped somehow. Why had he come to Hampstead? Was his death related to the homicide of his wife all those years ago? Revenge? That would mean someone was here, or had been here, who was involved in the homicide of Holiday/Noel's wife. Who? Was he or she still here?

And how did Caley come into this? She hadn't even known Holiday/Noel.

Susan took herself to bed and let her mind pick over the questions all night.

24

With the cat's help, Susan managed to drag herself out of the warm bed and stumble into the shower. The shower didn't do a lot, but she managed to pull on some dark blue pants and a white sweater. She dumped dry food into Perissa's bowl, and the cat sniffed it and gave her the how-could-you look.

The pickup groaned and grumbled before it finally caught. She sat shivering while it warmed up enough to move. It was even longer before the heater blew out hot air. Another dark, cold, clear morning. The stars, not knowing another day had started, glittered as brightly as though it were the dead of night. At the Coffee Cup Cafe, she got two sugar doughnuts to take with her. She thought of getting something for Hazel, but knew Hazel wouldn't eat it. Not healthy.

It wasn't yet six o'clock when Susan got in. Hazel was at her desk. Had to get up pretty early in the morning to beat her.

"The court records just came," Hazel said. "I put them on your desk. And I just made a fresh pot of coffee."

"Thanks, Hazel."

Susan threw muffler and parka over the coat tree, sat at her desk, and took a large chunk from a doughnut.

The trial records were slow going, and lack of sleep had her eyes glazing over. She must be getting old. There had been a time when she could go days with little sleep.

She skimmed through the jury selection and didn't start reading carefully until the trial actually got under way. It was immediately apparent that Noel's lawyer wasn't good at his job. He seemed to be out to lunch most of the time, letting inflammatory comments go by with no objection. The judge seemed to be a wee bit prejudiced too. With the defendant charged with murder in the first, this trial zipped through at great speed. The jury found Noel guilty and the judge sentenced him to life in prison with no possibility of parole. Bing, bang, guilty.

Bernadette Dalrumple, the prosecution's most damning witness, had testified the defendant had threatened his wife over and over, and she'd seen him strike her several times.

Where was Noel's lawyer when this trial was going on?

She got up for a coffee refill, then went back to the trial records. An hour later, Hazel buzzed. "Sheriff Riggs on the line."

"Jackson County, Texas."

"Right," Hazel said. "I'll put him through."

"Good morning to you." Deep voice, soft lazy drawl. "I've been kind of expecting this call. Your boy was one I sort of wanted to keep an eye on. Who'd he kill?"

"No one, as far as I know. He was the one who got killed."

Silence on the other end of the line. "Well, now, that kind of does surprise me and kind of doesn't. The bastard stabbed his wife about thirty times. Most horrible thing ever occurred in these parts. Blood all over the place. Near as we could figure out, she was sleeping. Perp just kept stabbin' away at her, tryin' to get her to die. Blood all over the bed. She fought. I gotta say that little lady musta fought like a tiger. Scattered blood all over the floor and walls, staggered to the hallway. Got stabbed some more, made it to the stairs, blood spattering all the way. Walls and floor. She rolled down the stairs, perp comin' after her and stabbin' stabbin'. She made it all the way to the kitchen, where she finally succumbed. Folks were all horrified. Tell you the truth, I had a hard time keepin' the son of a bitch alive till the trial, they were so outraged."

"How do you remember it so well?"

"I was brand-new then. First time I was involved with anythin' like that. You tend to recall the first one."

Yeah, you do, Susan thought. Her first was a baby. Beaten so badly its head was oblong like a watermelon, both legs broken.

"We tried the murderin' bastard, convicted him, and threw his ass in jail for the rest of his natural-born life."

"What was he doing out? Don't tell me he managed a prison break?"

"No, ma'am. He was set free."

"Why?"

"Sentence overturned on appeal. Prejudicial publicity. Little bitty town. Spread all over the paper."

"When was he let go?"

"Six months ago. Took Sonny that long anyhow."

"What?"

"Sonny Ward, his attorney. Name's actually Marvin; 'round here we call him Sonny. You know who killed him?"

"Haven't a clue. Why did he kill his wife?"

"He was the jealous type. They fought all the time."

"He beat her up?"

"Couldn't prove that. She was having an affair. With his best friend, is my guess."

"Who was that?"

"Name was Mat James."

Mat James? Well well.

"But that was never proved."

"James was married?" Susan asked.

"Sure was."

"Did his wife play into the investigation?"

"Kathleen, her name was. She died not too long after the murder. The file on her death is still open as to whether it was suicide or murder. Coming so soon after the murder, most folks assumed she killed herself because she knew something that would show her own husband was the guilty one."

"Did you think so?"

"Well, I gave it some thought, but she was always frail, unstable like, under a doctor's care."

"I see."

"And then there was others thought maybe we convicted the wrong one and maybe it was Kathleen herself who wielded the knife."

"What was your feeling?"

"Well, I tell you, there's lots to point to Noel, and I was always confident he did it. Kathleen James was Deirdre Noel's friend—best buddies, you know—and so distressed she maybe killed herself. Kathleen's death tore up Mat James's mother. She had to see a doctor there for a time."

Ettie?

"Next thing you want is Sonny's phone number."

"Exactly." She scribbled it down and thanked him.

"Good huntin' to you. Still gives me nightmares. Maybe now Noel is dead, I can put it to rest. If you find—that's to say, when you find who shot the bastard, I'd be purely glad to know."

"I'll give you a call."

She hung up and leaned back. The chair squeaked. Note to self, get WD-40. Tim Holiday was Branner Noel. Tried for murder, convicted, and sent to prison. Freed on a technicality, not found innocent. If the state of Texas had wanted to try him again, they could have, but after all that time, it wasn't likely.

She let the sheriff's information tumble around in her mind, then refilled her coffee mug and put in a call for Marvin Ward, Holiday/Noel's attorney.

"I knew I wasn't doing right by him," Ward said. "I'd never tried a capital case before, you see, and I didn't know what I was doin'. I got to tell you, I wouldn't be that much better at it now. We just don't get that much murder around here."

"Why did you agree to represent him?"

"Bran wanted me to. We were friends. Nobody was eager to take him on, such a heinous crime and all. I think he didn't believe he'd be convicted."

"Why didn't you file an appeal?"

"I've been filin' appeals for twelve years, tryin' to get him released. Just when I'm successful, he gets himself killed. I'm awful sorry about that. I liked him. You know who did it?"

"Not yet. What can you tell me that will help?"

A long silence. "Bran was charmin', a good talker, easy with people, liked by the ladies despite not being movie star handsome. He was, I got to say, a con man."

"Con man?" That surprised her.

"Yes, ma'am, I got to admit it, but only 'cause it might help somehow."

"Violent?" Con men generally weren't, but there was always the possibility.

"Shocked the hell out of me when I heard what he done. I knew them all my life. Him and Mat and Deirdre and Kathleen. We was all friends. Way back through grammar school and high school. After that we weren't so tight. I was always studyin' too much then to do a lot of hangin' with 'em. Maybe I lost touch."

"Them?"

"Bran and Mat James. Always together. Another reason I kinda' got let out; they always had money. I didn't."

"Where'd the money come from?"

"Can't tell you that."

"Are you saying they came by it illegally?"

He laughed. "That's what I can't tell you, but I'd be lyin' if I said otherwise."

"What were they doing?"

"For twelve years, I couldn't sleep knowin' I didn't have the skill to defend Bran back then. Then, when I finally make some bit of atonement, I hear he's killed. I sure am sorry, and I'm not goin' to say anythin' against him now to compound my first sin. No use you askin'."

She asked anyway, then promised to let him know when she found the killer.

Receiver in her hand, she stared through the window blind at the sky that was a cold blue with not a cloud in sight. She needed Parkhurst to bounce thoughts against. Hearing the recorded voice telling her to hang up, she pressed the button, got a dial tone, and punched in his number.

"Yeah?" His voice was so thick and hoarse she barely understood him.

"Susan. I called to see how you're doing, but I can hear you're not so good."

"Right. How's the homicide investigation going?"

"Just taken a giant leap forward. Get well."

"Right."

She hung up. Tipping the mug, she swallowed the last of cold coffee. Mat James was a friend of Tim Holiday/Branner Noel. He'd been having an affair with Deirdre Noel. The two men had a history of shady doings. How had it come about that Mat James was only on the periphery of this investigation? Was she finally getting somewhere?

She picked up the phone.

"Yes, Susan," Hazel said.

"Track down White, tell him to round up Mat James and bring him in."

Mat James sat relaxed in one of the plastic chairs in the interview room. He smiled and got to his feet when she came in. "What am I doing here?" he said in a voice with no worry in it.

"A few questions, Mr. James."

"Seems like a few questions might have waited until I got off for lunch. My whole staff thinks you've arrested me."

She didn't return his smile. "Sit down, please, Mr. James." He chose the end of the table.

She sat at a right angle to him. White stood by the door. All pals together.

"We just learned the real identity of the dead man found in your ex-wife's basement. Why didn't you tell us Tim Holiday was your old pal Branner Noel?"

Mat gave her a very good imitation of startled surprise. "I assumed you knew."

She tipped her head and raised an eyebrow.

"It hit me like a fist to the solar plexus. Bran dead. It doesn't get to me, you know? It's like he was gone to me when he was sent off to prison."

Eyes closed, Mat put his fingertips on his forehead. "I guess you never really know another person. I would have bet my life he couldn't do a thing like stabbing Deirdre." He flashed a rueful smile. "Maybe I shouldn't be so careless with my life."

"A witness testified that he hit her."

"I couldn't believe it. I couldn't believe it when he was found guilty and sent to prison. I couldn't believe it when he turned up dead in Caley's basement. I still can't get that in my mind so it isn't a shock when the thought comes around."

After a second or two, she asked, "How did you know the murdered man was Branner Noel?"

"Caley told me."

"She told you the homicide victim was Branner Noel," Susan said.

He shook his head. "She said Holiday, the guy who came to fix the furnace."

"And you knew Holiday was Noel—how?"

"He said he was using that name, the one time I saw him."

"And that was—?"

"About three weeks ago." He swallowed, swallowed again. "Could I have some water?"

Stalling for time? "Sure. You can have something else if you want. Soft drink? Coffee?"

"Just water." He seemed completely guileless. Con men were good actors.

When White returned with a glass of water, Mat took a gulp.

"Did you keep in touch with Branner after he went to prison?" she asked.

"I wrote sporadic letters and went to see him several times. He wrote to me even more sporadically. We called back and forth a few times."

"Did he let you know about his release from prison?"

Mat studied the water in his glass, shook it, and watched it swirl. "Yes. He called and told me. I said I'd come and pick him up, be waiting in a red convertible when he came through the gate. We'd go on a three-day drunk. He said no, he'd rather I stayed away, he needed time to be alone. He hadn't been alone for twelve years. He wanted to think. I told him to call me when he was through thinking.

That had the ring of truth, she thought. "Why did he come to Hampstead?"

"I was completely blown away when I found out he was here."

"How did you find out?"

"He came up to me one day when I was jogging. I didn't recognize him until he told me who he was."

"Why?"

Mat looked at her as though she hadn't been keeping up with the program. "Excuse me? Why didn't I recognize him?"

"Why did he talk to you?"

"Say hello, let me know he was free, say he was glad to see me." Mat didn't fidget, or scratch his leg, or glance away like people did when they were lying.

"And the two of you had a fight."

He looked at her. "No."

"I have a witness," she said quietly.

"We had a conversation."

"According to the witness, the two of you got very heated."

"Conversations can get emotional."

"How often did you see him after that?"

"I never saw him again. He was—he wasn't the same Bran I knew."

"Prison will do that," she said.

He rested a tight circle of fingertips against his forehead, as though he had a terrible headache. "I can't believe this. Bran dead? I just—" He took in a deep breath. "I can't take it in. Dead. Not incarcerated in some cell somewhere."

"Were you two working up a new scam?"

"Scam? I'm a hardworking bank manager. Banks are very conservative; they frown on employees involved in scams." He gave her a small smile that invited her to share in the best humor he could come up with under such sad circumstances.

"Maybe he wanted his share of the profits."

"Profits?" Mat shook his head, perplexed.

He took a look at his watch and got up. "I don't know what that means, but I know I've got to get back to work. If there's anything I can do, let me know."

"Oh, I will."

Had he and Noel gotten into an argument about the money stashed in the safe-deposit box and he'd shot Noel? Or simply shot the man to keep the money for himself?

25

Caley, seated at the kitchen table, shoved dirty breakfast dishes aside as she fumbled with the Advil bottle, almost in tears because the stupid thing wouldn't open.

"I'll do it, Mom." Zach took the bottle and twisted off the cap.

"Thanks. I don't know what I'd do without you. You are the greatest kid in the world."

He gave her a frightened look. "Okay if I go to the library with Jo?"

"Sure. Back by—" She squinted at the clock. The numbers danced. Ten o'clock?

"I'll be here by eight. You'll keep the doors locked, won't you?"

"Sure."

He slouched out.

What was wrong with him lately? She shook out a couple of tablets and washed them down with some orange juice one of the kids had left at breakfast. Looking around the kitchen brought up loads of guilt. What a mess. The sink was piled high with dishes, the peeling linoleum was covered with crumbs and spilled breakfast cereal and sticky spots that were God knows what. Zach had been keeping the dirty dishes under control and fixing stuff like hot dogs for the Littles and generally shoveling debris out when it got too deep, but she couldn't let him do everything. He was a kid, for God's sake. She transferred bowls of soggy cereal to the sink, then sat back down for lack of strength. Oh God, how long did this flu go on? How long had it been now? Did it ever go away?

When the television went on, she couldn't even rouse the necessary energy to yell at Adam to turn it off. Elbows on the table, she propped her chin in her hands. If she tried really hard, she could get up again. She knew she could. If she just rested a minute. Maybe she could put her head on the table and take a little nap.

She drifted off to sleep and dreamed. Two men dressed in black, masks covering their faces, were standing in the kitchen yelling at her. They gave her twenty seconds to tell them what they wanted. One looked at his watch. When he nodded, the other pointed his gun at her.

He pulled the trigger. She screamed.

The doorbell rang. She jerked up her head and tried to figure out where she was. Before she reached a conclusion, Adam called, "I'll get it."

She put her head back on the table and found herself running, trying to find a place to cross the river to get away from whoever was chasing her. She heard water running in the sink.

"You don't have to do that, Zach," she mumbled. "Go ahead and go to Jo's." He was humming Bach? Zach? Humming Bach?

She forced her eyes open. A man in jeans and a cable-knit sweater, sleeves pushed up beyond the elbows, was standing at her sink washing dishes. "Mat?"

He turned. It wasn't Mat. She should have known. Mat didn't wash dishes.

"Evan?" She squinted. Evan Devereau? Her boss? Church music director? Washing dishes in her kitchen? Hallucination?

"I didn't want to wake you."

She stood on wobbly legs. "You can't wash my dishes."

He turned, throwing a dish towel over his shoulder. "Don't worry, I'm an expert. I had a mother, three sisters, and a female dog we never referred to as a bitch. I'm excellent at dishwashing. I do other useful things too. Scrub floors. Laundry. Sweep. Dust. It's not only music I'm a whiz at. I'm all full of useful talents."

"Where's Zach?"

"According to Bonnie, he went off to meet his friend Jo, or maybe it's Sam. I didn't get that clear. Bonnie is, in case that's your next question, in her room writing a story to read to me later."

"You can't wash my dishes." Had she already said that? "You need to go."

He shook his head. "I'm your boss."

"The church is my boss."

"Well, I hired you. That means I tell you what to do. And I'm telling you. Go to bed." He took her elbow, turned her, and marched her along the hallway. "Where's your bedroom?"

"That one," Bonnie said, having come to see what was happening.

Evan propelled Caley, digging in her feet, to the end of the hallway, where she planted her arms on the doorframe. No way was she letting anyone see the condition of her bedroom.

"Go," he said. "Or I'll have to get tough."

"Okay, but—"

"Go. I'll have one of the kids wake you when I leave."

Tears threatened to gather up and spill over. Why was it she did just fine until someone was nice to her? Then she fell apart.

She dropped across the bed. It seemed only a moment later that Bonnie was whispering in her ear, "The good prince left and Daddy's here."

What was Mat doing here?

She pushed herself out of bed, splashed water on her face, and yanked a brush through her hair. When she stumbled out, not only did she find the kitchen clean, but the living room—except for Mat—and the bathroom were clean as well.

Oh, God, how could you ever face a boss who had cleaned your bathroom?

"What do you want?" she asked Mat.

"Hey, the house looks nice. I'm taking everybody out for supper. Where's Zach?"

She looked at the clock on the mantel. It was a basement find. She had been blown out of her mind when she discovered it still worked as long as she wound it every month. If it hadn't lost its mind the time was six-thirty.

She'd slept since ten this morning? Where was Zach? Oh, right, with Jo. Something was riling him. The awfulness of adolescence? He was due, God only knows. Such a good, responsible kid. She relied on him too much. She had to stop it immediately and start relying on herself. Zach was a kid. He was entitled to behave like a kid.

"What do you want, Mat?"

"I told you. I'm taking everybody out to supper. By the way, the house looks nice for a change."

"Get out!"

"Mommy!" Bonnie cried, her face stricken. Here was her beloved father come to see them at last and her witch of a mother wanted to throw him out.

"If we go, you won't have to cook anything." Bonnie looked up through her lashes beseechingly.

Caley took a breath. "Right." She gave Bonnie a hug. Germs, she reminded herself.

"Where is Zach?" Mat asked again.

"With friends. He won't be back until eight."

Mat made a fake growl at the Littles. "Hear that, guys? More for us. Let's go!"

Zach was late. He used more time than he'd intended, looking through his dad's apartment, and then he didn't find anything. Except Dad sure owed a lot of money. Zach put his bike away in the garage, ran to the kitchen door, and was inside the house with the door locked behind him before he smelled something wrong.

He wasn't exactly thinking, but he was expecting the usual

sounds and smells of home, the noise the Littles made and the clatter of Mom washing up after dinner. She wasn't the greatest cook in the world. Except for spaghetti; she was a wiz at spaghetti.

The kitchen was dark and empty and there weren't any sounds. No bickering from the Littles or Bonnie chattering to imaginary friends or Adam doing blow-up stuff, making machine-gun sounds.

"Mom?" He was headed for the stairway when an unfamiliar smell hit his nose. It didn't belong here. It was—pipe tobacco!

A hand grabbed his shoulder.

He screamed and wrenched away. He ran up the stairs. An angry voice growled something. While Zach didn't hear the words, he knew the meaning.

If he could just reach his room. He spared a glance over his shoulder. Baines was right behind him.

"The money, you little bastard!"

Panic squeezed him so hard he couldn't breathe.

A hand wrapped around his ankle. The pain in his chest was going to burst and kill him. The hand jerked him and he fell. His chin bumped against each step as he was dragged down. His teeth rattled against his tongue. Blood flooded his mouth, salty and metallic.

His cheek burned against the old carpet. Its mildewed smell choked him. He twisted, jerked up his free leg, and drove the heel of his boot into the guy's nose. Baines let go with a howl of rage.

Zach scrambled back up the stairs. He heard Baines pounding up right behind him. His bedroom door was at the end of the hallway. So far.

He reached the door, angled in, and slammed it shut. He'd just turned the lock when Baines thudded against the door. It didn't break open.

Zach slid up the window, climbed out, and jammed it shut. He climbed to the tree house, then across to another tree and from there to another.

He swung from limb to limb, getting closer to the ground. Baines tromped around shining a flashlight up through the trees, looking for him. When the light picked him out, without thinking about what was on the ground under him, Zach let go and jumped, arms widespread, mouth open. He hit the ground hard on his side, couldn't move, couldn't breathe. He heard Baines coming.

Rolling himself over, he pulled in air, gasping, lungs not working. Finally, he got a breath in and he stood, shaky, trying to get his senses working.

The flashlight beam cut toward him. He took off, melted into the shadows, and finally pressed up against the rough wood outside the garage.

"Hey, kid! I won't hurt you. All I want is my money. Give back the money and I'll forget I ever knew you."

Baines found the outside switch and flooded the driveway with light. While he stood blinking in the glare, Zach slipped by him into the garage.

Baines cursed and searched for the inside light. Zach grabbed the dusty old canvas covering the lawn mower and tossed it over Baines's head. With Baines coughing and choking and fighting the canvas, Zach jumped on his bike and pedaled as hard as he could to the street. Warm blood trickled from his nose. Wiping it with an arm, he put even more effort into moving his legs.

An engine roared, headlights popped up behind him. The black minivan! He pedaled harder. He couldn't see Baines's face, but he could feel those eyes staring into the middle of his back like a gun barrel.

Baines didn't worry about intersections; he just came smashing on through. Zach wasn't paying attention, either. He focused on getting farther ahead, but he kept losing ground.

At the next intersection he saw a pickup coming up on his left. He turned right and heard the pickup closing in on him. He knew he shouldn't, but he had to do something. He had to try. He had to.

He heard the truck picking up speed and felt it coming closer behind him.

Okay. Okay. He pumped his legs harder. It had to be perfect.

He risked one quick glance over his shoulder and swerved to the right, still pushing it as hard as he could.

The pickup was moving toward him with the roar of a jet engine. Faster. Faster. If he got it wrong— He'd heard the horrors. Do it wrong and he was road kill. Flattened with tread marks from top to toe, head squashed like a cantaloupe.

He reached out—inched closer—closer—

He eased to the left, putting everything he had into another burst of speed. Heart pounding in his throat, he clamped his fingers on the panel of the pickup bed. When the pickup gained speed, he was skimming along like a sailboat in the wind.

It was exhilarating! He held on for dear life, steering the bike away from bumps and potholes. The minivan was lost somewhere behind.

The interstate was coming up. He had to let go before the pickup tore onto the high-speed road. He was afraid. Grabbing hold was one thing; letting go, with the tires right there, biting into the road and pushing a ton of metal— A vivid image came to mind of what they would do to him if he fell underneath.

He had to let go. He had to let go. Now. Now. Now! The pickup took on speed, and Zach unclenched his fingers and jerked the handlebars to the right. The bike bounced up over the edge of the road, wheels shimmying and juttering, and he was airborne.

26

Caley's head pounded like a jackhammer. The Littles had a great time eating pizza with their daddy, who acted as though this were a regular thing and not a once-a-year event. Mat had been coming around an awful lot the last few days. What did he want?

Not that she wasn't glad for the kids. Although Zach might know Mat had some ulterior motive. Zach was no longer so easy to fool. And something was up with him. Oh, Lord, what was going on in her life? Maybe if her head wasn't so noisy she could figure out some of this stuff.

There was a period not too long ago when she would have been thrilled right out of her falling-apart jogging shoes that Mat was spending so much time with them. She had dreamed about the great return and her joyous welcome. And a magnificent one it would have been too. But she was a little smarter these days. Just how that had happened, she didn't know, but she was seeing her gorgeous ex-husband for what he was, not for what she had convinced herself in the beginning that he was: a prince on a shiny, dazzling-white horse. Or was that a dazzling prince on a dark horse?

She shuffled to the door and fumbled with the key. The Littles were shrieking with joy, pulling on Mat's arms and dragging him along. He swooped up Adam and tossed him over his shoulder. Bonnie tugged on his free hand. He set Adam down and, growling fiercely, ran after Bonnie, who screamed with pretend terror.

Well now, wasn't that just the picture of an indulgent daddy bringing his beloveds home after a dinner out? She unlocked the door, gave it a swift kick to unstick it, and went inside.

"It's warm," Mat said. "You must have gotten the furnace fixed."

She stared at him. Where had he been for the last three days? In a cave? Here she was, about to be arrested for the horrid murder of the repairman, and he made a comment about how nice it was to have the furnace fixed. If she killed Mat, surely any judge in the land would let her off. "She was just so provoked, Your Honor," her attorney would say. "Beyond human means and . . ." She sighed.

When Mat came in, a Little dragging on each hand, she shut the door behind them. She unwound her scarf and hung it over the newel post. "Zach?" She slipped off her coat and draped it over the scarf. "Zach?"

"I'll get these two monsters ready for bed," Mat said.

"They're perfectly capable," she said. "Thanks for dinner."

"I want Daddy to help me," Bonnie wailed.

"He can help me if he wants," Adam said.

She sighed again. Hadn't she been doing that a lot lately?

"When you get the place cleaned up like this," Mat said, "it doesn't look half bad."

She started to sigh and rubbed a hand over her face instead. "Okay, brush teeth. Right now." She pointed a finger. They scurried off to the bathroom. She called up the stairs. "Zach?"

She trudged up. His bedroom door was closed. Sleeping? The Littles had made enough noise coming in that they should have woken even Sleeping Beauty. She tapped on the door. "Zach?"

165

He didn't respond and she knocked louder. *"Zach?"*

When he still didn't answer, she tried the knob. Locked. She wiggled it and knocked again. "Zach!"

She ran downstairs. In the kitchen, she rummaged through the drawer filled with odds and ends, searching for a key. There were three, and any one fit all the inside locks.

She closed her fingers around one and went back up to his room. She opened the door and snapped on the ceiling light. The room was empty. She raced down the stairs and ran into the kitchen.

"Caley, what—"

Ignoring Mat, she picked up the phone and punched in the number. "Ettie, is Zach there? Have you seen him? He didn't call?"

She hung up and looked around for a note he might have left.

"Caley, what's the matter?"

"Zach isn't here."

"Maybe he snuck out to see a friend."

She pulled the address book from under the phone and looked up a number. "Mrs. Smith? This is Caley James. Is Zach over there? Have you seen him this evening?"

She asked Sam's mother to call her if Sam heard from him and went through the same thing with Jo Dandermadden. She replaced the receiver and ran her hands through her hair.

"Do you check on him at nights? Maybe—"

"Shut up, Mat."

"Maybe it's a regular habit. Goes to bed and when you think he's asleep, crawls out the window. He's only a kid. Kids do stupid things."

"Not this kid."

"Every kid—"

"You've hardly seen him the last three years. You don't know what a great kid he is. You don't know how reliable. You don't know—"

Mat went out the kitchen door.

She called the police.

When she hung up she hugged her arms across her chest. She'd known there was something bothering Zach. She should have stayed with him. She shouldn't have let Mat talk her into going out. She shouldn't have—

Mat came back. "Zach's bike isn't in the garage."

Susan asked Hazel to track down Demarco and have him meet her at Caley's house. His squad car was waiting at the curb when she got there. Leaving him with Mat and Ettie in the living room, she took Caley into the kitchen. In fits and starts, Caley told her about Zack being out with friends, going for dinner without him, coming back and finding Zack still not home.

The tap dripped. Susan got up to twist it off. It still dripped.

Caley, face a grayish color, scraped a fingernail at the rip in the vinyl tablecloth, red with white snowflakes and white Christmas trees. A misshapen mug with a stick figure drawn on it sat full of cooling coffee in front of her. A child's project, no doubt.

"Why aren't you out looking?" Caley's voice was frail and hollow, without heat.

"He's a twelve-year-old, very bright child, and he's gone someplace on his bicycle. Does he often go out at night on his own?"

"There was a murder in this house and now my son is missing, and you think I'm just a hysterical mom!"

"We're looking. We'll find him. He's only been gone a few hours and—"

"He's such a special kid." Caley blew her nose and blotted her face. "Oh God, please don't let anything happen to him." Her hands squeezed the mug until its jagged edges cut into her palm and blood seeped around her fingers.

"He said he wasn't feeling well." She grasped Susan's arm with bloody fingers. "Do you think he's sick? Collapsed somewhere? Too sick to tell anybody who he is? Delirious?"

Susan tore a paper towel from the roll by the sink and held it under the tap to get it damp. "Someone would call and let us know."

She pried Caley's fingers loose from the mug and wiped her hands. "Why did you go out? Are you feeling better?"

"Oh, Lord." Caley sighed wearily. "Sometimes it's easier just to go along with Mat. I didn't have the energy to say no."

Caley scrubbed her face with her hands, as though trying to rub away numbness. "If only I hadn't gone. I'd have known he didn't come home and I could have called sooner."

Eyes brimming with tears, Caley rose and pulled open a cabinet door. She pushed around cups and glasses and plucked out a small bottle. At the table, she twisted it open and tried to shake tablets into her hand. They spilled across the table.

Susan picked up one. "What is it you're taking?"

"Advil."

They didn't look like Advil.

Caley showed her the bottle.

Susan took it and scooped all the tablets back inside. "I'll get you some more."

Caley picked at a small rip in the tablecloth. "He had something on his mind."

"Zach did? What?"

"He's not a real talky kid, but if there was something on his mind and I asked, he'd tell me. If he didn't want to tell me, he'd just say so."

"He'd tell you something was bothering him, but that he didn't want to tell you what it was?"

"Yeah."

"You'd accept that? You didn't try to find out what it was?"

"I figure a kid has things come up in his life he doesn't want to discuss just like there are things in my life I wouldn't want to talk about. He's an intelligent person and entitled to be treated like one."

Susan thought not many parents had that attitude.

"Maybe he was hit by a car!"

"No one answering Zach's description has been taken to Emergency."

"Maybe he hasn't been spotted yet."

"Patrols are looking. We'll find him."

"That's what cops always tell hysterical mothers. 'We'll find him.' I've seen the TV shows. Months or years from now some pathetic little bones are found and—" Caley burst into sobs.

"Oh God, oh God, people go missing all the time. How many are found? It's so cold. He'll freeze. He could be lying somewhere. Like that poor old—" She jumped up. "The Littles!"

Susan took her hands. "The Littles are fine. Please, sit down. We're looking for Zach. We'll find him." She was thinking maybe she should call Dr. Cunningham for a sedative when Caley took a breath, blew her nose forcefully, and straightened her back.

"I have to go to the Littles. They'll be scared, and Mat isn't too used to the parenting thing."

"Sure," Susan said. "Ask Mat to come in here."

Mat James came in immediately. "Any word?" His face was pale and the lines around his eyes and mouth were deeper, and exaggerated even more by the harsh ceiling light. He looked defeated, a man standing on the mountaintop of middle age and seeing before him nothing but the same grayness of his life day after day.

"Not yet, Mr. James, but a lot of people are looking," she said. "Please sit down."

Mat got a mug from the cabinet, looked at the empty coffee carafe, and rummaged in the cabinet for instant coffee. He spooned crystals into the mug and filled the teakettle with water before he sat down.

"Zach is the child of your first wife," Susan said.

"Yes. That have anything to do with him taking off on his bike?"

"Does he know her family? Would he get in touch with any of them?"

Mat pinched the bridge of his nose. "Kathleen—his mother, biological mother—died."

Susan nodded.

"She didn't have any family. She was an only child. Both her parents died in a plane crash. They were going on a vacation to—" He put his hand on his forehead, then slid it down until it covered his eyes. After a moment, he brought it down to his chin. "I can't remember where. Somewhere in Mexico. She had a couple of aunts somewhere, but Zach doesn't know them."

"Where might he have gone?"

"To see a friend would be my guess."

"What friend?"

The teakettle shrieked, and he filled the mug with hot water, then held it out with a questioning look.

"No thanks," Susan said.

Mat took a sip, winced, set the mug down, and rubbed his lip.

"You never told Caley," Susan said, "about the death of Deirdre Noel, or your long friendship with Branner?"

Mat took in a breath and murmured, almost to himself, "Bran and I were going to get rich together."

"How?" She was hoping, with the stress of his son missing, he'd let something slip.

He shook his head. "Long in the past. The murder of his wife was a tragedy. I didn't understand it then and I don't understand it now. It happened twelve years ago. What does it have to do with Zach?"

Maybe nothing, she thought. A cop asked questions. "Why would Noel want information about Caley?"

"He didn't know her."

"Would he be looking for revenge? Felt all his years in jail were your fault?"

"Haven't we gone over this already?"

"The prosecution at the trial claimed you were the motive for the homicide. You were having an affair with his wife."

"It wasn't true. What does any of this have to do with Zach?" he said again, with more impatience.

What indeed? She had a homicide and a missing child. How were they connected? She asked more questions. Nothing came from any of them.

Finally, she said, "Ask your mother to come in here, please."

He rose, for a moment looked like he was going to say something, but simply nodded and left.

Ettie Trowbridge looked ten years older than when Susan first saw her. Nothing like adversity to take years off your life. Her face was drawn, her eyes red and bloodshot from crying. A lace-edged handkerchief was crushed in her hand.

"I am so irritated with Caley. If that child is hurt or lost—"

"Please try not to worry, Mrs. Trowbridge," Susan said. "We'll find him."

"If Caley watched these children like she should, this wouldn't have happened. She's negligent. Always has been. More concerned with her own goings-on than with the children."

"How is she negligent?" Susan asked sympathetically, implying that Ettie herself would never be anything of the sort.

"She lets them do whatever they want, go all over the place by themselves, and doesn't make sure responsible adults are present. She has men in the house." Ettie's breath caught on a sob. "If anything happens to that child, I'll—I'll just die, that's all."

"What men?"

"First a man in the basement and now that Devereau man and God knows who else."

"Evan Devereau, you mean? The music director at the church?"

"Yes, well, he shouldn't be here. She should know better. She should think of the children."

171

"And the man in the basement; Caley claimed he was only here twice and that was to repair the furnace."

Ettie waved that away and daintily blew her nose. "I'm sorry, pay no mind. I didn't mean it. Even Caley wouldn't take up with a man who has a tattoo. I'm just so upset—"

Susan's cell phone rang and she dug it from her shoulder bag.

"A bicycle's been found," Hazel said.

27

"Where?" Susan took pen and notebook from the shoulder bag at her feet and scribbled down the address Hazel gave her. Ettie watched with a fearful questioning expression.

"Is it Zach?" Caley stood in the doorway with Mat behind her. "Where is he?"

"A bicycle's been found," Susan said.

Caley sagged. Mat caught her and, when he pulled her into his arms, she didn't resist. She desperately needed someone to lean on right now; even an ex-husband would be better than nothing.

Susan gave Demarco a short nod and he followed her out. As they hurried toward the pickup, she pulled on gloves. He didn't even have his coat buttoned. Probably ate nails for breakfast.

"Learn anything?" Cold air clawed painfully at her throat.

He shook his head. "Mat needs money. That was apparent from a conversation his mother started. Mat shut her up. He's guilty of something. I don't know if it's the homicide."

It confirmed her own feeling, but didn't get them any further. "Dig into the man," she said. "His job, his extracurricular activities, his playmates. What he buys. How he gets his money, drives the car he drives, and lives where he does."

Demarco nodded. A man of a thousand words with nine hundred left. She got into the pickup and he headed for the squad car.

"And Demarco?"

He didn't click his heels, but he did spin on one.

"This isn't the military. Watch yourself."

A smile flashed across his face.

What had she unleashed by setting him on Mat James?

The bicycle had been located on Brooks Street, near the 4-H fairgrounds, but before she'd gone two blocks the radio stuttered at her.

"Yes, Hazel."

"Crenshaw found the James boy."

A rigid tension in her neck and shoulders that she'd been barely aware of slowly eased as she let out a long breath. "Can you patch me through to him?"

"Sure, hold on."

A series of clicks and then Crenshaw said, "Ma'am?"

"Is the child all right?"

"Mostly. He was trying to get himself and his bicycle home with maybe a broken ankle when he figured he better leave the bike and just get himself home. Marshall found the bike. I spotted the kid just around the corner. Paramedics took him to ER."

"What happened?"

"He says he was just riding when he hit a grate in the road. The bike did a somersault and he came down hard on his right ankle."

"Thanks, Crenshaw." Susan got Caley on the phone and told her Zach had apparently hurt his ankle in a bicycle accident and was at the hospital emergency room.

Trying not to wince, Zach lay back on the table. The technician jerked the bulky X-ray machine around and maneuvered it out of the cubicle. "The doctor will be back soon," she said.

He was really in trouble, Zach thought. Mom was going to go into liftoff and Baines was going to kill him. Why would the creepy hulk think Zach had the money? Because it was gone, obviously. Even a dumbass like Zach should be able to figure that out. Since he hadn't taken it and it was gone, somebody else blew away with it. Okay, who? How was he going to convince Baines he didn't have it?

Mom was going to explode in here like a tornado any minute, so he better get his story ready.

Sure enough, not twenty seconds later, she swooped in, his dad right behind her, and grabbed him in a hug. "Zach, I've been so worried."

As soon as she let go, his dad hugged him. "Hey, buddy."

"I'm okay," he said.

"Where were you?" his mom demanded. "You're hurt. The cop said something about your leg. What hap—"

The tired-looking doctor with black curly hair came in carrying X-rays. He whacked one on the view box and clicked on a light. A foot showed up. With about a zillion bones. Cool.

"What's wrong?" Caley snatched Zach's hand and kissed it, then held it against her face. He didn't yank away; she'd probably cry. She was almost there anyway.

The doctor saw him squirm and winked. "You're lucky, young man. There aren't any broken bones in the ankle. It's a severe sprain. But—" Taking a pen from his lab coat pocket, he traced a line on a bone in the foot. "See that? You fractured the shaft of the first metatarsus."

"He has a broken foot?"

"Toe, actually, but he's otherwise healthy, and the bone will mend in no time. Does it hurt?" he asked Zach.

Zach shrugged. "Some."

The doctor nodded. "We'll take care of that."

Zach swallowed some pills. He was told to put ice on the ankle at intervals tonight, keep it elevated, and: "Most important, keep off it." He was fitted with crutches and given an Ace bandage, his mom was handed more pills for him to take later, and his dad pushed him out in a wheelchair.

The pills were great. At first he pretended they made him dopey. Pretty soon he didn't have to pretend.

28

<hr>

"Don't be mad at Zach, Mommy," Bonnie murmured sleepily when Caley went in to check on her.

"Okay." Caley leaned down to kiss her.

Bonnie put an arm around her pillow and bunched it under her cheek. "He had something to do."

"What?" Tugging gently, Caley tucked the blankets around her daughter's shoulder. Very petite, Bonnie was. Tiny little bones that seemed so fragile, like a little bird's.

Bonnie yawned. "Help Daddy."

"Do what?"

Bonnie twitched her shoulder. "Dunno."

If Mat had involved Zach in any of his problems, Caley was going to yank out his heart and feed it to Mrs. Frankens's cat. She went into Adam's bedroom.

"Zach okay?" Adam asked.

"Yeah. He fell off his bike and broke his toe, but he'll be fine."

"He's neat, isn't he?"

"Zach?" She couldn't believe he was talking about his brother and thought he meant Mat. She could hardly trust herself not to blurt out what an idiot jerk his father was.

"That cop." Adam lowered his voice. "A Marine keeps everything neat."

"Yeah, he's neat." Sitting on the edge of the bed, she bent over and kissed Adam's cheek.

She snapped out the light and started to leave.

"Mom?"

"What, sweetie?"

"Are you mad at Zach?"

"I was," she said as mildly as she could. "Because I was worried and didn't know where he was."

"Are you going to ground him?"

Until he's thirty-five.

She looked in on Zach, sound asleep. Mat was in the kitchen sipping the last of the instant coffee. "You want this?" He offered it to her.

"What are you up to?"

"What?" He looked at her, and when she didn't respond said, "*What?*"

"What's Zach helping you with?"

He shook his head, letting her know she was way nuts. "What are you talking about?"

"Have you borrowed money again? Mixed Zach up in it?"

Mat smiled, that charming, sexy smile. "You're tired. Go to bed. I'll stick around a while so you can get some sleep."

"Go home."

"What?"

"Which one of those two words didn't you understand?" She snatched the mug from his hand, dumped the coffee in the sink, and banged the mug on the countertop, hitting it so hard the handle broke off in her hand and the rest of the mug bounced to the floor and shattered.

He put his arms around her and pulled her close. "Come on, Caley. You heard what the doctor said. He'll be fine. He just had a little accident. Kids do."

She pulled away and gave him a shove. "If you had something

to do with his getting hurt— If he's doing some stupid thing you asked him to do, I'll kill you." She got a broom and dustpan to sweep up the mess, thinking there must be something symbolic here. Tears obscured her vision. She swiped at them with her wrist.

"Here," Mat said. "Let me do that."

"Go home," she said.

"I want to help."

"Go. Home." She held the broom horizontally, like a spear . . .

"Caley—"

. . . and ran at him.

"Hey!" He jumped aside

"Go!"

"I'm leaving. I'm leaving. Let me know if you need anything."

"GO!" she screamed, and got caught in a coughing fit. You'll wake up the Littles, she warned herself. Bonnie'll have hysterics and Adam'll be on the ceiling.

"I'll call you."

"Of course," she said tiredly.

It was a good thing he went or she'd be flinging herself into his arms. He might be a rat, but now she was alone and she was tired and she had to sweep up this mess.

She didn't know how long she simply stood there, unable to get herself to move. Finally, she swept up the shards, dumped them in the trash under the sink, and shuffled down the hallway. Without undressing, she fell across her bed. Sleep circled around out there just past her fingertips.

At one A.M., Susan was still trying to take care of all the pearls and garbage piled on her desk. December 17, 18 really, since it was past midnight. On the 24th, she had a flight scheduled to go home. The 26th she had to tell her old boss whether she'd take the job he'd offered. Were it permanent, she wouldn't hesitate—she didn't think she would—but it was for two years. And she was no closer to finding Holiday/Noel's killer than she'd been two days ago.

Her cop instincts told her Mat James was guilty—of something—loud and clear. Demarco's had told him the same thing. Of what? Murder? Maybe. Mat James had an affair with Holiday/Noel's wife. Maybe Deirdre Noel had wanted him to divorce his wife and marry her. He'd refused. She'd threatened to tell her husband and/or Mat's wife. Mat had killed her to prevent it. Would he have picked up a knife and stabbed her thirty times? Would he have killed Branner Noel? Why? If Noel knew anything, surely he'd have brought it up at the trial. Maybe twelve years of brooding in a cell had brought something to mind.

If she could accept the reports of the Jackson County sheriff, there'd been no evidence of a break-in. No burglar or madman known in the vicinity. She wasn't sure she could accept the county investigators' work. They seemed to have picked up Noel and felt their job was done, dusted off their hands and gone home. They hadn't looked for anyone else, hadn't even seemed to look very hard for evidence of any kind.

Enough! Throwing down her pen, she grabbed her coat and went home, where she took a hot shower to thaw her feet. She pulled on one of Daniel's old sweatshirts, two sizes too large, and slid a stack of CDs into the CD player. It was a new purchase. When she brought it home, she'd relegated the cassette player to the closet shelf, sallied out and bought an armful of CDs. She got into bed before the cold claimed her again, and pushed the proper button. Bach filled the room. Perissa, the cat, came snuggling up, more for warmth than love, Susan suspected.

Tired as she was, sleep escaped her. Her mind wouldn't let go of the merry-go-round. Where had Zach gone and what had he been up to? He was one worried little boy. His mother had said he had something on his mind. She'd also said he was very bad at lying: "His daddy now, Mat, is a world-class expert. He could hand you a bowl of shit and a package of chips, claim it was the best dip ever made, and have you believing it."

Susan turned over and punched the pillow beneath her head. Perissa opened her eyes and glared at Susan for disturbing her.

Who killed the killer recently released from prison? Why? She'd take answers from anybody.

Porter Kane made a quick run to the river and dumped a box of ashes. Everything happened to him. It wasn't his fault the damn plane started giving him trouble. If he could of come up with the money to get it fixed, he'd of been okay. Then he got the ax from his job. Just a little time, that's all he needed. Fucking repair guy snooping around.

He went home, stripped off his clothes, and stumbled to bed. God, it must be near three o'clock. He bunched the pillow and tried to sleep.

"Roy, if you don't stop that tossing and turning, you can pick up your pillow and sleep on the couch."

"Sorry. Lots on my mind."

"Oh, Roy, she's your mother," Lillian said. "Nobody's going to think you pushed your mother off the porch and left her to die."

He grumbled something. If Lillian'd just shut up! Couldn't she see the whole thing bothered him? With everything on his mind, telling him he did the right thing wasn't helping. Couldn't she understand? Sometimes, on a night like this, he thought about snatching Jo and just taking off. Except then he'd never see Mandy again. He loved her just as much as Jo, but she was spending so much time with her friends that she wasn't all that interested in hanging out with dear old Dad.

He thought about Cindy and wondered if she was in bed alone or if Harley was with her. The son of a bitch. She'd told Roy she'd convinced Harley it was that furnace guy. Maybe the police would think Harley killed the guy and throw the bastard in jail. He wouldn't have to worry about Harley beating her up anymore.

Lillian had his mother's money all planned out. So much for this, so much for that.

He turned over and yanked on the covers, pulling a large share to his side. How could she go to sleep just like that? One minute telling him what to do and the next sound asleep. Didn't she have a conscience at all?

29

_____

At six A.M. on Sunday morning, when Susan rolled groaning out of bed, she realized she'd gone to sleep far too late to greet the day with glorious song. After a hot shower, she pulled on black wool pants and a gray sweater, scooped cat food into a bowl while Perissa rubbed against her legs and left beige hair all over the black pants. Susan gave them a quick swipe with a clothes brush and headed out.

The cold grabbed her by the throat and squeezed the air from her lungs. Her little brown sports car sat on one side of the garage, covered with dust, probably shivering and longing for California. She knew just how it felt. Why not get rid of it? Did she think she was going to drive it back? Probably. Hope and dandelions spring eternal.

The pickup needed coaxing, not wanting any more to do with this day than she did. At the Coffee Cup Cafe she got a large black coffee and headed for work.

Hazel was already there. "I heard you sneaking in," she said.

"This isn't sneaking. Bent over is the way I always look when I get up in the morning."

At her desk, she read reports that had come in during the

night. Joseph still missing from the crèche, another break-in. Whoever was responsible for this rash of burglaries they'd been plagued with was taking only cash or items that could be turned into cash quickly, like jewelry, credit cards, laptop computers. One woman complained because he'd taken her carton of cigarettes and the cookies she'd baked for her daughter's birthday party. Even the Lutheran church wasn't exempt. Reverend Mullett reported money missing from the donations dropped in a basket and used for refreshments at various functions like the after-services gatherings and Wednesday night Bible study.

It was after nine when she finally left for Robbin Pharmacy on Iowa Street. Elena Robbin, slightly overweight, black hair, wearing dark trousers and a striped shirt with a white collar, greeted Susan with a smile. Elena was a granddaughter of the Robbin on the sign. "I hope you don't have this flu everybody else has."

"Don't even suggest it."

"Everybody comes dragging in here wanting something to make them better." She waved a hand at the shelves of cold remedies, cough drops, and decongestants. "Fluids is the only thing. And bed rest, then just wait for the end."

Susan raised an eyebrow.

Elena laughed. "No, not the final end. The end of suffering from this particular virus."

Susan opened the bottle of Advil she'd taken from Caley James and shook two pills into her hand. "Can you tell me what these are?"

Elena took half-glasses from her lab coat pocket and settled them on her nose. She peered at the pills, then at Susan. "What is it you want to know?"

"Are they Advil?"

"No."

"What are they?"

"I can't tell you that. I could make a guess, but the only way to know is send them to a lab."

"I will, but it'll take a while. Guess."

"Okay. As long as you're not going to hold me to it. I'd say they're Halcion."

"Not Advil?"

"Definitely not. Have you been taking these?"

"I shouldn't be?"

"Definitely not."

"What is Halcion for?"

"Some physicians used to prescribe it for sleep, but it has heavy side effects. Nightmares, for one."

"What kind of side effects would result if two are taken every four hours or so?"

"Good Lord, don't ever do that. This isn't a good drug. It could cause amnesia taken that heavy. Have you been taking this?" Elena studied her.

"No."

"Whoever it is, tell her to stop immediately. Taken in those amounts, it's a wonder she didn't end up in a coma."

"Why do you say 'she'?"

Elena looked embarrassed. "Well, it's usually women who get sleeping pills. It doesn't make any difference. Man or woman, tell him or her to stop it."

"I will," Susan said. She thanked her and bought a bottle of Advil.

No wonder Caley James was so groggy all the time. How had she gotten Halcion? Given by a physician for sleep? Why was it in an Advil bottle?

When Caley opened the door, Susan stepped in and asked how Zach was.

"Doing great. Moving on those crutches like sixty. He zips around so fast, he scares me."

The house was quiet and the living room neat.

Caley smiled wearily. "If you're wondering why the decibel level isn't up to the ceiling and the place isn't a pig sty, it's because they're in bed and my boss was here. Let's go in the kitchen; I've got fresh coffee."

Susan wasn't sure she needed any more coffee this evening, but she followed Caley and took the mug when it was filled. She sat down, slipped the new bottle of Advil from her shoulder bag, and placed it on the table.

Caley picked it up and examined the label. She looked at Susan. "Was something wrong with the one I had?"

"Where'd you get it?"

Caley raked hair from her face. "So there *was* something wrong with it. What?"

Nothing slow about Caley James. "It needs to be analyzed before I'll know, but the pharmacist thinks it might be Halcion. Have you ever taken that?"

"No. What is it?"

"Apparently, a sleeping pill. You ever use anything to help you sleep?"

Caley rubbed her forehead. "Yeah, I think so, but I don't remember what. It was a long time ago. Anyway, I didn't put it in an Advil bottle."

"How could that happen?"

"You think I'm so scattered I'd do a thing like that?" Caley looked horrified. "What if I'd given it to one of the kids?"

"Do you ever give them anything like that? For fever or flu?"

"Zach maybe. Not the other two. They're too young. I only give them children's stuff."

"If you didn't put it in an Advil bottle, how did it get there?"

"I don't know."

"Who would deliberately try to harm you?"

"Nobody. Why would they? Oh, maybe one or two congregation members. They think I shouldn't be playing for church services because I'm divorced. We might as well be living in the dark ages around here. Hell, it makes me want to open a bordello in this house and advertise in the Sunday bulletin." She ran her fingers through her hair, making it stand on end.

"Your husband?"

"Ex-husband. Why? Get out of paying child support? He doesn't pay it anyway."

"Who comes into the kitchen besides you and the children? You said Evan Devereau?"

Caley flushed. "Only recently. He's been helping."

"Your ex-husband?"

"Yeah. I need some orange juice. Would you like some?"

"No, thanks," Susan said. "Coffee's fine."

Caley retrieved a carton from the refrigerator and plopped it on the table. "Does that feel cold to you?"

Susan ran a hand along it. It definitely wasn't cold.

"Shit." Caley grabbed a tissue from the box on the countertop and vigorously blew her nose. "I was hoping I was wrong and the poor old thing would rally 'round. No such luck. I tried putting stuff on the back porch, but . . . egg Popsicles."

Oh dear. Was there any way to get help for her? Caley looked like she'd just about reached her limit. Churches? They must have funds for those who needed help.

"Do any of your neighbors ever come in?"

"Sure. Pauline, across the street. The kids let her cat in and she comes over to take it home. Ida Ruth Dandermadden a time or two. I wouldn't put it past her. She's the leader of the get-rid-of-that-James-slut-before-she— I'm not sure what it is I'm maybe doing to the unsullied minds of the congregation."

"Why was she here?"

"She comes when I'm gone to spread her gospel. Ettie, in the interests of politeness, invites her in for coffee."

"So Ettie would be here."

"Sure. She takes care of the kids. Sometimes at her house, sometimes here. If they have to go to bed before I'm due home or stuff like that."

Halcion, Ida Ruth Dandermadden, and a tampered railing? What, for God's sake, was the connection? Susan would have Ida Ruth's blood checked for Halcion.

187

"When did you put that bottle in the cabinet?"

Caley looked at her. "You're joking, right? I can't remember when I brushed my teeth last, let alone put a bottle on a shelf. What does the stuff do to you?"

"Makes you sleep. Gives you dreams, sometimes nightmares." Susan didn't mention the possibility of amnesia.

Caley nodded. "Oh, boy, have I had those."

"How often do you take something to help you sleep?"

"Mostly never. I'm usually so tired I don't need any help. I had Tylenol with codeine when I broke my leg, but I maybe never did have anything for sleep." She poured a glass of juice and held it out for Susan. "It was cold yesterday morning."

"No, thank you."

Driving back to the department, she mulled over the Halcion in Caley's cabinet. Why was it put there? To embarrass her? By somebody like Ida Ruth? To make her fall asleep at the organ, play badly? Or to put her asleep when she was home?

Why? So he/she could get in and out of the house without her knowing? What about the kids? They'd know.

Ah, but maybe they did know. Bonnie had said that an evil prince had been in the basement moving things around. Nobody had paid any attention to her. At night the kids would be asleep, and with Halcion, Caley would never hear anyone coming in and out. Seemed very risky.

Branner Noel? To get in the basement? Pauline Frankens had seen him going in and out the basement door. The house proper? No reason for doing so that Susan could think of. The ex-husband? The kids wouldn't think anything of him coming in. Why would he want to come in without Caley's knowledge? To find something? What? If anything was hidden anywhere, the best place would be the basement. Without some clue of what she was looking for, she'd never find it. If—whether—it was still there.

Susan radioed Hazel, who said, "Nothing going on I can't handle, except the mayor. He called and wanted to know if you'd like to be a jack-in-the-box on the Santa float."

"I just may be coming down with the flu," Susan said darkly.

"You'd get to jump up and down the whole parade route."

She hung up and was pulling away when she saw smoke rising from Pauline Frankens's roof, white against a black sky.

30

—

$\mathcal{S}$usan reached for the mike and reported the fire to Hazel. While she watched, an orange glow started in the front window, then flames licked around the curtains. As she slid from the pickup she saw a small child race toward the house and disappear inside.

"Bonnie!" Susan ran after her.

It was dark inside; smoke filled the air. She coughed. Faintly, behind a great roar, she heard the child's voice call, "Ollie? Ollie?"

"Bonnie!" She was upstairs looking for the damn cat. Susan climbed the stairs. Smoke heavier up here. She followed the direction of Bonnie's voice. Smoke too thick to breathe.

She held her breath and tried to hear past the snapping crackling roar. Downstairs!

Too black to see. Stumbling through blackness so dense she lost all sense of direction, she strained to hear Bonnie through the roar. Dropping to the floor, she crawled. Bumped into a door that moved when she pushed. She felt linoleum under her hands. Bathroom. Feeling along, she found a cabinet and stood up. Faucet. She splashed water on her face and clothes. The fire's roar grew louder. Back on hands and knees, she made her way out of the bathroom. Kept crawling. Found the hallway.

Pain shot through her knees. She touched a bundle of clothes, clutched at it, and moved her hands along it until she reached a face. Bonnie.

Blind as a mole, Susan got a firm grip on the little girl. Air too hot to breathe. One arm grasping Bonnie, she scuttled along like a crippled crab.

The roaring grew louder. Screaming filled the inside of her skull. She didn't know if it escaped or went round and round, trapped inside. Panic tugged at her, urging her to drop the child and run. Run! Before it's too late.

Don't worry, Bonnie, she whispered in her mind. Smoke and heat scoured the membranes in her throat and clawed into her lungs. Hot wind slapped her face, tore at her hair and clothes. Pushing along, she fought to keep herself from leaving the child and escaping.

Keep going, keep going, she chanted in her mind. Bonnie hadn't made a sound or a struggle. Don't think about that.

A spark fell on her coat sleeve and sent up a little smolder of smoke. She tucked the arm under her body to put it out, thinking at the same time that might be stupid. She might burst into flames, a small fire waiting to welcome the large one coming.

She kept going and suddenly realized she didn't know where the door was. She was probably crabbing around in circles. She was going to die. The little girl was going to die, if she wasn't already dead.

An explosion smashed her shoulders to the floor. The roar of wind swept over her, sucking the air from her lungs, pushing the fire in. Her mouth gaped; hot air scored her chest. She clamped her teeth. Keep going.

Suddenly, she stopped. She heard the roar of God's own thunder. Flames billowed. Beautiful. Orange and red and black boiling up. Reaching out to welcome her.

A vise clamped around her ankle. No. Stop. I have to rise up and meet it. She kicked at whatever was dragging her back.

The vise got tighter. Pulled. No! No!

Her shoulders were grabbed and she was lifted. Somebody pried Bonnie from her hands. An oxygen mask was clamped over her face.

A deep breath set off a fit of coughing. She looked at the scene in front of her and thought she must be in a nightmare.

Smoke billowed up, gray against the black sky. Firemen, looking like spacemen, aimed hoses. Water hit the ground and froze. They skidded on the ice. Flailed their arms. Tried to hold each other up. They crawled with hoses snaked behind them. One man stood and fell hard on his elbow.

Flames shot up, forcing a retreat, lighting up faces of angry, frustrated firefighters trying to cope with the raw naked power of a force stronger than they were.

Susan pulled the mask from her face. "Pauline," she yelled at the fireman nearest her. That set off such a fit of coughing, she couldn't breathe. The oxygen mask was replaced on her face.

"You believe in miracles?" he shouted back.

No, she didn't.

Her chest burned and her lips felt blistered.

In amazement and terror, she watched a scene from Keystone Kops as firefighters fell and slid and staggered as they tried to get up. The ice on the ground melted into rivulets when the fire reached it. Paramedics lifted her to a gurney and slid her into the ambulance.

Hours later, when the grim madness of the dark turned into a cold bleak day, a weary and dirty fireman came in to see her. "What the hell were you doing in there?"

"The little girl." Her voice was raspy and deep, her throat raw. "I saw her go—" Coughing seized her.

"Don't talk," the fireman said.

"Didn't think, just—" Coughing clawed her raw throat.

"You realize you're a lot heavier than the kid, and you both had to be rescued."

"Thank you," she whispered.

He smiled. Very white teeth in a soot-blackened face. "That's what we're here for."

"Bonnie?"

"She's here. You did a pretty good job of protecting her. She's not burned any. You, on the other hand, got your hands singed."

Susan looked at the bandages on her hands. "Fire out?"

"Close. We're waiting to make sure."

"Mrs. Frankens?"

He shook his head.

31

———

*Th*roat still sore and raspy, voice sounding a bit like a bullfrog with a bad cold, Susan was released from the hospital on Monday afternoon. She was still subject to coughing fits, and her bandaged hands made it awkward to do anything.

Chet Mosler, the county arson investigator, was already at the Frankens house when she arrived. He was a tall, thin man with a long jaw, a lanky frame, and a heavy sense of humor. She'd worked with him before and was pleased at how good he was. A fireman, waiting to make sure hot spots were completely out, gave them hard hats and masks. "Be careful," he said.

She intended to. The front door was open, and when she and the arson investigator went inside, the temperature seemed to drop. That made it pretty damn cold inside, and damp. It smelled of burnt wood and soggy plaster and melted materials. A dark slime covered everything.

Straight ahead was what was left of the staircase to the second floor, on the right was the living room, and on the left the dining room. The kitchen was behind the dining room. She had been to fire scenes before, but had forgotten the bleak devastation fire left in its wake.

Blackened boards were everywhere, like debris smashed against the rocks of a seawall. Some lay as if thrown across the nearest skeletons of chairs and couch frames, or against the walls. Remains of furniture lay in black piles. Wires dangled from walls and ceilings, pipes protruded from walls at odd angles. The window frames and the stairs were trimmed with black icicles, like black Christmas tree trimming.

People in hard hats with clipboards were everywhere, poking into debris and taking measurements, collecting evidence and scratching through the black ice on the heaps of cloth.

Dr. Fisher spotted Mosler and came up with his hand outstretched. "Hello, Chet, Susan. Sad mess, this." He nodded at the chaos all around, then pointed at what had been the kitchen.

"Arson?"

"Yeah," Mosler said. "The fire was stronger in the back of the house. They think it started on that rear glassed-in porch. Probably why nobody saw anything until too late. Have you looked at the body?"

"Not yet," Fisher said. "I've been waiting for them to say it's safe."

Susan was all for safety. She flexed her cold toes inside her boots and shoved bandaged hands inside her pockets. The stench and the gloom and the sadness inside the burned shell of a house were the epitome of misery.

A fireman picked his way through the mess over to them and looked up. "It's okay now. Keep the hard hats on and try not to shake anything. The whole structure is apt to collapse into the basement."

Great. Just what she wanted to hear. Nothing like waiting for the floor to fall in to make you comfortable.

Mosler went first, then Susan, then Fisher moved across the shaky floor. The wooden cabinets in the kitchen were gone, a melted glob of what must be countertop hung next to the sink, the refrigerator door was open, contents black and melted. Shattered dishes from upper cabinets lay on the buckled floor.

She stuck as close as she could to the crumbling walls. The glassed-in porch behind was completely gone, ceiling burned away, wall between it and the kitchen nothing but a few jagged black boards. The floor was a gaping black hole. A ladder angled down into the blackness below. Glass and grit crunched beneath their feet. Her jaw tightened and her chest felt like the next breath might break something inside it.

Gunny had been pulled from class when the body was found sprawled in a doorway. One look and he started retching.

"Give me the camera," Susan said, knowing he wouldn't. Armed muggers would be turned down. With her bandaged hands, it was just as well. She couldn't click anyway.

He shook his head and started clicking. The victim was in the doorway of what had been the glassed-in porch. Clothed, though the fire had burned too much away to determine whether male or female. She assumed Pauline Frankens. It lay on one side with the forearms high and bent, like a fighter. Typical of fire victims. The heat cooked the arms, causing the muscles to contract. Clumps of burned flesh hung on the bones. The hands were black stumps. The face was grotesque, lips gone, teeth exposed in a ghastly grin, nose gone. A bit of muscle on the cheekbones. Eye sockets with eyeballs like a Halloween joke. Hair gone, top of the head missing.

Susan's stomach contracted. The coffee she'd had to keep awake did not sit well. Through the open ceiling, she saw a pearl-gray sky.

"My take on it," Mosler drawled, "would be, victim came running from the dining room, or headed to the kitchen and got caught. Shot maybe, or bashed on the head. Or just caught in the fire."

Susan didn't have a take on it, she went with the expert, and wanted to get out of this relic of a house and the misery it held.

"I'll need to poke around another hour or so, then it's all yours." Mosler ambled off.

Dr. Fisher studied the body. Susan tucked her hands in her armpits, trying to bring some warmth into them, and stared out at the backyard. A sparrow and a cardinal hopped around on the bird feeder hanging from a scorched tree.

"There's smoke around the nostrils," Dr. Fisher said, "and in the nose and throat."

That meant the victim was still alive when the fire caught her. Susan hugged herself.

He turned the body and indicated the cherry-red color. "The lividity suggests carbon monoxide in the blood."

She took a shallow breath, trying not to think it could be her he was studying.

He pressed a finger against a white spot that appeared in the red muscle. "Blanching," he said. "Means lividity isn't fixed. That white spot only appears for a few hours after lividity first develops."

She didn't watch anymore, just stood at the open porch wall trying to breathe fresh air. Every breath hurt, smelled of charred wood and death.

The paramedics loaded the body and carried it along the shaking floor out to the waiting ambulance. She went to the kitchen to find Mosler. The devastation there was worse than anywhere else. The roof was mostly gone and cold wind swirled through.

"This was a hot one," Mosler said. "See that deformed pipe?"

She nodded.

"Copper. It takes over eleven hundred degrees centigrade to melt copper like that."

"How did it start?"

He nodded at the propane tank against the far wall. "Found two of those so far."

"Arson," she said.

"Either that or this old lady wanted to stock up on propane. Porch area was stacked with highly burnable stuff too. Books and papers. Don't know why people do it. 'Course, in this case, it wouldn't matter. But all that junk just helped the arsonist."

Mosler shot her a look. "You could go, if you like," he said dryly. "Anything interesting turns up, I'll include it in my report and see you get a copy."

She had never figured him out. She didn't know if he had a sense of humor that was beyond her understanding or if he was making snide remarks about her intelligence, but she decided he was right in that she could go now. She went.

32

———

$\mathscr{I}$t wasn't until two o'clock on Tuesday afternoon that Susan was able to see Roy Dandermadden. Ida Ruth was still holding on, much to the amazement of her physicians.

"Should you be out in this cold?" he said. "I heard you were in the hospital. How are you?" He unlatched the storm door and invited her in, tucking the tails of his white shirt into his tan corduroy pants.

"I'm fine, thank you." The bandages on her hands had been replaced by small gauze squares, but her throat still hurt and she tended to have coughing fits if she talked much.

"A few questions." She sat on the couch and got out her notebook.

He looked startled at her raspy low voice. "You sure you should be doing this?"

"Despite the way I sound, I'm fine," she said. "Where were you on Wednesday of last week?"

"You mean when my mother got hurt."

A basset hound lumbered in, long ears flopping, and spread himself by Dandermadden's chair. Dandermadden reached down to pat the dog's side. "You asking for an alibi? You think I loosened that railing hoping my mother would fall?"

"Somebody loosened it."

"I was right here."

"All day?"

"Pretty much, I think. In the morning the girls and I went out to find their mom's Christmas present."

"In the afternoon?" She coughed.

"I was working on some shelves I'm putting up in the garage."

"Anyone else home?" Her throat was getting more sore and more hoarse.

"Only Harvey, here." The dog raised its head and thumped its tail. "My wife was at work and the girls out with their friends. When Lillian got off, they all went to a movie. I stayed home and watched television."

"Where is your wife now?"

"At work. She'll be back directly."

"What did you watch, Mr. Dandermadden?"

"Uh—an old movie. *It's a Wonderful Life*."

"You watched a movie at home rather than go to see one with your wife and daughters?" She swallowed to keep from coughing.

"Any law against it?"

He was beginning to get a wee bit angry with her. "No, Mr. Dandermadden, no law against it. Anyone call while they were gone? Come by? No? What time did they get back?"

"Close to midnight, I think. They went for pizza afterwards. My youngest one, Jo, she loves pizza. Gets her mom to take her every chance she gets."

"Does your mother have any enemies?" She spoke softly, trying to ward off the coughing fit she knew was coming.

"Enemies?" He bent down and rubbed the dog's ear tip between two fingers. "She has a sharp tongue, and some people maybe get irritated, but enemies?" He shook his head.

"Are you her heir?" She knew his anger was getting stronger, but he held on to it.

200

"Yes."

"Other relatives?"

"She has a brother. They haven't spoken in years. He pissed her off somehow."

"She ever get angry with you?"

Roy looked at her. "Don't think I don't know what you're doing, and yes, she got angry at me, but never so mad she wouldn't speak to me."

Who would be at her beck and call if she didn't speak to him? "Who else benefits from her death?"

The dog yelped, gave Dandermadden a dirty look, and paced off. "The church."

When she started coughing, she thanked him, told him to call if he thought of anything that might help, and left. In the pickup, she got the motor going, turned the heater higher, and searched through her shoulder bag for a cough drop. Roy Dandermadden, she mused, was guilty of something. The majority of suspects were guilty of something, but not necessarily the crime being investigated. Maybe his wife was tired of waiting for the old woman to die. Maybe he had an expensive girlfriend.

Roy held the newspaper open to the sports section, not reading, just trying to ignore Lillian's voice coming from the kitchen, where she was putting away groceries. She went on about how much easier it would be for Mandy to go to Stanford if they had money. They wouldn't have to worry about where every penny was going to come from.

"Maybe we could even take a vacation, Roy. You and I. How long has it been since we were anywhere together? Just the two of us without the kids."

Roy shook the page as he turned it. If asked, he couldn't even say how the Kansas City Chiefs were doing.

"Jo's always wanted to go to Disneyland—"

"For God's sake, the woman isn't even dead yet!" He flung down the paper and stomped into the bedroom.

A few minutes later, Lillian heard the car back out of the driveway. Leaning forward, she pressed an arm against her stomach to hold in the pain. He was seeing someone. She knew it. She didn't know who, but she knew there was someone.

Well, he couldn't just walk all over her. She'd pack up the girls and go as far away as she could get.

It'd been stupid of her to go on and on like she had. It wasn't even Christian. Roy was right; the poor woman wasn't dead yet, and she was his mother, after all. It's just that she was always so critical. No matter how much time he spent there, mowing the lawn, shoveling the driveway, cleaning the gutters, mending screens, painting window frames. She was never satisfied. He spent more time keeping her place fixed up than he did this one.

Lillian thought, bad as it sounded, it would be a relief when Ida Ruth passed. When he got back, she'd apologize. She'd been insensitive and she wanted him to know she was sorry.

Roy gripped the steering wheel to keep from pounding his fist on it. Where was his brain, calling Cindy from the bedroom? Lillian could have walked in. One of the girls could have picked up the extension. Thank God, Harley was working tonight.

What if somebody saw him sneaking over there? It'd be all over town, for God's certain sure. Lillian going on and on about Mom and him seeing her out there lying on the cement all night in the freezing cold. He just hadn't been able to stand Lillian's voice anymore.

He parked right in front of Cindy's house. That way they could say they had classwork to discuss. He walked as slow as the cold and his beating heart would allow him. She was waiting to let him in, and he enfolded her in a hug. She winced. He leaned back to take a good look at her.

"Cindy?"

She covered her face with both hands. "Don't look at me. I know I look awful."

He pried her hands away. "Did Harley hit you again?"

"No. He never hit me. I told you, I fell. I'm a lot better now. Oh, Roy, it's so good to see you." She snuggled gingerly against him.

"I had to see you. Just for a few minutes. I know I shouldn't have come, but I couldn't stay away." He drew her closer to the light and looked carefully at her yellowing bruises. "If Harley ever hits you again, I'll kill him."

"Roy, I told you. I fell. Just forget it." She twined her fingers around his and started to pull him toward the bedroom.

"We can't," he said. "It's too risky. I'm sorry I came."

She pressed a finger against his lips. "Never say that. At least you can hold me."

He did so, gently.

"How's your mother?" she asked when she drew back.

"Still the same. I can't talk about that."

She nodded. "I understand."

He stayed less than an hour, and when he left, he felt worse than when he'd come. If Mom died— If that woman cop found out about Cindy— Oh, hell, he'd just given her a motive.

Jo had put the receiver back very slowly and quietly. Dad was talking to Cindy? Cindy Wakefield the English teacher?

There was one way to find out. Telling her mom she was going to ride her bike over to the library, Jo wheeled it from the garage and swung on as it rolled down the driveway.

Even with her gloves on, her hands were cold. She wanted snow for Christmas. She wanted a lot of things this Christmas. Mom and Dad to stop fighting. Or whatever you could call it. They didn't exactly fight. They hardly spoke to each other, and when they did it was in such a polite voice, more polite than even you'd talk to a stranger.

She'd known something was going on with her mom and dad for a long time. She didn't think Mandy knew. Mandy was so busy looking at herself in the mirror and talking to her friends about going to Stanford that Jo could puke. Nothing else entered Mandy's head these days. Jo would be glad when she left. At least Jo wouldn't have to hear about it all the time.

She wished she could talk to Zach. Not that he could tell her what to do, but at least he'd be someone to be with and tell things to. She was worried about him. He was acting all spaced and weirded out.

Mrs. Wakefield lived on Cedar Street. From the end of the block, Jo could see her dad's car parked in front. What would happen if she just went right up to the door and knocked?

For one thing, her dad would be really mad at her. And what if they were—you know, in bed or something? She crossed the street and rode up on the sidewalk, then decided she wasn't the one doing anything wrong and went right out into the street just like she had every right to do. A better idea popped to mind. She pedaled to the far end of the block and left the bicycle propped against a tree trunk. Going through backyards from house to house, she got to the Wakefield house and hid in the bushes by the front porch.

The stupid bushes were dusty and had sharp things that pricked her jacket and stuck her right through the legs of her jeans. She felt cramped and cold, and she was going to sneeze. How long could she stay here? Her nose was starting to run and she couldn't find a tissue. What were they doing in there anyway? Never mind that, she wasn't sure she wanted to know.

Just when she thought she couldn't stay another second, the door opened. Scooting farther back, she pasted herself against the house. Her father and Mrs. Wakefield stood in the doorway. Over his shoulder— Jo gasped. Mrs. Wakefield's face was all purple and yellowish green. Like somebody had beat her up. Dad? No. He wouldn't do that. He wouldn't!

Jo bit her lip and crouched down as she peered through the

shrubbery and watched her dad walk, slow and kind of dejected, like he was really tired or discouraged, out to his car.

When he drove away, Jo stayed where she was a little longer, just in case Mrs. Wakefield was watching out a window or something, and then set off after her bicycle.

She started pedaling. Everything was going wrong in her life. Zach was looking over his shoulder all the time like something was chasing him. Mom was all tight and snappy. Mandy was dreamy about leaving for California. Dad was unhappy all the time. She couldn't talk to Mandy or her mom and especially not her dad, but maybe she could talk to Zach.

She rode all the way to his house. When she asked for Zach his mother smiled at her. "Hi, Jo. He's up in his room. Go on up."

He was sitting at his computer with his back to her. She came up behind him and whispered, "Hi."

He jumped twenty feet in the air, looked like he wanted to punch her, and tapped a key on the keyboard to make what was on the screen disappear. "Don't sneak up on me," he hissed.

"You want to go to my house and play Scream on my computer?"

"Can't. I have to go see a guy."

"Who?"

"A guy."

"I could come with you."

He turned on her. "You can't."

She took a small step back. "Why not?"

"You can't tell anybody, either." He glared at her. "I mean it, Jo. Nobody. Not ever." He waited to make sure she got it. "Promise?"

She didn't like this; he was acting really nuts. But she nodded. "How you going to get there?"

"Walk."

"You're supposed to stay off your sprained ankle."

"It's not that far."

He prodded her ahead of him and closed the bedroom door

as he came out. When they were outside, he told her he'd see her later. She got on her bike, and he took off down Hollis Street on his crutches. He'd wiped out the stuff on his computer screen pretty fast, but not so fast she hadn't seen it.

The name Porter Kane and an address.

With her bicycle, she had no trouble getting there before he did; all she had to do was be careful he didn't see her. That meant stashing her bike a block away against the side of a garage and hoofing it back to Kane's.

There wasn't much place to hide at his house. No trees or shrubbery or anything close enough to the front porch and the door so she could see. She had to settle for crouching down near the front tire on the far side of the minivan in the driveway. She had to wait forever.

Almost ten minutes passed before Zach came hobbling up on his crutches. He climbed onto the porch and knocked on the door.

Mr. Kane or somebody opened it. "What you want, kid?"

"You were out on Falcon Road."

"Yeah, so?"

"It was you," Zach said. "You took it."

"Whata' you talking about?"

"You had his tobacco in your jacket pocket. I smelled it."

"Anybody can buy tobacco." The door started closing.

"Anybody who is at the place where a pouch of it disappears, along with a lot of money? You think the cops might like to hear about that?"

A hand grabbed Zack's arm and jerked him inside.

Jo waited.

It got dark, and still Zach didn't come back out. She didn't know what to do. She had promised him she wouldn't ever tell.

She didn't like this. Something really bad was going on.

She waited.

She pulled in a breath with a big sigh and blew it out. Maybe this guy who had Zach was the killer.

Even very much aware that Zack might hate her if she broke

her promise, she had to tell somebody. If she told Zach's mom, Mrs. James would freak. Mrs. James was just that kind. If she told her own mom she'd get, I'm sure it's nothing, don't worry about it, or I'm sure it's nothing but we need to tell his mother, or we need to tell his mother right away. The first wouldn't help and the other two would take too long.

Jo breathed in and out on another sigh, got on her bike and rode to the police station. She told everything to the pretty woman police chief, except she didn't mention the name Porter Kane.

"I'm sure Zach's fine, but I'll check it out. What's the address?"

Jo made a big deal acting like she was embarrassed because she wasn't exactly sure where the house was. "But I can show you," she said.

No way was she just going home without knowing Zach was all right.

Chief Wren got in the back of a squad car and Jo sat in the front next to a cop named Officer Demarco so she could show him where to go.

33

$\mathcal{Z}$ach got dragged inside and tossed on the couch. Kane backed up to an overstuffed chair and lowered his butt on it, sitting hunched over with his forearms on his knees.

"You got something to say about cops, kid?"

Ignoring his heart slamming away in his chest, Zach straightened, leaned back, and rested one hand on the couch arm. "No," he said. "I'll never tell the cops."

"Doesn't matter. You got no proof."

"First off," Zach said, "I got E-mail set to go to Baines at eight o'clock tonight. That's when the post office closes."

"What do I care when the post office closes?"

"The E-mail says you have his money."

Kane squinted his eyes into narrow slits.

"Cops might need proof," Zach said, "but Baines won't. He'll come for it. If you don't hand it over, he'll hurt you so bad you'll wish you'd never seen the stuff."

Kane leaned back, hands behind his head like he was halfway amused, but Zach could tell he was listening. "That's what you came to tell me?"

"No, sir. I came to tell you that you have to give it back."

208

Kane made an explosive noise that was half snort, half barking laugh. "Assuming I stole anything, which I didn't, why would I go and do a damn fool thing like that?"

"If I get home before eight, I'll delete the message. Nobody will ever hear anything about the money. Not Baines, not the cops. If I don't get home, if something . . . happens to me, Baines will know at eight o'clock that you took his money."

Kane stared at him and made a rasping sound by rubbing a knuckle over the stubble on his jaw. "How you think this giving back is supposed to work?"

"We'll take the money to the post office and send it overnight mail."

"You think you got everything figured out, don't you?"

"Except how you knew the money was there."

Kane's teeth appeared in a wolfish grin. "Word gets around. You need money? Ask Baines, he'll lend it to you. Fellow like that has to have it coming and going. Understand?"

"Not really," Zach said.

"Kept an eye on the place. People comin' and goin'. Gotta be always takin' it or bringin' it back. Your dad, he was bringin' it back. And there it was, sittin' there for anybody smart enough to be in the right place at the right time."

Kane's face got a hard feral look. "And you're thinkin' I'll give it back?"

"Yes, sir, I hope so." Zach's heart was starting to leap around again, but this time because *it was going to work!* They'd package the money, get it to the post office, and Baines would no longer be waiting to ambush Zach and Dad wouldn't be in trouble. Everything would be just the way—

Kane's head went up, like a dog who hears something suspicious. He stood and looked out the window. "It's the cops! You lyin' little shit!"

* * *

Demarco started to get out of the squad car. A shotgun boomed. The windshield crazed. Screaming, Jo opened the car door, jumped out, and tore down the road.

He sprinted after her. The shotgun scattered dirt at her heels. He tackled her. They fell, his body shielding hers. Susan got on the radio and told Hazel to get all available officers at this vicinity immediately.

The shotgun boomed again.

34

$\mathcal{U}$sing the car door as a shield, Susan fired at the window on the side of the house where the sniper was shooting from. The shotgun thundered. Buckshot rattled along the road like sleet.

She fired back. He sent off another shot. Dirt exploded at her feet. Wind blew particles in her face like a handful of sand, filling one eye. Tears welled up, blurring her vision.

Sirens wailed. One squad car pulled in behind Demarco's and one ahead. Blue-uniformed officers spilled out, moonlight shining on eager faces. Probably everybody who wasn't out sick. They worried her. She didn't want any wild-man heroics that would get someone killed.

Spreading out across the front seat, she murmured into the car radio to keep the sniper occupied.

When the shotgun barrel appeared in the window, shots smashed into the frame and all around it. In a running crouch, she made her way to Demarco.

He lay still, one shoulder black with blood. Jo made mewling noises and struggled to get away from him. Susan touched a fingertip to the corner of his jaw. Her hands were so cold, she couldn't feel anything.

"Not dead," he muttered.

Taking a firm grip on Jo's arm, she told him, "Ease off."

A sharp intake of breath as he released his hold and shifted his weight. Susan pulled Jo out. Forcing the girl to stay crouched and shielding her with her own body, Susan, under the *crack crack crack* of handguns, ran Jo from the middle of the road toward the squad parked nose to nose with Demarco's.

White grabbed Jo and shoved her in. He handed Susan a Kevlar vest. "Ambulance on the way," he said.

In three minutes, the ambulance swerved in behind the squad car. Paramedics jumped out. From the rear, they grabbed a gurney.

"Keep him busy," Susan murmured into the radio.

Under the barrage of shots, the paramedics ran to the center of the road, dragging a gurney with a squeaky wheel. They lifted Demarco, buckled him on, and raced back, slowing only slightly when they reached the back of the ambulance. They tucked him inside and took off.

With the radio, she told Crenshaw, Marshall, and Ellis to go around to the rear. "At my signal, make a lot of noise. Break down the door if you have to."

She told Adler and White to come with her.

"Remember," she said into the radio, "this may be a hostage situation, so be careful what you shoot. And, guys, let's not shoot each other."

What she wouldn't give for five experienced cops. She held the 9-mm handgun ready as she approached the porch. Heart thudding loud enough to almost cover the creak of the boards, she went up the steps, eyes on the door. Nothing happened inside the house as far as she could tell.

Motioning Adler to go to the left of the door and White to get behind her, she cautiously moved up to the right side of the door. Standing against the wall, as far back as possible, she reached out and gently tried the knob. Unlocked. She pushed it open.

As it swung in, a round hole splintered the wood, and the

thunder of the shotgun made her ears pop. With the aftermath of noise crackling in her ears, she murmured "Now" into the radio.

Adrenaline kicked up, she went low through the splintered door, gun ready. She heard the noise as Crenshaw, Marshall, and Ellis came in the back. The living room was empty.

Expecting another shotgun blast, she peered around the door-jamb into a kitchen. Ceiling light on. Empty. Formica-topped table, four chrome chairs, white-painted cabinets.

When the shotgun roared again, her heart leaped into her throat. "Stay put," she muttered to Adler, and motioned White to follow her.

Back against the wall, she eased along the hallway to a stairway leading to the basement. She took a quick glance as she ran past. She waited for the shot. When none came, she moved slowly to the open door beyond the stairway. No sound from inside. She peered around the jamb and went in fast and low, gun ready. The room was empty.

There was a closed door across from the basement stairway. She stood to one side and listened. No sound. She called, "Police. Put down your weapon! Come out with your hands on your head!"

Her answer was a shot that splintered the door.

"You can't get away! Come out with your hands on your head!"

"Come in and get me!"

She wondered if the room was filled with ammo and he could sit there blasting away forever.

"Mr. Kane?" she called. "It's Chief Wren. We spoke last week."

She thought her answer might be another shot, but there was a silence that stretched out.

"So?" he said finally.

"What will it take, Mr. Kane, to get you to come out?"

"Ha! You think you can just sweet-talk me out of here?"

"Is there anything I can get you?"

"A million dollars."

"Anything else? Something to eat? A cheeseburger?"

"A million dollars and a helicopter."

"Hampstead Police Department doesn't have a helicopter."

She didn't know much about hostage negotiation—but "keep the barricaded suspect talking" was rule number one.

"I want a helicopter and a propeller for a Cessna 150."

Keeping her voice low, she told White, "See what's in the kitchen to eat. Don't waste time."

"Right." He went off to the kitchen and returned shortly. "Cans of soup, a loaf of bread, and some moldy cheese in the refrigerator, plus some beer."

"Where do you keep your can opener?" she called, not expecting him to reply.

"Lower cabinet, next to the sink."

"I'm kind of hungry. You mind if I have some soup?" She told White to warm up a can.

He answered with a grunt. She kept asking questions. Some he answered, some he didn't. "I don't like talking through a door. Why don't you come out?"

No response.

When White got back with a cup of soup, she said, "Soup's ready. Want a cup?"

"You can come in, if you want. Door's unlocked."

She twisted the knob and pushed the door slowly inward. Zach sat cross-legged on the floor at the foot of a single bed. Kane sat on the bed with a handgun at Zach's head. The shotgun lay beside him.

She kept her voice level. "You all right, Zach?"

"Nothing wrong with him," Kane growled. "Yet. Get everybody out or I'll pop him."

She motioned for White and Adler to move back.

"Tell 'em to leave!"

"Mr. Kane, you know I can't do that."

Zach coughed, tight and croupy. She could hear the wheeze when he drew breath. His eyes were looking above her shoulder, and his head moved a tiny bit as though he was keeping time to music only he could hear.

"You sure I can't get you something? A sandwich, soft drink? Coffee?"

"Get rid of the soup. Think I'm stupid? Let you waltz in here with hot soup and throw it at me?"

That was a possibility she'd had in mind. "I could set it on the floor. You could pick it up yourself."

He laughed. She eased closer to the doorway.

"Get back! Any closer and I pull the trigger!"

She stopped but didn't retreat. "You know a lot about planes?"

"Get rid of the soup! Get rid of it!"

She handed the cup to White and stepped just inside the bedroom doorway.

"Tell him to leave! Tell 'em all to leave."

"Take it easy, Mr. Kane."

He jammed the gun against Zach's temple. She motioned for Adler and White to move back. White sidled along the wall toward Crenshaw and Marshall in the kitchen entryway. Adler moved toward Ellis at the other end of the hallway.

"I saw on your minivan that you give flying lessons," she said. "Could you teach me? I've always wanted to learn."

Kane bared his teeth in a humorless smile. Zach started swaying his head and shoulders, barely moving, in time with his inner music. Kane grabbed one shoulder to make him stop.

Zach coughed.

"He needs a doctor," she said. "Let him go. So far you haven't done anything a good attorney can't take care of. Let me have Zach. I'll take him to his mom and—noo!"

As if *Mom* had been some kind of trigger, Zach uncoiled and lunged at Kane.

Kane fell awkwardly backward and rolled onto the floor.

Swinging her gun, she slammed it hard against his temple. With a grunt of pain, he got to his knees. As he rose to his feet, he smashed his weapon into her ribs.

215

Zach yelled. Throwing his arms around Kane's neck, he let his body go limp. The unexpected weight jerked Kane to one knee. His gun went off. Zach dropped like a stone, blood flowing from the top of his head.

The explosion in the enclosed space deafened her. She lunged and grabbed Kane's shirt collar. Fighting to retain her balance, she slammed her gun hand on his ear. He twisted to backhand her.

She struggled to get control of his gun while not losing her own. Kicking at his knee, she shoved her weight against his shoulder. He collapsed and she went down with him, landing beneath him.

Five cops swarmed in and made grabs at Kane.

She struggled to roll him on his back and get on top. Forearm hard against his throat, she shoved the barrel of her Sig Saur against his temple.

35

It was four A.M. when Susan limped into the interrogation room. Kane was sprawled in a plastic chair he'd pulled away from the table, picking with one thumbnail at the greenish black crescent in the other. His thinning brown hair stood on end, making him look somewhere between pissed off and deranged. White and Ellis were with him. She asked him his name for the record.

"Porter Kane," he growled.

She turned on the tape recorder, repeated the Miranda, and mentioned the date, time, and all those present. She reeled off offenses: kidnapping, child endangerment, discharging a weapon within the city limits, assault on an officer, attempted homicide, homicide . . .

He jumped to his feet. "I didn't fuckin' murder anybody!"

Ellis shoved him back down.

"I didn't kidnap the fuckin' kid, either. He broke into my house. I have a right to defend myself."

"What about Branner Noel? Were you defending yourself against him?"

"Who?"

217

"Tim Holiday." He didn't seem to recognize that name, either. "The man who repaired your furnace."

"That dipstick? Why would I kill him?"

"You tell us, Mr. Kane."

"I didn't kill anybody." He crossed his arms.

"We searched your house, Mr. Kane." She paused. He stared at her mulishly. "We found what appear to be cremated human remains. Is that why you killed Holiday? He saw the ashes and you had to get rid of him?"

Kane snorted. "What? You think you got yourselves a serial killer here? I never killed anybody."

"Why, Mr. Kane, do you have boxes of ashes in your basement?"

His skin had taken on a tired gray tinge. He slumped forward and scrubbed a hand over his face. "Paul Satterly Funeral Home, that's where they come from."

"Why do you have them?"

"Take 'em up, tip 'em out. They float through the air"—he rocked a hand back and forth—"to the river."

"You were supposed to scatter these ashes from a plane into the Kaw." She wanted to make sure she understood. "You were paid for this?"

"Would I do it for fun?"

"Why didn't you, then?"

His look of defeat took on a defensive edge. "How could I? Plane needs a new propeller. Landing gear doesn't always work right, either. Needs to be replaced."

"So you took the money and kept the cremated remains in your house?"

"Cremains," he said with derision. "Got laid off. Couldn't fix the fuckin' plane."

Oh boy, she could see humongous lawsuits looming for Paul Satterly Funeral Home from the relatives and loved ones of the dear departed. "Holiday saw these—uh, cremains?"

"Damned snoop. No reason for him to go in there."

"Is that why you killed him?"

"I didn't kill him!" He slammed a fist against the table.

She kept at him. Questioned him over and over. She had the sinking feeling he was telling the truth. If Parkhurst were here, she could bounce it off him.

"Cremains weren't the only things we found," she said. "We found two watches and a crystal clock with diamond numbers. Did I mention burglary in the list of charges?"

"I want a lawyer."

She had Ellis take him back to a cell.

Hazel brought in a mug of coffee. "What are you doing here?" Susan said.

"Drink the coffee. I got a call from the hospital. Ida Ruth Dandermadden died about an hour ago."

Susan sipped hot coffee, got her coat, and told Hazel she was going to Brookvale to check on Demarco and Zach James. She finished up the coffee on the way.

A Christmasy feeling hung in the cold, black sky, full moon, stars twinkling. Cold. Cold. Cold. She jogged up to the hospital doors.

They hissed open and she went into the warm lobby. The tree in the corner was all silver lights and red baubles. She said hello to the woman behind the desk and made her way down the hallway to the emergency area.

"I'm looking for Officer Demarco," she said to Mary Mason, the triage nurse.

"Room three."

Susan found Demarco lying in bed, shirt off, bandage around his shoulder. Crenshaw was lounging against the bed. "Chief," he said, springing to attention.

"How're you doing?" she asked Demarco.

"Feel like I been shot. We get the bastard?"

"We did. He claims he didn't kill Holiday."

For a long time Demarco was silent and she thought he'd fallen asleep, then, when two nurses came to move him to the OR,

219

he gave one shake of his head. "Doesn't seem his style. Creeping into somebody's house, shooting the vic, shoving the poor slob in the furnace."

She agreed. Reluctantly agreed. If Porter Kane hadn't killed Holiday, who had? Caley James? Mat James? She was no nearer to finding the answers than when she started. She had two homicides—maybe three, now that Ida Ruth had died—to clear before she left for San Francisco. In two days.

36

Caley James squealed into the hospital parking lot and pulled into a space marked PHYSICIAN.

"Hey! That's my spot."

"Find another one!"

She sped inside and stopped, confused. Which way? Down a corridor, she spied a desk and ran up to it. "My son. Zach James. Where is he?"

"Third floor. You go down this hallway and take the elevators—"

She didn't wait for the rest of it. Because she found the stairs first, she ran up to the third floor, not even short of breath when she got there. Waste of time, breathing.

"Zach James?" she asked a nurse.

"He's in three twenty-four, but—"

Three twenty, three twenty-two, three twenty-four. She stopped outside the door and took a breath. Pretending a composure she didn't feel, she stepped inside.

Fear dug claws in her throat.

Zach, eyes closed, lay on the bed. Face pale, head bandaged with a white turban, dark circles under his eyes.

Oh God oh God oh God.

"Zach?" She brushed his cheek with a kiss. "It's Mom, love." The catch in her voice made her swallow.

His eyes opened. "I'm okay, Mom."

"Oh, Zach." She wanted to grab him up, wrap her arms around him, and hug him tight against her. She picked up his hand instead and kissed it. "What happened?" Her voice was thick.

"He's a very lucky young man. Hardheaded too." A stocky man in green scrubs strode in and pushed buttons on the bed. With Zach lifted to a sitting position, he listened to Zach's chest, then to his back. Replacing the stethoscope around his neck, he held out his hand. "Dr. Sheffield."

"What happened?" Caley asked, struggling to breathe.

"A bullet rode right across his head." Dr. Sheffield traced a path over Zach's bandage.

"He was shot! Who? Zach—"

"Mom, calm down. I'm fine."

"But—"

Dr. Sheffield folded his arms across his broad chest and leaned against the bed. "He's fine," he repeated. "We'll keep him a couple of days. He's got a little spot of pneumonia, but—"

"Pneumonia!"

"We're taking care of it with antibiotics. It'll take longer for his hair to grow back. We had to shave it to look at the wound—"

Caley nearly dropped at the word *wound*.

"He'll have a great scar to show his friends."

Dr. Sheffield put his hands on her upper arms and looked directly into her eyes. "You have to limit your visits." She nodded. "Ten minutes. Right now I need to take a peek under that bandage."

She was ushered to the door, where a nurse took over and led her to a small waiting room. Brown tweed chairs, end tables with jumbled magazines, and a large fish tank built into one wall.

* * *

Susan turned from gazing at a dull blue-colored fish with big white teeth and handed Caley a cup of coffee, then took her arm and guided her to a chair.

"I just ran out"—Caley took a sip of coffee—"leaving Mat and Bernadette—"

"Bernadette?"

"Ettie. Mat's mother." Caley rubbed her eyes. "When Zach was little he couldn't say Bernadette. It came out Ettie and it just stuck."

"She uses the name Trowbridge. Did she remarry?"

"Third marriage. From James to Dalrumple to Trowbridge." Caley got up and went to the doorway. "Do you think they'll let me know when they're finished?"

"I'm sure they will."

"Mommy! Mommy! Mommy!" Bonnie barrelled into Caley, nearly knocking her down. "Did the evil prince hurt Zach?"

Mat and Ettie with Adam in tow came in. Mat swung Bonnie up in his arms. "How is he?"

Caley shrugged. "We can't see him right now."

"I saw him," Bonnie whispered in Mat's ear.

"Who, baby?" he said, distracted.

"I asked that. 'Who're you?'" She lowered her voice. "'The evil prince. If you tell, I'll kidnap you and take you far far away where you'll have to live in a castle.' Would I be a princess if I lived in a castle, Daddy?"

"You're my princess right here."

Adam got a kiss and a hug from Caley, and Ettie took his hand and led him to one of the tweed couches. Mat tried to get Caley to sit with them. She shook her head.

"Daddy?" Bonnie patted Mat's face. "You didn't ask what he wanted."

"What, sweetheart?"

"The pictures with the numbers," she said, proud to know something he didn't.

"Of course," Mat said with a great show of astonishment. "He wanted to paint."

Bonnie giggled.

Mat took Caley's elbow. "Sit down, Cal. Come on."

She ignored him and asked Susan, "Do you think they'll let me in now?"

"I'll check for you."

Susan fell into step beside Dr. Sheffield as he left Zach's room, and had to hustle to keep up. "I need to talk with Zach."

"I assumed that's why you were hanging around. Give it a minute until the bandage gets replaced, then okay." He gave her a severe physician's look. "Ten minutes."

"Yes."

When a slender young woman in white pants and flowered shirt came out and gave her a nod, Susan went in.

"You rescued me from that guy." Zach's voice was tight with embarrassment.

"With a lot of help from you. I don't know what we'd have done if you hadn't jumped the guy. That was a very brave thing to do."

He watched her, waiting for the rest of it.

"And very stupid. He had a gun to your head. You could have been killed."

"It's just that your way was taking forever and I had to—"

She eyed him. "Had to what?"

"Go to the bathroom," he admitted.

"Ah. I can see the problem. How did you get into that situation?"

He got a look on his face that she'd seen on one nephew or another over the years. It went along with, Do I have to?

"An officer got shot tonight," she said.

"Is he hurt bad?"

"He'll be all right. Talk to me, Zach."

Zach told her about seeing his father handing an envelope to Baines, seeing the money and almost being hit by Porter Kane, and being chased by Baines. He looked at her pleadingly. "Is my dad in trouble?"

"He might be."

"Sometimes he does things without thinking."

"Uh-huh. Like somebody else I know."

Zach grinned. "Mom said for a smart kid, I can be pretty dumb sometimes."

Susan nodded. "Like going to Kane's house."

"I wanted him to give Baines back the money. And he was going to. I could tell he was. Then you guys showed up and he just went into orbit. Totally blew. I thought I was dead."

"So did I, there for a minute. Were you ever in Ida Ruth Dandermadden's backyard?"

He looked sheepish. "Once. I wanted to tell her to quit saying bad things about my mom."

"Did you?"

"I didn't even see her. By the time I got there I figured it wouldn't do any good anyway, so I just left."

She squeezed his hand. "I'll probably be back, but right now your family is waiting."

Caley, Mat, Ettie, Adam, and Bonnie were all in the waiting room. Bonnie was singing.

> Itsy bitsy spider climbed up the water spout.
> Down came the rain and washed the spider
>   out.
> Out came the sun and dried the water up.

Mat put down the book he was reading to Adam. "After I see Zach, I'll finish it."

> Itsy bitsy spider climbed up the water spout.
> Down came the rain and washed the spider
>   out.
> Out came the sun and dried the water up.

Itsy bitsy spider climbed up the waterspout.
Down came the rain and washed the spider out
Out came the sun—

"Bonnie, darlin'," Caley said. "You've been singing that for five minutes. Your grandma has heard it enough. Find another song."

"Have you, Grandma?"

"Yes, sweetheart, I think I have. What else can you sing?"

"Itsy Bitsy Spider" was maddeningly running through Susan's mind as she headed down to the second floor to stop in on DeMarco.

He was back from surgery, settled in a bed, sleepy from all the drugs he'd been given. Blood dripped into his arm from the unit on a pole. "Hi," she said. "It looks like you're here for a while."

"Nothing major damaged," he mumbled.

"Good. You did a courageous thing, protecting that little girl."

He started to shrug and winced. If he hadn't been so dopey from the surgery he probably would have said, Just part of the job.

"I'll stop in later to see if you need anything."

"Itsy Bitsy Spider" ran through her mind as she headed back to the department. She snapped on the radio and wiped it out with *"Eine Kleine Nachtmusik."*

Hazel grinned at her when she came in.

"What?"

"The mayor left a message. Al Wily has the flu. Our mayor wants you to take his place in the parade."

"What was Al Wily supposed to do?"

"Al's a clown."

"What?"

Hazel laughed. "Won't that be fun? You'll get to paint your face and—"

Susan went to her office. As she worked on the folders stacked on her desk, something kept trying to touch her conscious mind, like the soft flitter of a butterfly wing.

She gulped a mouthful of coffee, then told Hazel to have

someone pick up Mat James and bring him in. "He was at the hospital a few minutes ago."

In the interrogation room, Mat sat with his back to the one-way glass and rose when she came in. He looked tired, deeper lines in his face, bloodshot eyes, unshaven, clothes wrinkled.

"Thank you for coming in, Mr. James," she said.

"I wasn't given a choice. What's this about?"

She clicked on the tape recorder, stated the date, time, and names of all those present. When she recited the Miranda warning, he looked up, startled.

"Should I have an attorney?"

"Up to you. Would you like one?"

He hesitated, then sat down. "I'd like to know what I'm doing here."

Susan sat across from him. White stood with his back to the door. "Can I get you something, Mr. James? Glass of water? Cup of coffee?"

"Coffee would be nice."

He was soon to find out how wrong he was. "Cream or sugar?"

"One sugar."

She nodded at White, who left and returned a minute or so later with a thick white mug of coffee. He set it down in front of Mat and Mat took a gulp.

"You gave Will Baines a large amount of money," she said.

"Forgive me for saying so, but that's none of your business."

"You killed Holiday/Noel because it was you twelve years ago who murdered his wife. Not Noel. He came here for revenge. Or did he have some evidence that didn't come out at the trial? Was that it? Something that showed you were in the house the day she was stabbed?"

"None of that's true," he said tiredly.

"No? Then you won't mind telling what the money was for."

"I was paying back a loan."

227

"With cash?"

"That's how Baines does business."

"Why did you borrow it?"

He put a hand on his jaw, thumb on one side, fingers on the other. "I got behind on some bills and needed to take care of them before they got delinquent."

"What bills?" Susan asked.

He moved his thumb and fingers together at his chin, as though wiping something off. "There's no reason I need to answer that, but just to make sure you don't get the wrong idea, it was for car payments and furniture I bought for my apartment."

"How do you know Will Baines?"

"I've known him for a long time. I knew him in Kansas City."

"Have you borrowed money from him before?"

He smiled. Even though he was tired and the smile was ragged around the edges, it was still charming.

"Once again, Chief, I don't have to answer that."

"Why did he move to Hampstead?"

"You'll have to ask him. I believe he came to see me once and liked it here. Now, if that's all you have in mind, I'm leaving."

Susan thanked him for his time and watched him walk out with a confident, everything-under-control walk.

The damn itsy bitsy spider came back and spun away at her sanity.

37

———

$\mathcal{H}$is name is Martin Thackeray," Ellis said. "He runs the rare book and sewing machine place that Will Baines bought."

"Oh. Right." Susan leaned back in her desk chair.

"The place was closed, but he was working on the inventory and heard somebody up in Noel's apartment."

"Break-in?"

Ellis nodded. "The guy wasn't even subtle about it. Took a crowbar and went at it. Tore the hell out of the door. I called for backup, and when Adler got there we went in and found him."

"He say anything?"

"Naw. Just that we were making a mistake."

She shuffled the folders on her desk until she found the Branner Noel case file. Taking out the two snapshots she'd found in Noel's apartment, she put them side by side on her desk. Snapshots of Mat James with two different young women. Flipping them over, she looked at the numbers on the back.

"Come with me," she said to Ellis, pushed her chair back, and stood up.

Mat was standing with his back against the table. He straightened and sent her his engaging smile when they came in. "We meet again, Chief Wren?" The smile was less captivating now than it had been when she'd had him here twelve hours ago. After very little sleep last night, a day at work, and then breaking into Noel's apartment, Mat was starting to look a little frayed; his age was showing with more pronounced lines around his tired, bloodshot eyes. Even his skin was beginning to look slack, and stubble covered his jaw. He was still wearing a suit and tie, but his white shirt was less than pristine and he'd loosened the tie.

"Sit down, please, Mr. James."

He moved a chair around to the head of the table and sat down.

She clicked on the tape recorder, stated the date, time, the names of all those present, and repeated the Miranda warning.

"Mr. James, what were you doing in Branner Noel's apartment?"

"He was an old friend. I felt I had to see where he'd been living before he died."

She raised an eyebrow. "That doesn't sound even slightly likely."

"Yeah, you're right." He leaned back and hooked an elbow over the back of the chair. "I was looking for a key."

"A key to what?"

"Safe-deposit box."

"Where is this box?"

"Bran asked me, if anything ever happened to him, to take care of whatever needed taking care of. I wanted to see what needed to be done."

"That didn't answer my question." She waited. "The only key we found was for a safe-deposit box in Woodsonville. Is that the one you were looking for?"

"Woodsonville? That may be it. I've got it written down somewhere."

He was playing games with her and she was tired of him. "There was a great deal of money in that box. Is that what you were after?"

He looked astonished. "Money? I had no idea what was in there."

"Or were you looking for snapshots, Mr. James?"

She placed one on the table in front of him. "Who's the woman?"

"Kathleen," he said softly. Cleared his throat and said, "My wife. First wife."

She put the other snapshot in front of him. "This woman?"

"Deirdre—"

"Yes?"

"Noel. Deirdre Noel, Bran's wife."

"The one you had an affair with, causing her husband to kill her."

"No," he said.

She didn't believe him. "Why were you trying to steal these photos, Mr. James?"

"A lawyer might argue they belong to me. Bran gave them to me and asked me to keep them safe while he was in prison."

"How did they get into Noel's apartment?"

"Bran must have taken them from my basement."

"Why take them? Why not ask?"

"I don't know." Mat got to his feet. "I have to get back to the hospital."

"Sit down, Mr. James."

"I'm leaving."

Susan shook her head. "I can arrest you for the murder of Branner Noel."

"I didn't kill him."

"Convince me."

"What can I say? I didn't kill him. I don't know how to convince you."

Susan turned over one photo. Mat froze for a split second. If she hadn't been watching so closely, she wouldn't have caught it.

"Is that what you were looking for, Mr. James?" She flipped it back before he could memorize the numbers.

"I don't have any pictures of Kathleen. I wanted it for Zach. One day he might want a picture of his biological mother."

"How did you know Noel had taken the snapshots from your ex-wife's basement?"

He bent one leg and rested the ankle on his knee.

"That's what Bonnie was talking about at the hospital, wasn't it?"

He flashed a quick smile. "She's the only one who looked at those old albums."

"You're under arrest—"

"For what?"

"Come come, Mr. James, surely you didn't think you were getting away with it. Breaking and entering. Grand theft—"

"Grand theft? A couple of old snapshots?"

"It's not the snapshots you were after. It's the account numbers on the back. You wanted to get at Noel's money."

"It isn't his," Mat said, dropping all pretense of not knowing what was going on.

"You want to tell me whose it is?"

"Ours." Mat looked a bit more weary and wilted. "I had those photos all these years and didn't know the numbers were on the back."

"Yours and Noel's."

"Yeah, it's all in the Cayman Islands."

She looked at him.

He grinned. "Hey, if it's good enough for gangsters . . ."

"How'd you get this money?"

He shook his head. "That I'm not going to tell you. I want an attorney now."

She told Ellis to let Mat make a phone call and then put him in a cell.

Demarco's digging into Mat's life had turned up some very interesting information; it showed just how clever Mat and Branner Noel had been. Under the name MB Publications, they purchased access to a database of credit card numbers from Prairie

Central Bank, over two-and-a-half million names. MB Publications and various other businesses, MJB Care, BNJ Services, B&M Bill Inc., then billed the cardholders for small amounts every month, $19.99 and under. They used five different merchant accounts to process the transactions. The imagination boggled at how much money they racked in, staggering amounts. They'd been so slick; they were never arrested or charged with any crime. There'd never been enough evidence.

Branner Noel, she speculated, wrote account numbers on the backs of the old photos so he wouldn't forget. Whatever papers there were besides those in the safe-deposit box had been destroyed. The two accounts in the box held numbers that were the dates of his wife's birthday and his own birthday, no problem remembering. Those he dipped into because he needed funds.

Credit card fraud wasn't her job. Finding Noel's killer was. As she went to her office, the itsy bitsy spider crawled back into her mind.

38

All day Susan chipped away at the pile of work on her desk. Her head ached, her eyes were gritty, her throat dry, and her entire being longed for sleep. Apparently, an all-nighter was beyond her. The itsy bitsy spider kept playing through her mind. It was December 23, seven o'clock in the evening. Around three tomorrow afternoon she was scheduled to leave for San Francisco. That gave her roughly twenty hours to clear three homicides and pack her suitcase. All the coffee she'd had was sloshing uneasily in her stomach, and the caffeine jangled her nerves.

She scribbled her name, closed the folder, and tossed it to the other side of her desk. As she was reaching for the next folder, the itsy bitsy spider that had been tapping at her subconscious finally broke through. Spider tattoo!

Leaning back, she examined the thought, turned it over and looked at it from the other side. Her heart started pounding with the high she always got when pieces started falling in place. All she needed was evidence.

Right. Her balloon of excitement started leaking.

After another ten minutes of thought with nothing developing, she picked up the phone and told Hazel to have White call her.

* * *

Ettie Trowbridge sat at the long table in the interview room, looking so serene—platinum hair perfect, makeup discreet, tan pants
and tan shirt with brown swirls spotless and unwrinkled—that severe doubts started eroding Susan's brilliant idea. White and Ellis,
one on either side of the door, nodded when Susan came in.

"Mrs. Trowbridge," she said. "Can I get you anything? Coffee?
A soft drink?"

"Nothing, thank you, dear. But you can call me Ettie and tell
me what this is all about."

"You'd better call your attorney. You're going to need him."

"Attorney? I don't even know one. At least not here. Why
don't you just tell me why I'm here?" She sounded as though she
was going to reach out and pat Susan's hand. There, there, there,
tell me about it.

Susan recited the Miranda warning. Ettie looked bewildered.

"Are you waiving your right to an attorney?"

"I guess I am. At least for the moment. Now, dear, please
explain."

"Why did you come to Hampstead?"

"My son was here, and my grandchildren."

Susan nodded. "You told me they meant everything to you.
You'd do anything necessary to keep them safe."

"Certainly."

"Anything," Susan repeated, "including perjury. You lied at the
trial twelve years ago when you said you'd seen Branner Noel hit
his wife many times. You swore to it because you knew your own
son killed Noel's wife."

"Nonsense," Ettie said.

Susan sat on a corner of the table, one leg dangling. "No? Was
it you who killed Noel?" She leaned forward and rested her elbow
on her knee. "When he was released, he came to Hampstead looking for you."

"Preposterous."

And Susan was beginning to think it was.

"Noel spent twelve years in prison. Twelve years of hell for something he didn't do. Then he got released and came looking. Was it self-defense, Mrs. Trowbridge? He came to make you admit your lies, threatened you, and you killed him before he could kill you?"

"What rubbish, dear," Ettie said, her demeanor as perfect as when she'd come in. "Now, if it's all right, I have some gifts to wrap."

So much for threats. With no evidence to hold her, Susan had to let her go. After Ettie had gathered her coat and purse and scarf, she nodded pleasantly at Susan and walked out.

"All right," Susan said to White. "Here's what we're going to do."

Susan sensed change coming. Or maybe it was just the excitement of getting close and it had been so long since that had happened she'd forgotten what it felt like.

The radio in the pickup crackled. "Suspect leaving residence."

She was a block south and moving parallel with White. She hoped he wouldn't get too close and spook the suspect. She had told him if he lost her, he was dead.

"Headed north on Ellington."

Silence. "East on Oak."

The suspect zigzagged through town as though suspicious, and she started to get nervous.

"Turned north on Falcon Road."

Her heartbeat picked up, she hit the overheads and mashed the accelerator, sped down Ninth and went right on Iowa out to the county road, another right and right again on the far end of Falcon Road. She doused her lights, cut her motor, and slid from the pickup. The temperature had dropped; the always-present wind simply gained force and got worse. Her nose, throat, and lungs were held in a vise grip of cold. It seeped through the soles of her boots. Not a fit night for man or beast. Moonlight let her walk along the road without stumbling.

When headlights popped up, coming at her, she dropped behind prickly shrubs. The vehicle stopped, the suspect got out. A flashlight flickered through the trees as the suspect made a descent down the slope toward the river.

"Now," Susan whispered in her radio.

White came roaring up, lights going, siren wailing. He rocked to a stop, tumbled from the car, and thrashed down the slope. "Freeze! Police!"

Susan scrambled down the embankment. Ettie, caught in the blaze of White's flashlight, froze, one hand shading her eyes, the other holding up a gun.

"Drop the gun!"

Ettie fired it, whirled, and ran. Moonlight glistened on the black water. She stumbled and dropped the gun as she scruffled her feet searching for purchase. She fell, banged her head on a rock, and slid swiftly toward the river. A loud splash followed.

"Get an ambulance!" Susan yelled.

Ettie made a strangled squealing gasp. Her arms flailed. Susan waded in and lost her footing in the rush of the current. Chunks of ice bumped against her. The cold took her breath away.

"Give me your hand!" She grabbed at Ettie, who was panicked, choking and sinking, then bobbing up and splashing away at the water.

Susan thrashed, grappled for the bottom with her toes, lost her balance, rode the current. She had to get Ettie and herself out of the water or they'd die. The low water temperature would send their bodies into shock, shutting off all functions. Clothing would act like an anchor and muscles would cramp.

"Ettie! Don't fight!"

With a gulp of air, Susan lunged for Ettie, and her fingers clutched the edge of the woman's jacket. Ettie spluttered, made wild lunges. Susan tugged on the jacket until she had both her hands on Ettie's arm.

The river pulled them around a curve, sweeping them under a fallen tree. She clutched a branch. It broke with a sharp crack and they floated helplessly on. Susan rolled onto her side, kicked, and groped with one arm toward the bank.

When she realized she could feel the river bottom with one foot, she dug her boot into the mud. Moving slowly, one foot, then the other, she struggled toward the river's edge until the water was shallow enough that she was able to stand. The cold wind hit.

Ettie choked, gasping and coughing.

Shaking so hard her teeth clacked together, Susan arrested her for the murder of Branner Noel.

39

———

$\mathcal{S}$now started falling at ten A.M. on December 24. With no warning and the fury of Moses destroying the golden calf, the worst snowstorm in fifty years swept across the plains of Nebraska and Kansas, shrieked across the entire Midwest, and whipped all the way to the East Coast. Nothing moved. Roads were blocked, airports closed, people stayed inside.

In Hampstead, the parade was canceled and the power was out. Wind screamed down the chimney, making the cat's hair stand on end. Around six, Susan braved the dark and the snow torn around by the howling wind and floundered to the garage. She gathered the last few pieces of firewood in a bucket and flailed back to the house. Plunking the bucket on the hearth, she put logs on the grate. Swearing and grumbling, she crumpled newspaper and shoved it in with the poker. After more newspaper, she finally got a fire going. Very cozy Christmas Eve.

Using a flashlight, she tracked down candles and lit half a dozen, put some on the mantel and the rest on the end tables by the couch. Courting a house fire, she thought. But with no holiday decorations, at least they gave some hint of festivity. She checked the batteries in her little radio and turned it on to carols. Wrapped in a blanket, a book in her lap, she sat on the floor and tried to read. The flickering flames gave off a strobe effect that made reading difficult and threatened to give her a headache. She gave up and stared at the fire.

Tears clogged her eyes. All alone on Christmas Eve. Her closest relationship was with a cat. The wind freaked Perissa. She streaked through the living room into the dining room, backed into corners, and pounced on shadows. The clock on the mantel struck eight. Five hours ago, she was to have boarded a plane that would take her home. It had been three years since she'd been there.

Perissa stalked into the living room, oozed under the coffee table, and growled. Someone pounded on the door. "It's probably Santa Claus," she told the cat, and went to answer it.

Parkhurst, looking like the abominable snowman, stood on her porch with a leather satchel in one hand, a lantern in the other. The lantern sent out an eerie glow against the night and swirling snow. Weary traveler of the eighteenth century making his way to the inn.

"Have you recovered or am I talking to the ghost of Christmas past?"

He clapped snow from his hat and stamped it from his boots. "Let me in. It's freezing out here," he croaked, remnants of the flu still in his voice.

"It's not much better in here," she rasped, her own voice still harsh from smoke inhalation. "Do you have heat at your place?"

"No."

"Then come on in."

He went to the kitchen and took thermos bottles from the bag. "Hot soup."

"How'd you manage that?"

"Coleman stove." He shrugged off his coat. "It's from Hazel, in case you're worried. To combat the flu. She gave me enough to last out the winter."

Susan took his coat. "I don't suppose you brought hot coffee."

"Got that too."

"My house is your house." She draped his coat over the shower rod in the bathroom, trotted upstairs, snatched a blanket from the guest room, and brought it down.

He removed his boots and stretched out on his back, stockinged feet toward the fire. "I didn't know if you had any wood. So I filled up the Bronco."

She tossed him the blanket and he spread it over his legs. Perissa crouched on a couch cushion, growling like a pit bull.

"I hear you cleared the homicide," he said.

"Hazel tell you?"

"She said I should forget work and concentrate on getting well."

"You well?"

"Well enough," he rasped.

"Finished up last night." She lay down next to him with her own blanket and, when he looked at her, she felt the pull of attraction, the crackle of electricity.

He looked at her a moment too long before he turned and stared at the fire. "What led you to Ettie Trowbridge?" he said, voice hoarse.

"Bonnie's song." Susan thought her voice sounded thin. She cleared her throat, then told him how it had stuck in her mind. "Holiday/Noel had a small tattoo of a spider on the back of his neck, just below the hairline. Ettie claimed she'd never seen the man, but when I questioned her she said Caley would never have an affair with a man who had a tattoo."

"The spider did her in."

"She saw it when she shoved his head into the furnace."

"She's the arsonist too, I suppose?" he said.

Susan stared at the fire. "Pauline had a photo album underneath her when the fire got her. It had 'Grandma's Brag Book' on the cover. The only thing left was a fragment of the cover with GRA on it. She was trying to save photos of her grandchildren, or maybe trying to tell us something about Noel's killer."

He snorted. "Dying clue?"

"Maybe. Ettie is Zach, Adam, and Bonnie's grandmother. Pauline saw Ettie let Noel into Caley's house and it puzzled her. She knew Mat had taken the children and Caley was sick. She thought maybe Ettie was there to take care of Caley and that Noel—although she didn't know his name—had come to see Caley. But if that were so, why was Ettie letting him in the basement door instead of through the front door like a bona fide guest? Pauline told all this to Ida Ruth."

"And Ida Ruth, never one to let opportunity go by, called Ettie and what? Said get your Jezebel daughter-in-law away from the church organ or else?"

"More than that," Susan said. "Ida Ruth, being a little sharper and having a meaner take on humankind, realized this made Ettie a strong suspect for murder. She told Ettie what Pauline had said and that it was her, Ida Ruth's, Christian duty to inform the police. Why she didn't do that first, only Ida Ruth knows and she's beyond asking."

"Some people like to take a needless poke at rattlesnakes."

"Ettie loosened the railing. I think she would have banged Ida Ruth's head against the concrete a few times if the woman hadn't had the stroke that left her with almost no speech."

Stomach to the floor, Perissa crept over to Parkhurst, rose on tiptoe, and hissed in his face. Startled, he jerked back. The cat fled back under the couch and resumed growling.

"Jesus! That is the meanest cat I've ever seen."

Susan laughed. "That's true." She paused. "Wherever Pauline Frankens is, I hope she knows her Ollie wasn't hurt in the fire. That big loving cat is now snuggling up to the James children."

"Hazel said something about Halcion in an Advil bottle."

"Ettie was afraid Caley would get custody of the children and take them away. If Caley were proved unfit, Mat would get custody. Since he's not exactly the fatherly type, he'd turn them over to her."

"You didn't have anything even remotely resembling evidence."

She grinned. "I know. That's why I tried to shake her up a little. Sure didn't look like I'd succeeded until we caught her trying to dispose of the murder weapon."

Parkhurst shook his head. He got up to get a pillow from the couch, tossed one to Susan, and lay back down. He shoved the pillow under his head. "Game to the very end, that little lady."

They were quiet, listening to "Silent Night" on the radio.

"Mat claims he didn't kill Noel's wife," Susan mused.

Parkhurst raised on one elbow and looked at her. "Don't tell me you believe him."

"I do. He's not a great guy, he's a cheat and a con man, but I didn't sense any violence in him."

"So the White Water sheriff got the right guy after all?"

"Noel was another thief, charming, according to his lawyer, but Caley didn't find him charming. She saw him as creepy and menacing. Prison probably changed him."

"And the scar on his face," Parkhurst said dryly.

She nodded. "Ettie found him pretty menacing. He hung around Caley until Ettie showed up, then followed her to learn where she lived. He rang her doorbell and pushed his way in. Scared her. She had no idea he was even out of prison."

"Threatened her?" Parkhurst got up to put another log on the fire.

"Apparently. She wouldn't tell me exactly what he said, but he made clear his only reason for living was to find out who killed his wife."

Parkhurst poked at the log, sending up a shower of sparks.

"He called her Sunday afternoon," Susan said, "and mentioned the children, how easily something could happen to them. He hoped nothing would. His only purpose was in tracking down his wife's killer. Ettie told him to come to Caley's house, she had something to show him that might help him."

"So she let him in, showed him the gun, and shot him."

"Yeah."

She stared at the fire. "You know, I think he was innocent of his wife's murder."

"Somebody killed her. Took a knife and stabbed her thirty times."

"Somebody did that all right," Susan said. "I'd bet my money on Mat's first wife. Kathleen. She was mentally unstable. I think she felt Mat was leaving her to be with Noel's wife and she stabbed the woman."

"I guess it doesn't matter now, does it? Not with both of them dead."

"Yeah," Susan said. "He ordered a headstone for his wife's grave from that catalog that was in his post office box."

Parkhurst gave a short laugh. "Well, then, how bad could he be? How's Demarco?"

"Grumbling about having to stay in the hospital. Probably doing calisthenics in the hallway. I think the physician's going to boot him out soon just to get rid of him."

They listened to "The Little Drummer Boy," then Parkhurst said, "You going back to San Francisco?"

She took a breath and opened her mouth. Finally, she said, "I don't know."